THE STORK TRAP

Piri Shepherd

The Stork Trap

Cover art by Fred Seddon
Set in Arno Pro by Carnegie Book Production

ISBN 978-1-7384311-0-6
Printed in the UK by Halstan.

THE STORK TRAP

Piri Shepherd

Author's note

This story contains Inuit characters. I wanted to tell a story about global warming in the Arctic, and this meant that Killaq and Amaruq were Inuit when they turned up in my head. I have tried to write my indigenous characters with humility, and without any intention to offend or to appropriate. If I have failed in this aim I am sorry, and any cultural or factual errors are mine alone.

WINTER

Killaq

January 2062

Snow dusted the back of the musk ox. She scraped at the bare ground, looking for lichens or mosses that might have taken precarious root here now that the ice was gone. Not far beyond her hooves, on the seaward side, the land fell abruptly in a steep rubbly talus to steel-grey waves groaning and crashing far below. In the long coarse drapes of her brown pelt she was impervious to the wind hurling across the high scarp, but her woolly calf huddled into her for shelter, safe on the lee side.

Then a sharp, whiplash sound, deafeningly loud, snapped across the steady thrum of the wind. A crack in the earth snaked like lightning along the cliff edge, behind the musk ox, cutting her off from the land behind. She dipped her head, lowering the wicked curved horns, as if to protect her calf. For a moment everything was still. Then the cliff top vanished in a deadly avalanche of tumbling boulders, surging down the slope faster than a man could run.

Afterwards, a friable ochre scar marked where the cliff edge had been, and below the fresh rubble lay in a mud-brown fan on the grey talus. The musk ox and her calf were gone.

Note shoreline vulnerable to landslip after permafrost melt??

/file/save/BearingWitness/

/exit/

It was hacked drone footage, uploaded directly from the house server to the sensory inputs in her brain via the portal implant which sat under the skin, just underneath the base of her skull. She was collecting images of melting, flooding, landslides; the piece-by-piece evidence of the changes being inflicted on the Arctic, on her land. Killaq saved the viz, and lay back, looking at the arched interior of the console lid she had been using to access full-spectrum VR. Fear ran down her spine. This was the future: not just for the musk ox and her baby, disappearing in a jumble of hooves and boulders. It was the future for her; for everyone.

Annie

January 2062

Annie felt the sweat in the crease of her elbow as she linked arms with Tom and threw her body weight into the crush. The police were forcing them backwards with heavy plastic riot shields and she braced her feet and leaned her body into the press of protestors. She was in the second row back, squashed close up behind the man in front; he was a bit taller than her, and she could see the rough, peeling skin where his t-shirt rubbed, and the familiar pucker and lump where his upload portal must be. The mass of people rolled back a few steps and her feet left the ground but she was safe, held in place by everyone around her, and she felt a huge exhilaration and a widespread impersonal love for all the protesters, all her brothers and sisters. She was part of a great beast, a great battling creature; she was a soldier in a great army; together they were in the right and they would be victorious. She felt as if she had a strength and a focus which she had never known before and if she died under a police baton charge it would be all right because she would have known this day, everything magnified in the sunlight, everything important and clear, all of it somehow exemplified and made talismanic by the sharp detail, the man's neck, his tattooed scalp, the patterns writhing over the depilated skin: somehow this was truth, this was all that mattered. 'SAPA ARE BASTARDS!' she yelled, waiting for the ebb and flow of the shout, catching the crest of the slogan as the wave of sound rolled past her and adding her voice along with everyone around her. It was orchestrated, she knew it was co-ordinated by direct link, but it felt organic, spontaneous: the great beast of protest lifting its head to howl.

'SAPA ARE BASTARDS!' yelled Tom next to her, and he caught her eye, and grinned, and then they were forced back so sharply that she stumbled and nearly fell under the tattooed man's boot, and the man's weight came onto her but Tom hauled her up and for a minute he was holding her and then she jumped and he swung her up and she was on his shoulders, looking out over the pushing, shoving crowd.

The convoy was coming through. It had forced its way through the mass of protesters blocking the grand steps and entrance to the SAPA Building, and she saw, over the heads of the swaying line of human riot police, the security droids in their matt black high-threat armour, and the vehicles crawling in the middle. Her view swam and there was the tell-tale shimmer of an energy screen; they must be bringing someone in, someone important enough to have to be there in the body. The lead car held back, leaving a space for the second one to pull up parallel to the foot of the steps, and a door opened. Over the crowd she caught a glimpse of a small, scurrying figure emerging, maybe a clerk or a secretary. The important person must be coming next. Then she felt Tom grip her thighs and he was shouting something, and she turned her head to see the reflective black surface, only centimetres away from her, of a security drone with a gas nozzle extended, and she had time to think 'Shit!'

She woke up in the containment facility, lying in a shallow, faintly lit rectangular space. Coffin boxes, they called them. She had been in one of these before. For a minute she just looked at the ceiling, a hand's breadth above her face. Printed on the grey surface was the Australian coat of arms, with its kangaroo and emu, and beneath it a disclaimer in bold type.

YOU HAVE BEEN DETAINED FOR YOUR SECURITY AND/OR ON SUSPICION OF COMMISSION OF AN IMPRISONABLE OFFENCE. NO ASSESSMENT HAS BEEN MADE OF YOUR SUITABILITY FOR DETAINMENT. THE COURTS SERVICE IS NOT LIABLE FOR ANY INJURY WHETHER PHYSICAL OR EMOTIONAL SUSTAINED OR ALLEGED TO BE SUSTAINED IN THE COURSE OF YOUR DETAINMENT.

IF YOU HAVE BEEN RESTRAINED AND/ OR SEDATED YOU MAY FEEL THE AFTER EFFECTS OF THESE PROCEDURES. THIS IS NORMAL.

YOU WILL SHORTLY BE CLEARED FOR ALGORITHMIC ASSESSMENT. PLEASE WAIT PATIENTLY.

THIS FACILITY IS ADMINISTERED BY THE SINO-AUSTRALIAN PACIFIC ALLIANCE ON BEHALF OF THE DEPARTMENT OF CORRECTIVE SERVICES OF NEW SOUTH WALES.

There was an unpleasant smell in the coffin box. Someone had been sick in here, not too long ago. Annie tried to breathe through her mouth. They used to have panic buttons in the boxes, but then when setting off the panic button became a mode of protest in itself, they stopped that. She guessed they could tell if you were truly claustrophobic just through the life-signs monitoring process.

The wait seemed to take longer than usual. Then there was a voice.

'You are registered as Annie Patricia Ling, date of birth 22 November 2040, registered competent adult, social security reference 08SP573APL013. Do you confirm your identity?'

Annie drew a breath and the reek of the stale air in the box filled her nostrils. 'I protest the actions of SAPA in claiming illegal ownership of Antarctic territory,' she said in a clear tone.

'If you do not confirm your identity, it will take longer to verify you and clear you for release,' the voice said. 'Your period of detention may be unavoidably prolonged. Do you understand what I have said?'

'I protest the actions of SAPA in claiming illegal ownership of Antarctic territory,' Annie repeated, louder this time.

'You will have to stay here longer if you do not tell me who you are,' the voice said, dropping down a level of linguistic difficulty. 'Do you understand?'

'SAPA have no rights in the South! The mineral heritage of the South belongs to humankind!'

'If you do not tell me who you are you will be sedated until a human operator can process you. Do you understand?'

'I assert the right of protest,' said Annie, before she heard the hiss of the gas release and her field of view became dark.

Many hours later, after she had been hauled out of the box and had stood in line to be presented to the human operator, who looked exactly as bored and unimpressed as you might expect him to be having spent the day issuing warning certificates of criminal infringement to protesters, and after she had repeatedly refused to confirm her identity or sign for her possessions or provide an address, she was forcibly imaged and a blood sample taken, and she was informed that the record of Annie Patricia Ling had been marked with a potential infringement which might be activated against her should she be brought before the court for any other reason within the next calendar year. Then she was let go. She stood in the institutional foyer with its grubby pale green decor and stained brown synthetic floor and ran her fingers through her short hair, considering. She could take the protest further, maybe if she lay in front of the automatic exit, blocking the safety system; she could get herself rearrested. But hey, she decided, honour was satisfied, and anyway she needed a beer. She turned to the door camera and found the menu in the heads-up display that scrolled along the top of her vision.

/door access/exit request/

Outside it was dark, the warm, slightly heavy dark of midsummer in Sydney. There was a floodlit area in front of a chain-link fence and another exit portal, and then a road bordered by industrial units, dusty and abandoned-looking now that the working day was over. Down the road was a bus stop and under the perspex shelter was a queue of other detainees, looking stooped and sorry. She didn't like that idea much, jolting on the bus back into town, having your destination recorded. Her location was available to the authorities all the time anyway, just as everyone else's was, but she thought they paid particular attention to released detainees: paranoia on her part maybe. She headed in the direction of the bus stop, taking care to look as worn-down and slow as everybody else, but doubled around the end of the queue and kept walking into the humid night. Round a corner and then another, before she could square her shoulders and lift her head up. She had Chinese features; dark hair chopped into a shaggy crop; and a petite, athletic figure: today for the protest she had on anonymous denim shorts and a grey vest, although when she wasn't planning to get arrested she liked to wear a tight, colourful sheath dress or sometimes, in private, the freedom of just body paint, jungle-patterned or channelling some high mountain landscape, changing around her as she moved.

Annie took a breath and started jogging. She wouldn't activate her implanted portal until she thought the facility might have given up on listening to her. For now she had to find her way to the waterfront without her maps overlay, but this was something she had practised before. All the detention facilities were in unremarkable light-industrial neighbourhoods, much the same as each other, but this one – yes, she thought this was Badgery Creek. She would run for half an hour or so and then pick up the Metro and lose herself in the Saturday night crowds. Ahead of her the streetlight came on, behind her the light went out, as she kept a steady pace, finding a satisfaction in the match of the stride and the breath, the rhythm of the footfall. She hopped on the Southwest Overground at Leppington and sat, swaying, listening to the rattle of the wheels and watching the nighttime city outside. As the train neared the city centre the carriage filled up, mostly party people heading for bars downtown, with shaved heads and swirling skin art, strategic nudity covered with moving body paint. A woman strap-hanging above Annie was wearing a shift dress crossed over one shoulder in an eye-watering mustard yellow; over the other exposed breast and shoulder, and up to a wavy line crossing her face diagonally from chin to brow, images of massed insects crawled, wings and antennae repeating themselves, seething over the small nipple as the woman herself rocked blank-faced with the motion of the train. It was impossible not to watch. After a moment Annie made an effort and turned her head, leaning her cheek against the warm plastic of the window and looking out over dark streets and lighted walkways, neon bars, moving hoardings. The bistros and clubs started to give way to formal civic buildings, galleries and exhibitions, and the party crowd drained away: Annie got off at Museum.

Time to leave the Overnet. Annie wandered into Hyde Park, trying to look purposeless, and slumped down at the base of one of the tall fig trees which bordered the ANZAC memorial. The park was full of strolling crowds: crazy roller boys; engrossed couples; sedate opera goers, both men and women wearing flowing gowns that she guessed would cost a month's pay or more for most people. Hopefully she just looked to them like a girl who might have overdone it a bit on a Saturday night. She closed her eyes, leaned back on the rough bark, and accessed VR through her portal. Here in the city there was full strength access wherever you were – if she had been out in the sticks somewhere she might have had to use a console.

Hey Shaz, she messaged randomly, *soz not gun make it to Harry's, overdid the carachas!!!*

Hey Anniegirl, came back the reply, *seeya tomorra girlfriend.*

Seeya at the unit, Annie sent, confirming the entrance code triggered by the word 'caracha.' She had chosen it to sound like a cocktail (actually, she had found, when she looked it up many months later, it turned out to be a skin disease of llamas). In front of her a door appeared. She selected her identification icon and applied it to the lock. The door opened.

Annie swung through the door and chose a programme, RabbitRun, hit activate, paused VR and came back to her body under the tree. RabbitRun would move her Overnet ID randomly around the city, making a plausible trace if anyone ever investigated, leaving her free to move unseen, although she still had to be careful about cameras so as not to trigger an exception by being imaged in one place when RabbitRun had her somewhere else. She opened her eyes and looked around. Thankfully none of the passersby were worried about the little drunk girl propped up against the base of the fig. She stood up and stretched. She never got over that feeling of sudden freedom, of being unobserved: it was like a breath of mountain air in the muggy Sydney night.

/Darknet/connect/messages.

Hey girl, gotta cold beer with your name on it.

It was Tom. She sent him a thumbs up. She had a hoodie which was good for avoiding the cameras, here in the city; better not to run, either, so it would take her an hour to cover the 4km or so. She drifted off, strolling with the crowds, heading east whenever she could. It was after one in the morning when she finally neared home. Here in Double Bay the rising tides had been fatal to what had once been a seaside district of boutiques and bars. Some of the beaches had been recreated further inland, but the ocean now threatened the high rises, and a sea-barrier snaked around the base of some of the more expensive real estate. The other side of the barrier was where Annie was heading, to the half-drowned beach huts and apartments which had been abandoned as too costly to preserve. This was where she had to be careful. The top of the barrier was permanently lit and imaged, but her group had infiltrated one of the cameras with a routine that would erase the image of the climber. Ok, here, this was the place.

/Darknet/connect/AnnieLing/

/welcomehome/AnnieLing/

That was it, she was in. She had three minutes before the camera would revert to normal. She ran up the ornate metal stairs to the top of the barrier, where some effort had been made to make it look like a tourist structure, with sculptures and small trees in planters. Then, quick, one leg over the railing and down, fingers finding the chipped holds in the smooth surface, jumping down into the shadow at the barrier's foot.

It was low tide and a half-moon gleamed wetly on the buckled surface of the old road. Sand had drifted up between the houses in long rippled tongues, covering what had been decks and front gardens, sweeping garlands of flotsam into doorways, and in other places the running tide had scoured out the pavement and the subsoil, leaving the corners of buildings leaning unsupported over dark water-filled vacancies. Already windows had fallen out and roofs subsided, and where she was standing, seaweed grew thickly over what had been a wall bounding a small forecourt. Annie took off her boots and tied the laces round her neck: there was no way of traversing this next bit with dry feet. She wriggled her toes on the gritty surface.

Two blocks along and three towards the sea, the water deepening as she went, until she turned around a corner, out of the moonlight, and ducked under what had been a roller door, stuck half-open now, into the true blackness of a car port. She waded confidently into the dark space, finding the door to the right which gave onto the wreckage of a kitchen, faintly lit by moonshine through broken windows, the once-chic units stained and warped by the sea. The bottom of the stairs had rotted away; a leap took her three steps up and she ran up the flight to the short landing and banged on the door. 'Hey,' said Tom, her big, blond, dependable bloke, letting her in, handing her a beer, and here was Aleigina, curvaceous and dark-eyed, playing chess with Misha by lamplight in the far corner, and Noah, with his skinny build and his anxious, fidgety manner, his Black face focussed in concentration on the text scrolling in front of him. This was her cell, her group of protesters, brought together for different reasons: some passionate about the climate fight, some running from intolerable lives or who knew what problems. For now this squat in the flooded building was home, until the government made good on their promise to clear the ruins; then the group would have to move on. It was a large, long room, once a trendy first floor living space, now divided up into tented areas, with blankets and sheets tacked up to make private spaces, and here in the communal part there were woven rugs and mounded cushions, and the snaking cables running power to the three console chairs against the back wall. They could generate all they needed, pretty much; these houses had all had solar pvi, and they had their own wave turbine which they could let out on an anchor in a running tide.

Annie grinned and reached for the beer that Tom passed her. 'Hey,' she said.

How We Got Here

Climate change has caused substantial damages, and increasingly irreversible losses, in terrestrial, freshwater and coastal and open ocean marine ecosystems (high confidence). The extent and magnitude of climate change impacts are larger than estimated in previous assessments (high confidence). Widespread deterioration of ecosystem structure and function, resilience and natural adaptive capacity, as well as shifts in seasonal timing have occurred due to climate change (high confidence), with adverse socioeconomic consequences (high confidence). Approximately half of the species assessed globally have shifted polewards or, on land, also to higher elevations (very high confidence). Hundreds of local losses of species have been driven by increases in the magnitude of heat extremes (high confidence), as well as mass mortality events on land and in the ocean (very high confidence) and loss of kelp forests (high confidence). Some losses are already irreversible, such as the first species extinctions driven by climate change (medium confidence). Other impacts are approaching irreversibility such as the impacts of hydrological changes resulting from the retreat of glaciers, or the changes in some mountain (medium confidence) and Arctic ecosystems driven by permafrost thaw (high confidence).

From IPCC Summary for Policymakers, 2022

Killaq

Killaq was curled up in her tiny bedroom in the prefabricated pod house she shared with her mother and brother. Her father had died in a work accident, many years ago; she barely remembered him. She was working on 'Bearing Witness', her climate blog. The plan was for a three-parter on the history of climate change: 'How we got here' was the provisional title. She scrunched her fists into her eyes. It was important to spell it all out, she knew it was, even though it was hard to believe that everyone didn't know this already. After the municipal council had had to abandon the Centennial Library, where Killaq had had a Saturday job when she was younger, because on bad days storm waves came crashing across the road and battered at the entrance? When whatever world news you streamed you saw governments building flood defences? When your inbox was filled with charity appeals for people dispossessed from low-lying lands?

She sighed and started making some bullet points. She would start back at the beginning of the century; she could find a Canadian government report or statistics, and then maybe an interview with a politician from the Age of Denial. Something pompous. Then some science, something to explain how methane in permafrost had turned out to be the crucial thing, the carbon source that risked tipping them all into irretrievable warming, bringing in its wake high sea levels, species extinctions, and refugees crossing and recrossing the globe in search of habitable lands. She checked her notes. It had been the MARS initiative, measuring methane by satellite from space, that had been the start of political awareness of the problem, back in the 2020s. And then (moving on to the second instalment) there had been the botched attempt to legislate for carbon risk, so she would drop in something from the Global Carbon Treaty from, when was it? She should know this. 2029, right, 2029. She drew a finger under her bullet point list. *Week three,* she wrote in mid-air with her finger, and underlined it with a wavy line. Would she attempt to tackle the infamous Schedule III which had tried to apportion carbon risk financially between nations? Too complicated for a weekly blog, she decided; that was a whole different story: how Canada and Russia had set up new independent states, the Arctic Nation and the Siberian Federation, supposedly in the name of devolution and indigenous rights, but actually to hive off the rising carbon cost of melting permafrost. Maybe she could do a separate article, get some interviews with some of the elders who remembered the old days.

She would deal with week three later. Now she started looking for imagery: news items from the early flooding events; documentary clips about sea level rise. And something for the heartstrings, to finish. Everyone knew the famous image of the last polar bear sinking in the open sea, but they knew it from the music video:

Killaq hunted around and found a contemporary documentary showing the same footage. She stripped off the cheesy commentary (they called the bear 'Biffy', for Christ's sake), and layered it in at the end.

Killaq sat back. To tell the truth she wasn't sure about this last polar bear thing. There were persistent stories, here in the North: no one had seen a bear themselves, but they had maybe met an old hunter who had seen one; or they had an uncle who, in a gathering snowstorm, had felt an unmistakeable looming presence; or someone had eavesdropped in VR on a community gathering in Siberia, and *they* had said ...

Forget about the bear. She had just time for some console time before supper.

/enter/DesertWarrior/

Ambra Di'capria lay across the sandstone boulder, the sun-warmed stone gritty under her stomach, and stared out over the plain. As far as her scope would focus was pale, whitish-brown, baked terrain and an overarching cloudless sky. Immediately in front of her the bluff fell away in a steep jumble of tottering, eroded boulders and far below she could just make out the serpentine trail that had brought her here, winding between bizarrely wind-carved rock towers and arches, to the foot of the uplands where she had started her long climb. Away in the distance she could see the ochre swirls of a sandstorm on the horizon, but it was distant enough not to worry about for now. Over the whole arid landscape nothing moved except some sort of carrion bird, a condor maybe, turning in slow circles in an updraft. There was no wind and the heat was punishing.

Her heads-up blinked, showing a red warning for heat exhaustion. She slid down from the boulder and huddled in a little patch of shade at its foot. It was still as hot but easier to endure, out of the direct sun. Beside the heat warning shone the thirst icon, steady red as it had been since the beginning of the ascent. There was no water on this high plateau. She pulled her sheish closer around her face, cutting out the glare in folds of muslin fabric. She wore the loose trousers, tunic and turban which marked her as a member of the Marahani Hesh and a hardened desert fighter despite her young age; her elongated limbs, exaggerated hips and waist, and sloe eyes pointed to an Accent ancestry, maybe, at any rate not human basic. A broad leather belt carried an array of pouches and hand-weapons, her crossbow was strapped to her thigh, and across her back was slung her great scimitar, Starmaker.

The scope had showed no sign of the Al-Siloch, but she knew it was following. Cautiously she raised her head from behind the boulder, keeping as low a profile as possible. Holding her breath she extended her scope out over the plain. The sky had darkened; as she watched a sandstorm came roaring towards her, already blotting out the furthest of the rock arches, and in front of it the ground roiled, heralding the approach of danger.

'Ah, plucky indigenous girl fighter takes on soil-eating monster,' said a sarcastic voice behind her.

She spun around. A figure was lazing against the nearest boulder. It was a young man in his twenties. He had thick dark hair and wide Inuit features, and he wore padded trousers and kamiks, high sealskin boots. A sealskin sleeveless jacket laced over his bare, hairless chest. It was her brother, Amaruq, in his usual stylised-Inuit body normal, and he was grinning in his particularly insolent irritating way.

'How *dare* you hack my VR!' she yelled. 'I fixed the access, after last time!'

'Can't outcode me, li'l sis,' he replied, still grinning.

'Never, never, never do that again,' she started, and then, finding that her voice had become squeaky and indignant and not befitting a hardened desert warrior, simply drew her crossbow and shot him. The image of Amaruq broke into fragments spinning across the sky. She watched for a moment, then, satisfied, turned back to the view from the bluff.

On the stony ground behind her a dot appeared. It looked like a raindrop on the dusty soil, although the air was as dry as ever. The dot started to widen, darkening the rock it had fallen on, until the whole surface shone with a black gloss like human hair. Next to it another dot fell and spread, covering pebbles and a long strip of gravelly sand in a pale flesh-colour. Another drop washed a crenelated boulder with mottled grey: it looked like fur: dark, short-cropped fur: sealskin. Percussively the dots fell on the landscape like rain and where they landed colour splashed and rippled, leaving a patchwork of black and pale colours, textured or smooth or bearing enigmatic jigsaw fragments of detail. It almost began to look as though a shape underlay the new colours of the soil and rocks: an outline: the shape of a man, sitting crosslegged. Then with a sudden shift in perspective the outline became three-dimensional. Sensing something, the girl glanced over her shoulder. 'I hate you!' she shouted, whirling round and reaching to draw Starmaker. Amaruq stood up out of the painted surface, shaking himself, and the girl lunged at him with the huge, curved blade.

'Shield,' said Amaruq, holding out a hand casually. In his fist appeared a long, oval shield, which met Starmaker's swing with a crashing impact. He moved forward in an ironic, exaggerated fighter's stance, holding the shield in front of him.

'You are so annoying!' The girl hefted her scimitar again, this time in a high two-handed grip. 'I am going to *kill* you.'

As she paused at the start of the downstroke the ground trembled. She hesitated. Little pebbles started to skip on the sandy soil, and then one of the larger boulders rocked. A huge gobbling noise filled the air. Over them loomed the vast bulk of the Al-Siloch, its octopus body towering into the air, its wide suckered tentacles gripping the edge of the bluff and its evil, intelligent eyes shining with a red light.

'Shit,' said the girl. She dropped Starmaker. 'Interrupt.'

The Al-Siloch froze in place, one thick tentacle still in mid-air.

'Now see what you made me do,' she complained. 'I am going to get terminated and I will *never* get to the end of this episode.' She stooped and picked up Starmaker from the dust.

'You said you were getting bored of Desert Warrior, anyway,' said Amaruq, still crouching behind his shield.

'Actually,' she said, complacently, looking down at her long legs and tiny waist, 'I quite like the Ambra character.'

Amaruq rolled his eyes. Then, quickly adjusting his expression, he held out his hand.

'Killaq. Ma sent me to fetch you. You can't stay in here forever. It's dinner time.'

'It isn't anybody's business how long I stay in here, and anyway there won't be anything I can eat.'

'Just murdered fellow creatures, right?' And then, as the girl's grip tightened on Starmaker, he added 'Actually, Ma said she made a bean casserole. Vegan. All the veggies from the co-op greenhouse.'

'I don't believe you. You told me that before, and it was walrus.'

Amaruq grinned. 'You liked it, though.' He jumped up on a boulder out of the way of Starmaker's scything blade.

'Come on, Killaq. Ma will be worried. And if all the rest of us have to forsake our cultural heritage and eat nothing but vegetables, you might as well be there to get the benefit.'

She looked at him untrustingly, then sheathed Starmaker in a single sweeping movement. 'All right, ok. But for Ma, not for you. And if it's walrus again I will *pulverise* you.' She brought up the end-of-episode menu, stopping only to add, as an afterthought, 'And I don't see what's so fucking *cultural* anyway about eating farmed walrus.'

/exit/

Killaq hit Open and the console lid swung up above her. She propped herself on an elbow and rubbed her eyes, looking down ruefully at her sturdy body in its black tracksuit. She missed Ambra's lithe strength and fluid movement; the swirl of the muslin headscarf; the feel of the desert sun on her skin. Here in Iqaluit, just south of the Arctic Circle, it was dark, and it would carry on being dark most of the day until the spring wore on, and gradually the dim midday sunlight would start earlier and last longer. That wouldn't be until after the clocks changed in March, though, and now it was still January, the dark of the year; the sun would rise only briefly in the middle of the day and illuminate the piled, drifting snow, the low windowless houses and the crashing waves in the bay. Killaq had never been anywhere else, outside of VR, and the long cycle of the year as it swung from darkness and snow to the light nights of summer was second nature to her, but VR gave her a taste of sunshine in the indoors days. She could never decide if that was a good thing, or not.

She perched on the side of the console, wriggling her toes, then stood up, looking around the little bedroom. It was a prefabricated unit snapped onto the side of the house. The whole house was made of units locked together: pod houses, they called them, standing on adjustable stilt legs, made to be taken apart and moved if the frozen ground they stood on became unstable. In the old days the town had been built on permafrost, solid as rock – you couldn't dig to bury a body or run a sewage pipe – but now unpredictable thaws were setting in, creating treacherous ice swamps that would pull you down if you tried to cross without flotation, and every year sinkholes opened up when unseen pockets of melting transformed the ground to rocky slurry. You could lose your dog, your car, a child even. Killaq's grandma had said that she remembered when the bay froze in winter all the way across, and the hunters' dogsleds used it as a quick crossing to find seal and walrus, but now the safe trade routes over the ice had vanished and the waves of the Arctic came right up to the town, even in the depth of winter. And though the ice was gone, in exchange there was much, much more snow, sometimes over the tops of the houses, so that the town was buried under it: white, heavy, lethal. That was when people stayed home and went sunbathing in VR.

She put the console on standby and padded through the corrugated pod link to the family room. Ma was there, a stout Inuit woman in her middle years with a cheerful expression, wearing one of the bright-coloured tracksuits that she always wore, and there was a White man too sitting at the kitchen table, a stranger.

'Killaq, this is Mr. Sanderson, from SAPA, and he is here in Iqaluit to meet some of the people, isn't that nice?'

'Please, call me Aubrey,' and the stranger stood up and held out a hand. He was an unprepossessing figure, slight and a bit stooped, with thinning curly hair and pale, protuberant eyes. He might be forty, Killaq thought, although it was hard to tell. He was wearing a sober corporate outfit, although hanging up were brand-new winter overtrousers and anorak, hired maybe, or bought new. The accent was British.

'Uh, hi,' said Killaq, nonplussed. Ma was setting out a coffee pot and the good china; Killaq sat down on the edge of a chair, wondering what was going on.

'Mr. Sanderson – oh, *Aubrey*,' said Ma, 'says that SAPA doesn't know enough about our culture and community in the North, and he is here on a fact-finding mission?' She looked at the strange man for confirmation.

The man cleared his throat. 'Yes, that's right, just part of our general outreach commitment. We try to interact with the lives of communities so that we in SAPA are aware of needs that may exist. We have quite an extensive grant-funding programme. It's – is it Killaq, did you say?'

Killaq nodded from behind her dark fringe.

'Well, Killaq,' the man said, drumming his fingers softly on the table surface, 'I wonder what you think of facilities for young people here in Iqla – Iqaluit? I bet you could tell us a thing or two about how things might be better, eh?'

His tone was off, somehow, the condescending question at odds with an intensity in the pale blue stare.

'It's ok,' said Killaq.

'Very loyal of you to say so, I'm sure, but there must be things you and your friends would enjoy? Recreational facilities? I was just telling your mother here that SAPA is considering Iqaluit for one of its medical assistance grants. We are often able to assist with upgrading medical facilities in areas where we are in land-partnership with the local administration.'

Killaq said nothing.

Ma reached for the coffee pot to interrupt the silence. 'More coffee, Aubrey?' She raised an eyebrow at Killaq behind the visitor's back.

Like most people Killaq kept her VR message link permanently open. Now the message icon flashed in the corner of her vision.

/Darknet/message/Amaruq/

Keep him talking till I get there.

What about???

God knows, ask him about SAPA, just keep him there. And give me audio and viz.

'Um, Mr. Sanderson,' Killaq blurted out.

He accepted a fresh coffee from Ma, and turned to her.

'Um, tell us about SAPA?'

Ma sat down with an expression of relief and refilled everyone's coffee.

'It's very gratifying that you should ask. Many people I am afraid are just not engaged, even though SAPA brings economic benefits to communities, almost without exception.' He turned his thin smile on Killaq. 'Only this week, in Australia – but you wouldn't be interested in that. What would you like to know?'

Ask him about land partnership.

Ask him yourself!

'I guess I wondered how SAPA got to be in the North, here. Didn't you start out in the Pacific?'

'Why, yes, Killaq.' He cleared his throat and took on a speech-making tone. 'You know of course that SAPA was the first of the great trans-governmental trade partnerships, commercial alliances overleaping the petty restrictions of nations to forge bonds based on benefit, mutual profit, freedom of trade.'

'And now you're a supra-state.'

'Exactly, SAPA is a body with the rights and status of a nation state, but based on commerce, not geography.'

But not democracy.

Shut up, I can't talk to you and him at the same time.

'You're quite right, of course, that we started out in the Pacific quadrant, that's where the name, the Sino-Australian Pacific Alliance, came from originally. But nowadays we consider ourselves to have a global remit. Here in the Arctic Nation we see the potential for involvement, to the benefit of course of communities. Look, perhaps I can show you what we have accomplished recently in Peru.'

The man drew a square shape in the air and one wall of the kitchen immediately vanished, to be replaced by a crisp view of attentive small children in smart pale-blue uniforms sitting in rows.

Nice image control, I wonder how much that costs.

Shut UP!

'This is an interactive recording, so you can ask the children about their experiences. Go on, think of a question. The interface will translate.'

Fortunately Killaq was saved from having to interrogate the images of Peruvian pre-schoolers. A chime sounded and the man looked momentarily vacant, accessing his messages online.

'I'm sorry, but I'm going to have to leave you, that was an urgent call which I have to take. Mrs. Nan- Mrs. Nanoortalik, thank you so much for your warm hospitality. I'm sorry I have to dash away, but I hope you'll come to the presentation I'm putting on in the Community Hall, just really to give everyone a flavour of what SAPA can offer and to allow people to ask questions.'

The Peruvian children vanished, leaving the kitchen wall looking somehow less real.

Shit, keep him there.

I'll try.

But two heavyset men had already appeared in the kitchen and were helping the man into his kapok anorak and overtrousers. It didn't seem to be gear he was familiar with. Then he was hustling out into the pod porch and his assistants were operating the outer door. There was a brief view of dark and wind outside and the landing lights of a VTOL personal transport. Ma hurried out to check the door seal after him.

'Well, that was a bit strange,' said Ma. 'And I wonder why SAPA is interested in the Arctic Nation all of a sudden. Not that many outsiders care much about our culture and what we need.'

She picked up the empty coffee pot. 'I do like a man who likes a nice cup of coffee, though.'

'Ma,' asked Killaq, warily, 'how come he was here in the first place?'

'Yes,' said Ma, 'I don't really know the answer to that. What he said was that his team at SAPA contacted the Council of Elders, and asked for the names of some typical households, because they wanted to talk to some normal people, for their outreach programme, SAPA I mean. And we were on the list he was given.'

Killaq hesitated.

'I wondered at him coming to talk to us like that. He seemed maybe quite important in SAPA. Did you see he had his own transport?'

'I guess maybe they all do, Ma, they live different lives from us.'

Ma paused from stacking the good china and came and put an arm around Killaq's shoulders. 'It was nice you could come and talk to him, little bird, I was glad you took the trouble. Sometimes I feel I don't know where you are for half the day.'

'That's the idea, Ma!' said Amaruq, leaning round the kitchen door in his outdoor gear and footwear.

'Oh, you! Take those boots off before you come inside! Where have you been? Have you eaten?'

Amaruq swung in, leaving his boots on, bringing a breath of wind and snow with him. 'No coffee left?'

'No, that Mr. Sanderson had three cups. You would have been interested to meet him, he's been telling Killaq all about SAPA.'

'I bet,' said Amaruq. 'Ma, after dinner, can I borrow Killaq? I need to talk to her.'

Amaruq and Killaq had a den, when they were small, only just old enough to use VR and far too young to have portal implants. Amaruq had made it, testing to its limits the kids' construction programme which was all he had had access to. They had kept it online, along with a lot of other childish forgotten stuff, although Killaq thought that Amaruq still tinkered with it sometimes; last time she had been there it had seemed somehow different. That was where they were now.

They sat under the overlacing wicker branches in the round hollow deep in a tangle of brambles, on a floor of moss, where they had played and argued and hidden many times. Shafts of light shone through chinks in the branches. Killaq was the dark-eyed five-year-old Inuit girl that she always was in this place, although she had added to the character each of her tattoos when she had first worn them: the tear-drop bracelets; the wide double V on her forehead; and the leaping orca. By her side was her Husky puppy, Ila. Amaruq was in body normal as he always was: she didn't think she had ever seen him wear a VR persona. He was questioning her about the SAPA man.

'Anyway, why do you care?' she ended up saying. 'It was a bit weird him turning up in the kitchen like that, but SAPA doesn't have anything to do with the North, really. I thought all that outreach stuff was just bullshit.'

'Look, Killaq,' Amaruq started, and then he hesitated, abandoning his usual bantering tone. 'There's stuff I have to tell you, sometime. I think SAPA are more of a danger than most of us know. Not just me, other people think that. I've been trying to keep you from being dragged in, but we might need your help.'

'Other people? Seriously?' Killaq laughed. 'What is this, a SAPA conspiracy theory?'

Amaruq laughed too. 'Maybe.' He held out a hand. 'I'll tell you sometime soon, if it doesn't get sorted out. Meantime, come hunting.'

Killaq disapproved of hunting and rejected its significance in Inuit culture with all her vegan heart. But this was a virtual hunt, something Amaruq and she had done together ever since she could remember. She took her brother's hand. The tightly woven branches around them vanished in a heartbeat, and they were in their dogsled, tearing across a white unbroken landscape with the wind in their teeth. The sun was brilliant in a clear sky and the dogs' sharp shadows raced alongside them. Killaq gripped the dogwhip in her mittened hand and felt that, of all the places she might call home, this was the place, here with the sway of the sled, and the clean sound of the sled-runners cutting through the new snow, and the boundless view before her to the far white horizon.

How We Got Here

And here we have the Arctic, this tremendous reservoir of natural resources, and are we saying that we should just leave these minerals in the seabed?

> But some people say, don't they, Minister, that the damage to the planet, if we exploit the Arctic, will be greater than we can repair in a lifetime, perhaps in many lifetimes?

Well, of course mistakes have been made in the past, but doesn't that mean we can learn from those? The technology, the human ingenuity which we can bring to bear on these problems – well, why shouldn't we have the capacity to use these resources, and do it in a way which won't hurt the environment we live in?

> Isn't it the case, Minister, that the methane locked up in the sea floor is said to be one of the most potent potential sources of atmospheric carbon enhancement? I have here some research published last week –

Well, Carlotta, for every great technological advancement there has always been someone sounding the note of doom. When railways were brought in they said that it would addle our brains if we travelled at more than twenty miles an hour! Have you been on a train recently? Is your brain addled?

> But Minister, this research appears to be saying –

Really, Carlotta, I'm surprised at a programme of your stature lending its voice to this sort of anti-prosperity agenda.

From British news archive, 20.4.25

Annie

Annie lay with her head on Tom's shoulder, drowsing and listening to the rhythm of the waves beneath them. It was mid-morning: high tide. A live-message icon chimed and she considered ignoring it; she was so comfortable here, watching the sunlight through the red and brown weave of the hanging blanket which separated their sleeping space. It was already hot.

/messages/connect/

Hey, Annie.

Then the link flickered and crashed. Shit. She sat up, running a hand through her hair, ignoring Tom rolling over sleepily into the space she had left. Most people accessed VR direct, through their portal, for messages and day-to-day tasks, but used a console for lengthy time away, say playing a game or joining a meeting. You were safer that way: the link was hardwired and everyone else understood that you were away from your body. Annie rolled herself lightly onto her toes and, pushing aside the red and brown blanket, walked naked across the communal space to the consoles on the back wall. No one else was up yet. She lay back on the cracked synthetic fabric of the console chair, scavenged in sections from city waste disposal and cobbled together, and hit access and ID.

/messages/reconnect/

Hey, Annie. I saw the protest last week. Looked good.

It was that bloke, the one whose Darknet character was some sort of Eskimo. Annie had come across him fleetingly in forums before.

Hey – she consulted the ID prompt – *Amaruq.*

D'ja have a long time in the tank?

Long enough!

You got time to talk about some stuff, SAPA stuff?

Well – she thought about rejoining Tom in the tangle of sheets, in the morning heat –

Never mind, take me surfing instead.

Surfing?

Despite herself Annie started to laugh.

You're in Oz, you go surfing, right? Take me with you!

What, now?

Now!

Well, hell, Annie thought. Why not? No one else was going to be up for hours yet.

I don't know about the link transfer, she warned him. *The upload may be a bit dodgy once I leave the console.*

I can fix that, sent Amaruq.

(Really? she thought).

No surfing anywhere near, take me a while to get there, she cautioned.

Give me a takealong link, give me a ping when you get there. Wherever there is.

Shit, Annie sent, *why not. Giving you viz and audio. Or no, wait, gotta put something on.*

Go as you are, said Amaruq.

Really? she sent. *Gonna get me arrested.*

/exit/portal link on/

You still there?

Told you I could fix it.

Annie crept out of the communal room and reached for her shortie wetsuit hanging on its peg over the stairs. Then she stopped. This was crazy. She tiptoed back into her bedroom area, where Tom had now rolled onto his back, deeply asleep. There was no point waking him. She grabbed a hat and drew off fresh water into a long pouch, then crept down the stairs and pulled her surfboard down from where it was stowed, clamped to the ceiling of the old kitchen. She must be insane. This Amaruq, he could be anybody. Fired with recklessness she floated her board out of the half-open roller door, wading alongside it. The heat of the full sun outside struck a fierce glare from the water surface.

There was no surfing at Double Bay, especially now that the littered ruins slowed the waves, and the tides rose sloshing into abandoned rooms. It would have to be the other side of the headland, where the South Pacific sent its rollers breaking on the first land for thousands of miles. Annie waded round the back of the house to the collapsed lean-to where their dinghy, the *Cleo,* was hidden, tied her board on at the back and shipped the oars. They had an outboard, too, that the group used for actions, but she wouldn't be able to justify the carbon cost – they had raging arguments as it was about whether the shock value of a protest could outweigh the use of a fossil fuel, even when the fuel had been stolen from the SAPA depot.

It was hot, crazy hot. Annie leant back into the stroke, feathering the blades expertly to take them around the corners of buildings and sunken obstacles. Suddenly the ridiculousness of her taking an Eskimo surfing struck her and she laughed out loud.

What?

Not much ice around here, arctic boy.

S'right, I'm getting my sunshine fix, just being here with you.

Yeah, right, sent Annie, and concentrated on rowing. Once she was clear of the houses she unshipped the oars and hoisted the small sail, taking the *Cleo* along the coast. An hour's untroubled sailing took her to the old lighthouse: this was a tourist spot and there would be nowhere to moor, but further back from the point there was a café cantilevered out over the cliff, where she knew the owner. Betty would let her tie up for a couple of hours at the little jetty, no questions asked.

/messages/Tom/

Hey girl, where d'ja go?

Took the Cleo, gonna catch some waves.

Didn't wait for me <sad face>

You were snoring!

She broke the link before he could ask her to give him viz. Somehow that felt complicated.

The afternoon sun caught the ripples in front of her as she paddled out, lying on the board, dipping one arm and then the other in an easy rhythm. It was second nature to her: the sea smell and the sun and the salt drying on the backs of her knees where the wetsuit ended. She sent her passenger a takealong ping – *Here now!* – but it seemed to her that he might have been there all along, or maybe somehow he didn't need the ping to catch up with her.

She got to the place where the waves were starting to break and waited, floating. Then she felt the swell live under her and the tug of the wave lifting the board and she turned and with two strong strokes sent the board forward, and then it was that moment and she swung her feet beneath her and stood up, fast and light, swinging up her arms and then tucking down into an easy surfer's stance as she shot down the whorled green side of the wave. Above and behind her the wave was already breaking and she carved her bottom turn, staying ahead of the wave crest, heading back up the wave, hitting the wave lip, shifting her weight in a white flourish of spray and cutting back down.

Wooo!

She allowed herself a smile. So, the Eskimo liked to surf. Then the next turn claimed her concentration.

They spent the afternoon riding waves. He was an easy companion: he didn't chatter, but she could feel his focus on the wave, and his elation at the speed and the spray and the fast movement. It was almost as if he was there next to her, or sitting on his own board watching her, waiting in the slow swell for his turn.

Finally she was tired. She sat with her legs hanging either side of the board, easily balanced on the swaying ocean.

So, you like?

Thank you, wave riding lady, I do.

Reckon you're the first surfing Eskimo?

Abruptly the link was dead. She tried to follow the meta-data back but there was nothing there.

/Darknet/reconnect/

Nothing. That was strange, it was as if he hadn't been there at all. She shrugged and leaned back on her elbows, looking up at the late afternoon sky. Then there was a shout in the distance and she peered towards the shore.

'Hey!'

It was Tom, dear Tom on his own board, with that powerful, lopsided paddle stroke, she would recognise it anywhere. She waved back and sat, idly watching him paddling out. Soon he reached the wave break and without pausing he duckdived beneath the oncoming wave and came up beside her, sweeping his long wet hair out of his eyes.

'Hey babe,' he leaned alongside to hug her, 'saw the Cleo at Betty's, knew I was on the right lines, you'd be here somewhere.'

'Crazy man, how d'ya get here?'

'Mostly walked, took me all afternoon. Reckoned I'd find you and we'd come home in the Cleo.'

'What if you didn't find me?'

'Have to walk back again!' He smiled at her. 'You been out here all by yourself?'

'Not quite.' She hesitated. 'I tookalong someone I knew, someone from the Carbon Free World group.'

'Oh, takealong.' Tom shrugged. 'S'not the real thing. Maybe you got audio and viz, but s'like a picture, s'not *surfing.* Might as well stay home and do it properly in VR.'

'Yeah,' she said, and tailed off. She was a bit uneasy. Now she came to think of it, it hadn't been like takealong, not like it usually was. Normally, you gave someone audio and viz, so they saw and heard what you were seeing and hearing, and they might message you, but it wasn't like you were aware of them being there. This time – she remembered Amaruq's reactions, she knew he had been surfing with her. That was impossible. When she got back, later, she would have a proper look at the link record – by rights she should be able to find the traceback and get his link ID. Something was weird.

'Never mind,' said Tom, 'gonna ride a few waves with your old man?'

She leaned over as if to kiss him, but then turned and, throwing herself forward, sent her board into the wave. 'Gotta catch me first!' she yelled over her shoulder.

Later that evening, after they had taken the Cleo home in the luminous dusk, and they were sitting cross-legged on cushions at home, eating Aleigina's stew with couscous, she told the others, 'Been surfing with an Eskimo today.'

'Ouch!' said Gina. 'Can't say that!' She swept her dark wavy hair over one shoulder.

'What can't I say?'

'Eskimo! They're Inuit, or, or I think there's some other names. Eskimo, it's like calling someone an Abo.'

'I read somewhere,' said Noah, who was into this sort of stuff, 'that the term was being reclaimed by the indigenous people.'

'Yeah,' said Gina, launching into the discussion, 'so it's probably ok for someone from the community to use it. Like if *you* used the word –'

'Don't even say it.'

Annie broke in. 'I don't suppose he's really an Esk- ok, ok, an Inuit. S' just his Darknet character.'

'Don't guess he liked it much, all the same.'

'Well hell,' said Annie, remembering the way the link had suddenly gone dark.

'Listen up, anyway,' said Gina, stacking stew plates. 'Noah got into a SAPA comms chain today. It's all broken up, it's reconstructed from a data dump, but you can hear what they're saying well enough. It's a bit disturbing. Noah and I thought we should take it a level up, to Group, see if we want to get involved.'

'It is the North,' Misha drawled, running a hand over the narrow plaits that covered his head. He had an eastern European accent, Polish maybe. 'We have enough work to do, here in the South. We cannot fight for the whole world. Even though it maybe needs fighting for.' He leaned back, improbably elegant in a leather jacket over his bare chest and worn-out jeans.

'Yes, but,' began Gina, but Noah broke in. His dark, chiselled face had an anxious expression.

'Just let them listen, Gina, then we can decide.' And, glancing around the group, 'Ok?'

'Here, listen. I'm sorry, I don't have viz.'

A crackly voice filled the room. It was a middle-aged man speaking; he had an Australian accent and a patrician tone.

'So, Aubrey, you old devil, did you get well in with the natives?'

'I think we might say we are making some progress, yes.'

The second voice was lighter, with a British accent.

'Wampum and tobacco, eh?'

'I think the community was persuaded of the benefits of the new hospital facilities, yes.'

There was a chuckle.

'How quickly can we move now, would you say?' said the first voice.

The recording cut off, but Noah held up a finger. 'Wait.'

'... bound to be a certain amount of resistance,' the light voice was saying.

'Nothing PR can't deal with,' said the first voice dismissively. 'If the Inuks don't like getting fucked in the ass then they should live somewhere civilised.'

Another break.

'... get down to brass tacks.' It was the first voice again. 'We've got the deal with Ardsen for the miners, but it's volume dependent.'

'Have legal got pipeline accesses sorted?'

‘They tell me it’s in place, if it isn’t I’ll hang ’em by the short and curlies. Everything depends on the methane market. That Sherborne, though, I don’t think he has the balls for the job. Talking to me about remediation. Remediation! As if anyone cares if there’s a huge fucking hole in the tundra.’

There was a snicker. Then the recording cut off.

There was a silence in the lamplit space. Underneath them was the sound of the sea washing in the deserted rooms.

‘Shit,’ said Tom. ‘Ardsen? That’s strip mining.’ Frowning, he shut his eyes and selected the search icon in his heads-up.

‘I don’t get it,’ said Annie. ‘What do we think they are going for? If it’s somewhere in the far North, far as I know all the mineral rights are owned by the Arctic Nation, or by the Russians.’

‘Or Finland,’ said Misha.

‘Permafrost, it’s permafrost mining,’ said Noah. ‘For methane. Like he said, it depended on the methane volume price.’

Annie looked at him, appalled. ‘But shit, the carbon cost, that’s astronomical.’

‘Right,’ said Gina. The lamplight shone on her crochet wraparound, striped in faded rainbow colours. ‘And illegal. They must have swung some deal with the World Court.’

‘All the rights of a nation, none of the responsibilities,’ Misha said in a sing-song voice. It was an anti-SAPA slogan from the early days.

‘Fuck you, Misha,’ said Annie, rounding on him.

'What is this, because it's in the fucking North it's not our problem?'

Misha leant forward and put a flame under his hookah. 'Annie, sweetheart,' he said, 'you know that I think it is all broken already.' He took a long draw. 'All we can do is enjoy the days that are left. I like to live here, with you lovely people. I like to protest, because it is, hmm, dangerous. It makes me feel alive, sexy.' He fixed her with his grey eyes. 'I have never believed that we can change anything. If SAPA are going to dig up half the north and let the carbon free, how will you stop them? You, with your little dress and your surfboard. Any of you?'

'I notice you don't say, any of *us*,' said Noah. Misha inclined his head, smiling ironically.

'Wait, look,' cut in Tom. He pointed, and an image filled the space between them. It showed a great machine in a barren landscape. It looked at first sight a bit like a combine harvester, but then the image focussed in on the slaved trucks swarming alongside, dwarfed by the machine, like beetles around a dead thing. This was much bigger than a combine. If you watched the image for a moment you saw the miner moving with terrible slowness over the rocky ground, relentlessly processing everything in its path and spitting out a slurry of waste. Behind it a long swathe had been carved out of the land, hundreds of metres deep, the dark churned track reaching into the far distance. The view zoomed in to the Ardsen logo, gold on a blue ground.

'Ardsen brings you the Dreadnaught,' said an enthusiastic voice. 'A kilometre long, the Dreadnaught offers new efficiencies in the world of mineral extraction. The ability to mobile-process on site and connect immediately to your supply chain will revolutionise your bottom line.'

Tom killed the infotorial.

'Shit,' he said. 'Just, shit.'

How We Got Here

Super-solid methane, locked up in remote locations – tundra; the floors of deep, cold lakes; the sea floor itself – this is the reservoir of climate-forcing gas which makes the earth system vulnerable to rapid temperature shifts. In recent years research has focussed on the workings of the so-called clathrate gun and the mechanisms by which, in the recent geological past, violent releases of methane from clathrate storage in all likelihood brought the earth's climate out of ice age conditions into the warm interstadial we enjoy today. Where next, was then the question? How much methane does the earth system hold in reserve and what is the risk of its release over the next two hundred years? The search for these answers is what led to the recent creation of the Whole Earth Methane Survey (WhEMS). Today we report on the latest results from WhEMS and the geopolitical and strategic dilemmas which these data bring in their wake. How must we prioritise the risks, increasingly focussed in the far North, of development on permafrost compared with deep-water mining, or of raft settlement compared to tethered ocean communities? More importantly, does the global community have the appetite for the exercise in restraint which may be urgently needed if the clathrate gun is not to affect all our futures?

From *Science Today* editorial, 2.9.26

Killaq

Killaq lay back and stared at the ceiling in frustration. She was trying to follow Amaruq in VR. Normally the privacy override and trace functions were no problem for someone of her coding ability: she had taught herself when she was twelve, eavesdropping on Annelie Phillips' corny virtual romances. She had told herself it was ok because Annelie was so intensely dislikeable, but even at twelve Killaq had had a practical streak, the ability to put aside conscience or convention if she wanted to get something done. In Amaruq the same trait was stronger, ruthless even.

One more try, she would give it one more try. She had expected strongly coded security and she knew a lot about how to deal with that sort of barrier. Amaruq's coding was challenging, but that wasn't the problem. It was as if the security itself, with its puzzles and hoops to jump through, wasn't actually the thing; even when she could open the doors, the links were tenuous, his whereabouts uncertain. It was like breaking through a gateway guarded by monsters and finding nothing on the other side but mist.

She called up her own cloaking functions – much good it would do her, she was sure Amaruq would know she had been testing his defences – and started the first sequence again. Half-way along, she paused. This particular manoeuvre, it had a kind of asymmetry. When she had been here before, she had been focussed on getting through. Now she paused. There was a, a sort of soft place, an overlap. She looked more closely. It looked like nothing, like a duplication in the code. Amaruq never duplicated his code. Ah. She leaned on the soft place. There was nothing there. Suddenly out of instinct she summoned up all her sense of her brother and called to him.

'AMARUQ!'

She fell whirling into the dark and landed hard, face-down on gritty soil. All around her was crashing noise, the sound of a massive explosion. She cowered, terrified, arms shielding her head; this didn't feel like VR. It was cold, very cold, and her arm hurt where she had fallen on it. Then there was the sound of gunfire.

'Amaruq!' she screamed. 'Help!'

There was a hand on her shoulder. She opened an eye. She couldn't see anything. Then flaring light filled the sky. In the brief instant before it was dark again she saw the face of an Asian soldier, looking drawn and mud-stained.

'God and all his fucking angels, Killaq,' said the soldier. 'What are you doing here?'

Abruptly the battle scene vanished and she was in a white space. She cradled her bruised arm, sobbing. Gradually she regained her self-possession and her sobs abated. She tried to make sense of where she had been, of that brief, violent fragment of experience, but with no success. Then she tried to look around, but there was no around to look at. It was just white, like the white there was in a construction programme before you started building, except that in that case you would have come with a toolbox; here it was just white. She started to panic: maybe she had fallen into some loop in Amaruq's code and she would be trapped here and her body in its console would fail and after some immeasurable time in whiteness she would just go out like a candle when her body died and no one would ever know.

Calm down, calm down, she told herself. They would put your body on life support. Anyway that isn't going to happen because Amaruq will come looking for you. She couldn't shake off the image, though, of Ma looking sorrowfully down at the unconscious girl in the console. When I get out of here, she thought, I will be a better person, I will spend more time with Ma.

After another while she started to be bored. She tried to sleep but it didn't seem to be possible. If she shut her eyes it was still just white. She wondered how long she had been away. It was impossible to get an idea of time passing. Maybe it had been a long time already. Her panic started creeping back.

At this point a black dot appeared on the white in front of her. She was so bored and frightened by now that she was captivated by the dot. Slowly it elongated and became a rough-edged mark, like a line drawn by a child with a black crayon. The line swept up and around, making a circle. Then the circle hinged open and a figure appeared crouching in the doorway. It was a dark, scribbled shape, as if the child had coloured in an outline of a person but had not been too careful about keeping its crayon inside the lines. It swung its legs down and pushed the circle shut behind it. The door vanished. Killaq tried to shrink back but there was nowhere to retreat to. Then the figure shook itself and it was Amaruq.

'Amaruq!' Killaq ran to him, but he held his arms to the side and wouldn't return her hug. A little roughly he pushed her away.

'Sit down, Killaq.' A chair appeared behind her. Obediently she sat.

'Do you mind telling me, sis, why the *fuck* you apparently thought it was a good idea to follow me into a war zone? You put us both in danger. I had no idea you knew that level of code.'

'I don't,' she faltered. 'I'm sorry. I was seeing if I could track you, just as an exercise, I didn't think I would be able to. I'm sorry, I know I shouldn't have.'

She looked up at his cold, frowning face. 'I was afraid!' she said. 'What was that place? And then you left me here, for hours and hours, and I thought I was lost and I would never get home and I would *die* in my console.' She started to cry again.

'Oh, Killaq,' said her brother. He came across to her and put his arms around her, and she buried her face in his chest and kept on crying.

'Look,' said Amaruq, after a while, 'I want you to *promise* me that you will never follow me like that again.'

'I promise,' came the choked, tearful voice.

'Seriously?'

'Seriously, truly, I promise. But –'

'*But* what?'

'But, I'm not a little girl any more. You can tell me stuff.'

Amaruq sighed. 'If that's the price of not having you drop into takealong with some Korean soldier who doesn't know you exist, then yes, I will tell you some stuff. But not here.'

He held Killaq away from him and said 'Home.' She opened her eyes and looked up at the inside of the console lid. The time-away counter was just coming into the red.

'Killaq,' said Ma, putting her head round the door. 'Good, you've finished working. Come with me, I want some help with the display for the craft fair.'

Amaruq was away from home for three days. Ma never worried, even though it was February and a windstorm had been raging all week. She said it was natural for a young man to be out and about with his hunting buddies. Then on the Thursday he showed up, looking cheerful, wearing his snow boots into the kitchen.

'Ma,' he said, hugging her, 'Killaq. Come and eat poutine.'

'Oh you,' said Ma, laughing. 'Whoever wants to go and eat poutine in this weather. I doubt the Shack is even open.'

Killaq was on the point of saying that poutine wasn't vegan. The chips were probably cooked in animal fat and the curd cheese was obviously a dairy product and who knew what was in the brown gravy. She looked dubiously up at Amaruq.

'Come on, sis!'

She did want to make it up to Amaruq. Maybe she could get them to leave off the cheese. She got up and started putting on her heavy outdoors gear.

It was dark outside, and even though she knew to expect it, outside the gale hit her like a body blow. She staggered and Amaruq caught her arm, steadying her.

'I've got the truck,' he yelled above the howl of the wind.

'What?'

'The truck!'

He dragged Killaq into the lee of the building. You could breathe a little better here, and the snow was less deep; on the other side, the wind side, it had drifted and been blown nearly up to the roof. What he called his truck was parked there: it was a solid, low-slung all-terrain with fat tyres and a winch for getting out of difficulties. Some of the original red colour still showed between the dents and scrapes. Snow was already plastered along the windward side.

'Get in!'

Killaq leapt in, laughing, covered in snow. With the heavy door shut you could hear yourself think again. Amaruq was already gunning the motor, forcing the vehicle backwards over a drift of snow. Then they were in the road and with a momentary skid he started off cautiously down what would be the middle of the street if any of it was visible. Even with the powerful high beams on they could only see driving snow ahead. Amaruq turned on navigation but kept driving control on manual.

'Ok, where are we really going?' said Killaq.

Amaruq turned on her a face of injured innocence. 'To eat poutine, of course.'

Killaq just smiled. 'Have it your own way.' But after ten minutes of the truck slithering through deserted streets, and one bad moment when the wind hit them from both directions at a crossroads and Killaq thought that even the solid all-terrain might tip up and be blown over, Amaruq pulled up and killed the growling engine. Peering out Killaq thought it did look like they were at the Poutine Shack, although snow was covering what was usually a flight of steps leading up to the door. There was a light showing.

'Door'll be open. You go – I'm going to put an anchor in. Wait, I'll help you get out.'

Killaq couldn't open her door from inside against the pressure of the wind. She waited for Amaruq to grope his way around to her side and put his weight on the handle. The door flew open and brought the roar of the outside into the cab. Killaq tightened her hood around her face and stumbled into deep snow. Somewhere under here were the steps. Half-crawling, braced against the wind, she floundered up them and banged on the door. Amaruq was already behind her. He threw the door open.

Inside it was quiet, although the wind was shaking the little café and making the walls creak and tremble. It was fuggy and warm. A brazier glowed in the middle of the room, and the six plastic tables were lit by soapstone oil lamps, each sending up a greasy dark spiral of smoke. Outside the wavering circle of light cast by each lamp the room was dark. The generator must be down.

/connection not available/

No VR, either. There were no other customers, but Jean-Louis, the owner, was calmly drying a tumbler behind the counter. He was a solidly built White man in his early forties, with a stained apron around his broad waist and long dark hair kept back with a leather tie.

'Tabernac!' he said. 'This weather! What're you having? The choice is poutine, or poutine.'

'We didn't think you would be open,' said Killaq, taking off her mitts and heavy outer jacket.

'Hah!' said Jean-Louis. It seemed he was about to say something else, but he vanished behind the counter and came up with two plates. 'Electric is off, but I had the fryers on earlier. Been keeping these warm for you with the back-up battery, Captain.'

Amaruq raised an eyebrow but took a fork from the mismatched collection in a mug on the table and dug into his poutine. 'Ah,' he sighed, 'this is the stuff!' Killaq poked dubiously at hers. Chips with curd cheese and brown sauce: this was the legacy of French Canada in the North. It was hot, glutinous and greasy, and the cheese ran into the sauce so that she couldn't separate them. She extricated a few chips from the bottom of the pile where the sauce hadn't reached and made an attempt at eating. After a minute she gave up.

'Why did you call him Captain, Jean-Lou?' she asked. Jean-Louis looked at Amaruq, who gave an almost imperceptible shake of the head. 'Just my way,' Jean-Louis said.

'Men!' thought Killaq. It would be some boys' secret they had, something to do with hunting or liquor running. She got up to go to the ladies, leaving her poutine uneaten on the table. The toilets were chilly and by the time she had struggled out of her overtrousers and back into them again, she was glad to head back to the stuffy warmth of the restaurant. Amaruq's plate was clean and hers had vanished. Jean-Lou was sitting in the chair where she had been. Both men were leaning over the table, talking softly; their expressions were grim. As she watched Jean-Lou passed a small package over to Amaruq who without looking at it stuffed it in a pocket of his overtrousers.

'Ready to go?' Amaruq asked her. He slapped Jean-Louis on the shoulder and he and Killaq started getting back into their outside clothes. 'Thanks for staying open for us, man. First class poutine!'

'Best in the Nation,' Jean-Lou replied.

When they were back in the truck Killaq asked Amaruq what had been in the package. 'Oh, nothing,' he said. He had the grace to look sheepish. 'Actually, don't tell Ma, but Jean-Lou asked me to keep some episode records for him in hardcopy. His wife wiped them off the console at home.'

'What,' said Killaq, 'porno stuff?' She turned up her nose.

'Don't ask *me*,' Amaruq said, as he gunned the heavy engine and set the truck in motion, fishtailing out from the snow-covered parking lot. 'Really, don't ask me.'

How We Got Here

Delegates today celebrated the first meeting of the Council of the Sino-Australian Pacific Agreement (SAPA). 'This is a great step towards maintaining the friendship and co-operation of our two great nations,' said the appointed Secretary, Mr. Zhang Quiang (pictured, left, with Trade Secretary Amos Reece-Findart). 'Now in the Year of the Metal Dog, and for many years to come, trade will flow and wealth will be created unrestrictedly between us, and prosperity will flourish without the hindrance of nationalist agendas.'

moneynews.com, 24.2.30

#SAPA set up today to overrun our democratic freedoms and allow big business to rule our lives.

@tellitlikeitis, 24.2.30

Annie

/connect/forum private message/Amruk/

Hello? Amruk? Are you there?

/connect/Amaruq/

Amaruq? Are you there? I need to tell you something, something urgent. It's about SAPA. I can't put it on open link. Can you get in touch?

/reconnect/Amaruq/

Amaruq, been trying to find you. I need to talk to you badly. It's about SAPA. My group don't know I'm trying to contact you. Please get in touch?

/reconnect/Amaruq/

Amaruq, please get in touch, it's important.

/reconnect/Amaruq/

Amaruq? I'm sorry I called you an Eskimo.

How We Got Here

English

The States and Supra-States party to this Treaty,

> *Affirming* the need to deal justly with the cost of the climate remediation works needed for the continuance of the prosperity of nations and the survival of the planetary environment, to the benefit of all;
>
> *Declaring* their resolve each to bear a proportionate share of those costs taking into account both the wealth of the State Party or Supra-State Party and the share of Carbon Risk arising from that Party's territory or activities;
>
> ...
>
> *Have agreed as follows:*
>
> ...

Article 3

Each State Party and each Supra-State Party shall contribute to the Global Carbon Fund annually a proportion of that Party's GDP calculated in accordance with the formula set out in Schedule II hereof and based on the Carbon Risk identified by the WhEM Survey in its most recent iteration at the time of payment.

From the Global Carbon Treaty, 2029

Killaq

She had thought they were going to the den, but when Killaq opened her eyes she was on a beach. She squinted against the strong sunlight. She was sitting on flat, rippled sand, which stretched either side of her as far as she could see, and in front the waves ran in to the land, curling and crashing in synchrony. She thought she could smell the salt, but that couldn't be right, there was never any smell in VR.

She looked down at herself. The little Inuit girl looked wrong in this setting. Bringing up the menu she ran through a list of personas. She didn't have a regular character which was any good for the seaside; maybe she would have to make one. In the meantime she chose Librarian Girl and conjured up a blanket for her to sit primly on with her straight skirt and her seamed stockings. She took off the pale grey heels with their little button detail and lined them up neatly next to her on the blanket.

Amaruq pulled himself out of the waves and came wading in to the shore. He shook himself and he was dry. He was wearing the same laced sealskin jerkin and trousers as always, but in concession to the beach setting he had made the trousers end in a ragged line at knee-height, and his feet were bare. A tattooed line of curling script, Inuktitut syllabics, ran from his ankle bone up the side of each shin. Killaq thought that she couldn't remember when she had last seen Amaruq's feet bare, not since they were kids, she guessed.

'Hey, sis. Don't you own a bikini?'

'Very funny. What are we doing here?'

'Well,' said Amaruq, suddenly looking less confident, 'I'm learning to surf.'

Killaq leaned back on her elbows and threw her head back and laughed.

'You? Surfing? Like there was any sea within a thousand miles of us that you could go in without freezing!'

'No,' said Amaruq, sounding uncharacteristically earnest, 'just here in VR. See, I got it wrong the first few times, I didn't realise there was a difference between the different boards. This one,' – now he was leaning on it – 'this is a Fish, but I think it's not really a beginner's board.'

'Wait,' said Killaq, 'you're really learning? Experientially?' VR could give you the learning environment to pick up any sport, but unless you wanted to do it for real outside VR most people just loaded a programme that gave you some fancy moves. Experiential learning was the no-shortcuts version which allowed you to transfer your skills and muscle memory to the outside world.

'Well, you know what Ma always says.'

'If something's worth doing, it's worth doing well,' Killaq chorused.

Amaruq shrugged. 'That's what I thought.' He held the board out and it vanished. 'Listen,' he said, sitting down on the blanket in a quick, springy movement, 'I said I would tell you what all that was about, the time I fished you out of my code last week.'

'The time you left me in a loophole for hours to punish me, you mean.'

'You weren't there for hours, it just felt like it, and how did you get there in the first place, Miss? Maybe next time I'll leave you there.'

Killaq turned her back on him and sat looking along the beach. Not much attention had gone into it; she could see where the ripple pattern repeated. Amaruq nudged her with his shoulder.

'You want me to tell you about it, or not?'

Killaq carried on looking along the beach. There was a faint blur where the beige sand ran into the horizon. Amaruq leaned around her and looked up into her set expression.

'Never mind,' he said, and swinging himself onto the other side of the blanket he started piling sand onto her feet, seamed stockings and all.

'Hey! Stop that!'

'You speaking to me now?' he asked, carefully squaring the corners of the sand pile. It was going to be a fort, Amaruq always built forts. Killaq wriggled her feet and the pile collapsed.

'All right,' she said. 'But I'm still cross with you.' Amaruq came back to her side of the blanket and she leaned on his shoulder.

'See,' he said, 'I have been trying to work out how to take your consciousness with you into VR.'

This wasn't what she had expected. She looked at him, startled. The belief that you could live, permanently live, in VR was the province of lunatics on forums and conspiracy theorists who insisted that the government – or the World Court – or a secret hereditary ritual society – already knew how to do this but were concealing the knowledge from everybody. No one sensible gave this any credit. The phenomenon of consciousness was very well researched, but whilst the areas of the brain that produced the sensation of self had long ago been mapped and indeed could be manipulated, no one had succeeded in creating a truly aware observer, or in moving anyone's awareness to any other location than their own brain. It was beginning to be said that in some way which wasn't yet understood, consciousness was an organic property which would never be replicated digitally.

'I know,' he said, with a wry smile. 'Fruitcake stuff, right? But I think people have been looking at it the wrong way.'

'Fruitcake stuff, all right,' said Killaq, who was beginning to lose her patience, 'and what does that have to do with that battle scenario I fell into, and that soldier, was that you?'

'Wait, wait. I have to explain it from the beginning. Bear with me, li'l sis.'

Killaq folded her arms in a long-suffering way. For this she was using her console time-away allowance. First *surfing,* and now this.

'Ok,' he said. 'How VR started, it was all about games, interactive games on a physical screen, wasn't it. And those original coders got better and better at making the detail of their scenarios realistic, but the person playing the game was on the outside, controlling it with, I don't know, little switches and things.'

Killaq knew this already. She probably knew more about the history of VR than he did.

'So then the next stage was that they learned to make better sensory information, and those first scenario builders used a visor, or a helmet, to give the wearer the impression of viz and audio, like little kids do now.'

'Like Ma still does.'

'Like Ma still does,' Amarúq agreed. 'And then they located the sensory reception areas in the brain, and learned to build an upload portal, implanted in the body, so that the digital world could be experienced directly, uploaded directly to the brain's sensory input, so that it would feel like the person was actually in the digitally coded scenario, at least as far as audio and viz went, and we all started using VR for all our messaging, and watching subscriber narratives, and everything.'

'Yes,' said Killaq. 'Is there a point to all this?'

'Don't you see, sis? So far, it's all been about making the sensory experience of VR faster and more interactive and more creative and sexier, but the person experiencing it is still living inside their own brain, and the fact that VR exists at all is just a way of extending that person's senses, it's just another remote, really. And you can't change that by making VR itself better. At the end of the day the whole experience of VR is down to the console interface.'

'The roots that net the dreaming head,' said Killaq, using a phrase that often came up when people were talking about the reliance of the VR industry on hardware and portal implant technology. She didn't know where the phrase came from.

'Yes, yes,' said Amaruq, 'but look.' He picked up a stick and drew a line on the sand. 'This, this line, is the portal interface. And here, on this side, is the organic brain,' – he drew a circle – 'and *here*, on the other side, is VR.' He drew a square. 'Now look.' The line became a piece of black cord. Amaruq picked it up and rearranged it on the other side of his VR square, meticulously tucking in the ends to make a curve. 'You aren't moving the consciousness, you're moving the interface.'

Killaq looked at the cord and the symbols doubtfully. 'I don't think I really understand what that means. And if I did understand it, it *must* be impossible to do, to do for real, I mean. Mustn't it?'

'That's just it,' said Amaruq. 'I've been experimenting.'

Killaq was beginning to be uncomfortable. All this was a long way from the Amaruq she knew and trusted. She had heard of people having psychotic episodes after too long in VR; it was one of the dangers everyone got harangued about in school. She looked intently at him, but he seemed completely normal.

'Look, ok,' she said, 'but what has this got to do with the soldier? And then I have to go.'

Amaruq grinned. 'You think I'm losing it, don't you? Can't blame you, sis, sometimes I think I'm crazy myself.' He pulled a ferocious crazy face, sticking out his tongue and bugging his eyes. She threw a handful of sand at him.

‘Ok, enough about the theory of consciousness. So what I have been doing, to try and find out more about this, is working with, ah, with surrendered rights, I bought some surrendered rights. On the Darknet.’

Killaq leapt up. ‘Snuff gaming? Is that what that was?’ She was truly horrified.

‘Sis, sis, calm down.’ He took one of her hands, pulling her back to sit back down next to him, but she wrenched her hand away. ‘Look, I’m trusting you with this. At least hear me out.’

‘Snuff gaming, I can’t believe it.’ She looked at him in distress. ‘I’m going home now, right away. I’m going home and I’m going to tell Ma.’

First world countries and supra-states had largely automated their military capacities. In Australia, say, to announce that you were joining the army probably meant that you were a games theorist, a tactician, a psychologist, or a specialist in the pathology of airborne diseases. You would be unlikely to be an infantryman. All around the world, however, warfare continued between lesser nations, rebel groups and religious affiliations, and those brutal, small-scale conflicts were fought by human soldiers. It was a natural step for Darknet programmers in the mid years of the century to send agents to persuade those soldiers, in exchange for sums that were worth a year’s pay in the local currency, or for ill-defined promises of asylum for widows and families, to have an upload portal fitted or upgraded so that the soldiers’ experience – maybe, their death – could be used as material for online battle scenarios. This was, of course, illegal almost everywhere.

'I'm going home,' Killaq repeated. She raised her hand in a gesture of warding off, of revulsion, and brought up the exit menu from her heads-up.

'Wait,' said Amaruq, and then, holding his own hand out palm forward, 'Wait!' Killaq's arm, with its librarian's puffed sleeve and little pearl button, froze and was held immovably in place. She couldn't load the menu. She tried to bring up the online escape option, the panic button that was always there, but there was nothing.

'You can't do that!' Killaq yelled at him. 'Let me go!'

'Will you listen to me now?' Amaruq asked. He had a distant, impersonal look.

'Yes, yes, I'll listen to you, just let me go!'

Suddenly she could move again. She stood, rubbing the arm that had been frozen, although there was no pain, looking at him untrustingly.

'Sit down, sis.' He looked up at her with a half-smile. 'Please?'

Killaq made herself a different blanket and sat down facing him, knees neatly together, tucking her feet underneath her and smoothing her straight skirt. She wrapped her arms around herself and watched him from behind her fringe. She had never felt afraid of Amaruq before. Now she wished she had her thigh crossbow with her, or better, Starmaker. This was his scenario; she doubted she could call for them without his seeing it. Very cautiously she brought up the first menu.

Amaruq sighed and put his head in his hands. Without her having called for it, Starmaker appeared on the sand before her, complete with leather shoulder harness.

'Look, sis, I'm sorry. I didn't mean to twist your arm. It's just, this is important, and if you won't listen to me, who will? Have Starmaker, make yourself safe, leave whenever you want to. I won't force you, I was wrong to try.'

Killaq slowly reached out and put her hand on the scimitar's familiar, well-worn grip. Gradually she let go of the librarian persona and let herself become Ambra, the alteration flowing over her as the prim kitten heels changed to Ambra's tall thigh-boots, stained with the dust of innumerable journeys. Like a wave riding in to the beach and turning the dry sand dark, a wash from a different colour palette swept over the dove-grey skirt and cream blouse, and then she was wearing Ambra's wine-red tunic and her hair wound itself back into the narrow braids which went under the muslin turban. She sat at ease now, more athletic, fearless, clasping the ankle of one leg bent in front of her, the other leg stretched out on the sand. She checked. Her escape button was back. She sheathed Starmaker, looking at Amaruq warily.

'I'm going home now. Don't try to stop me. Give me a link to this place, and if I feel like it after I get home, I'll come back and you can explain whatever it is that you think you want to explain to me.'

'Ok,' said Amaruq, humbly. He handed her a conch shell, the size of his palm, white and turreted on the outside, its pearlescent pink interior smooth as a lake at sunset. 'Here's your link. Hold it to your ear: you can hear the sea. It will bring you back here.'

'But I don't guarantee to *be* here,' he added, sounding more like his normal self, 'depending on how long you decide to take.'

Killaq just shook her head.

/exit/

Killaq wandered into the kitchen. It would do him good to wait for her a bit, serve him right. Ma was watching the news on a 3-D projection focussed over the kitchen table.

'Will you look at this,' she said. A squat Asian man in a military uniform was standing at a lectern, gesticulating. Behind him a banner bore unfamiliar lettering. Killaq pointed at the lettering and the translation interface supplied the words in Roman script.

'Democratic People's Republic of Korea'

'The Great Step North'

The view shifted to soldiers parading in a square. Ma looked troubled.

'They're saying that the Koreans, the North Koreans, have announced that they have ancient territorial rights in the North.'

'Same as we do,' said Killaq, flippantly.

‘Well, no,’ said Ma. ‘Not like we do. They want land, of course, all theirs is getting flooded.’ Ma looked thoughtful. ‘The Siberian Federation will never just give them a Northern Homeland, just because they say that their ancestors came from there, thousands of years ago. War in the North, that’s what it will come to.’ She hoisted herself up, puffing, and began to lay the table for dinner.

How We Got Here

[The view is of empty ocean in a flat calm. The sun is low on the horizon. Occasional patches of floating white might be ice fragments. The shot narrows until we can see a V of travelling ripples. It is a bear, swimming slowly, with only its snout above the water. As we watch the bear stops swimming and starts to sink. With a struggle it raises itself to the surface again and swims for another few strokes. Then it lifts up its muzzle for a last breath and lets its head fall beneath the water. The camera watches the white outline becoming indistinct under the waves.]

Well, viewers, what a sad moment. As our regular signers-on will know, our camera drone has been following Biffy, who was tagged by Enviro volunteers two years ago and has been believed to be the last wild polar bear in existence outside of zoos and DNA programmes. These bears evolved to hunt on the ice and with the last remnants of the Arctic ice now gone, the bear's habitat has gone with it. Inevitable maybe, but today we mourn the passing of a species, never to return to its free wilderness life.

[Melancholy music]

From Wilderness World, 'The Far North' special programme, December 2054

Annie

The edge of the heavy bolt cutters cut into the palm of her hand as she leaned her full weight on them. Then the wire gave and another strand was gone. Next one. She could hear Tom breathing next to her in the darkness. Misha was supposed to be behind them with the trolley generator and the searchlight. She leaned again into the bolt cutters.

This was the perimeter fence of SAPA con 17, one of its Australian research establishments, and the idea was to paint the façade with a repeating slogan, 'Hands off the South.' The images themselves would last only seconds before SAPA security found the breach and arrested the activists, but the instant upload of the action would go viral in VR. They hoped.

It would be easy, of course, to upload footage of the con 17 building overlaid with a slogan, without ever going near it. 'The whole thing is entirely pointless,' Misha had said, laconically, drawing on his hookah. 'Of course I will be there with you.' But for her group, for her and Tom, the physical side of the action, the physical risk, was essential, an article of faith. You could say what you liked on forums, but the only true protest was to put the body in harm's way, to walk the walk.

Another strand gone. There was an unpleasant smell in the hot night, something rotting in the bramble-filled ditch they were crouching in. 'Misha!' she hissed. 'Misha!'

'Can't see him,' Tom muttered next to her. 'I'll go back.'

'Shit, that fucker,' Annie whispered, before putting all her strength into the next strand. Tom abandoned his own cutters on the ground by the fence support where he had been working and slid away. The strand gave under the pressure of the heavy jaws. Annie moved to the next one. Then she froze. There was a light coming towards her, a circle swinging backwards and forwards on the ground, the flashlight of a perimeter guard. Annie took a shallow breath and ducked her head down. She was wearing camo body paint which hid her heat signature, but if he came close enough to see the broken strands, it would be hopeless. She could hear his feet on the gravel the other side of the fence, a slow casual stride. A routine patrol. Now he was close enough that the flashlight played briefly over her bodypainted arm and she could hear him humming wordlessly in the back of his throat. Annie held her breath. The flashlight swung over her and the heavy footsteps came by, very close, not stopping. She thought he was past. She risked a look. There he was, already two steps beyond her. She risked breathing out. The guard carried on, his boots crunching in his slow stride, the far away compound lights shining faintly on the wicked black neutraliser slung by his side. Annie started slowly to reach for the cutters.

Then the guard stopped. He held up his head, listening. 'Received,' he said, aloud. 'Standing by.' There was the sound of an engine in the distance. The guard turned towards the fence, his hand reaching to his side. Annie shrank away, heart beating. He was too close, if she ran now, he would shoot her. The guard started scanning along the base of the fence, flashlight painting the ground. She would have to run anyway. Now, now, no, wait. The vehicle she had heard was pulling up with a screech of brakes, scuffing the gravel. It was a squat truck. The guard went over to the driver's side and talked through the window. She couldn't hear what they were saying. She started to move her exposed arm back underneath her. She shifted her weight back. Her foot squished in something in the bracken-filled gully. The driver was getting out. She slithered back, excruciatingly slowly, still keeping low. The further back she could get before they saw her, the better. The two men went round to the doors at the rear of the truck. She moved back again. Now she was crouched in the bottom of the gully. She couldn't see what was happening. Then she heard the clang of the truck door opening. All of a sudden there were barks. Dogs, shit. She got her weight on the balls of her feet, poised to scramble out of the other side of the ditch and run. Then everything happened at once. There was a dog, a big attack dog, squeezing through the half-hole that she and Tom had made, and Tom was by her side, shouting, pulling her up the bank, and there was a bright light, painfully bright, and then she was up the other side and the dog was through behind her and she was running along the perimeter road and she couldn't see, it was black dark, and suddenly the dog was on her, its teeth were in her thigh, and she yelled with the pain and fell down, shielding her head with her hands, and the dog was on top of her, snarling. Then there was a noise and the dog went limp and there was Tom, no, it was Misha, pulling the dog away and she tried to get up but there was blood everywhere and her leg folded under her and then someone had his arms under her armpits and was dragging her, it was Tom, he hoisted her in a fireman's lift, and they were running, running, and behind them were shouts and lights. Finally they were at the edge of the dead ground that surrounded the facility and there were buildings here and Tom eased her down.

'Can't stay here,' said Misha crisply. He looked awake, his cynical manner abandoned, his eyes shining.

Tom looked around wildly. Behind them the shouts were getting closer. 'You shot the dog?' he said.

'Come *on*!' Misha replied. He stooped by Annie, arranging her arm over his shoulder. 'I'll take one side,' he said. 'You can't carry her like that for long. She's hurt.'

'He shot the dog,' said Tom, incoherently, but he bent down and took Annie's weight, gripping Misha's forearms, holding her between them. They started to shuffle down the street.

'Ah,' said Misha, looking at the manhole cover on the corner. 'Got it.'

A long time afterwards they were sitting in the lamplight with Noah and Gina, back at Double Bay. Tom was leaning back on one of the VR consoles, holding Annie against his chest, and Noah was frowning in concentration as he cleaned and disinfected the ragged wound in her thigh and sutured the long oval tear made by the dog's teeth. Annie was semi-conscious, knocked out by a shot of something Noah had produced from his illicit medical kit, but awake enough to moan and turn her head into Tom's shoulder when what Noah was doing sent sharp stabs of pain through the injured leg.

'So you hid in the sewers,' Gina was saying. 'And what, you came home that way, underground?'

'It didn't go anywhere, not anywhere that a person could get through. We just waited as long as we could, all day. We needed it to be dark again before we tried coming out. To start with we could hear them walking overhead but then it seemed to die down. So in the end Misha gave it a go, and we all came up like rats out of a trap, and limped along until we could get far enough away to call for help.'

'It was horrible,' said Misha, looking over the top of his hookah. He had managed to clean himself up and was back in his leather jacket and jeans. 'Never again do I want to have to cross a residential suburb with a girl that can't walk, and all of us covered in crap from the sewer and the remains of camo body paint. Every time there was a camera we had to go into the Darknet and make it safe, or try to. It took forever. And my cigarettes were ruined.'

'Actually, man, I know it was you that shot the dog, but we couldn't have made it through there without you. So, you know, thanks,' said Tom.

'Yes,' said Misha, with a flash of anger, 'I shot the dog. What would have been a better thing to do?'

'Ok, so, Misha,' said Gina, carefully, 'what I don't understand is why you had a weapon, at all.'

Their group adhered to a policy of non-violence. If they were scrupulous about never putting themselves in a position where one of them might be accused of damage to persons or property, was the reasoning, they could continue to protest publicly without drawing down on themselves the draconian anti-terrorist powers of the Department of Correction. It was a fine line at the best of times.

Misha shrugged, looking back at Gina with an opaque expression. 'It was just as well that I did, I think.'

'Where did you get it from? And where is it now?'

Misha held Gina's gaze but didn't answer. Then, abruptly, he put down the mouthpiece of the hookah and stood up. His manner was still as smooth but now his voice held an edge.

'Not everything I do, darling children, is answerable to you.'

'Whoa, man,' said Tom. 'Easy.'

'The trouble is,' Gina began.

'The trouble *is*,' said Misha, 'that because I was armed, and could save little Annie from being eaten by an attack dog, some of you will now have to be outside the law for real, and cannot go home to Mummy at the weekend.'

He picked up his jacket and went out. They heard his steps going down the stairs, a pause, and then a splash.

'He does have a point,' said Noah, putting down the suture gun.

'Yes, but,' said Gina, helplessly.

It was simple. Killing the dog had crossed the line. Annie and Tom were traceable by the DNA on the abandoned cutters, in Annie's blood on the road. As registered Australian citizens Annie Ling and Tom Carter had to cease to exist.

Misha, it seemed, wasn't traceable. But then no one was sure if the identity he used, Misha Simonovsky, Australian registered alien, was a true identity in the first place.

Noah picked up a tin of nano wound sealant, and started painting Annie's leg in long stripes. 'We can't do anything about the breach, as far as Annie and Tom go. They should be safe enough here, in the short term. When Annie is better we need to take stock, see whether we need to split up, move maybe.'

'Shit, Noah,' said Tom, distractedly, 'where did you get that from? Military grade, looks like.'

'Never mind that,' said Noah. He strapped a soft dressing over the wound. 'There, done. As good as I can do, anyway. So,' he carried on, 'want to see what happened with the real action?'

The protest at con 17 had not exactly been a diversion. The facility had been on the group's hit list for a long time. Mineral exploitation in the Antarctic was a legitimate target. The group hierarchy, the largely unknown organisation above them that they could only contact through a Darknet avatar, had approved. Other 'Hands off the South' actions had been timetabled simultaneously for maximum impact in VR. All it was, was that Noah and Gina had taken the opportunity to set up a side action at the same time. Noah drew a small bowl of rainwater to wash his hands and ran the recording.

It was a conference space in VR, an unremarkable business meeting room, and around the table were avatars of the delegates in the usual way. Time was too short and carbon too expensive for anyone to spend time physically travelling to meet colleagues in other cities. The convention was for business purposes that the avatar should be body-normal and resemble the person attending, within reason. At the head of the table was a White man of medium build with pale, protruding eyes and a fidgety manner. As he sat, waiting for the meeting to begin, he had crossed one ankle over the other knee and was running a hand up under his trouser cuff to scratch his shin. His beta labelled him as Aubrey Sanderson, head of Growth Environment for SAPA.

'S'him,' slurred Annie from her place on the console. 'We saw him, it was him.'

'Shh,' said Tom, cradling her.

'Was him, they brought him in that day. Day I got arrested.' Annie closed her eyes again and Tom held her and stroked her dark hair.

One after one the delegates' icons lit up. Head of Security for SAPA. Head of Security for Ardsen. Head of Dreadnaught PR, for Ardsen. Head of Carbon, SAPA (Acting). Head of Facilities, SAPA. Head of Extraction Technology, Ardsen. A thin woman whose beta labelled her as an Industry Liaison Facilitator with the Canadian government.

'This is me, now,' said Noah.

Charlotte McFall-Spalding, Ardsen Liaison for Environmental Safeguarding.

'Wha?' slurred Annie. 'Whaddya mean, s'you?'

'In takealong,' said Gina. She couldn't hold back from a triumphant look.

'Right,' said Tom with a slow grin, 'so it's not ok to kill a dog that was biting my Annie, but it *is* ok to set up a completely unauthorised unconsented takealong past god knows what level of firewall?'

'Cool, huh?' said Gina, ignoring the bit about the dog.

'Listen,' said Noah. 'This is her now.'

She was asking the Canadian government for assurances that what she called the 'tribal folkways' of the Inuit would be respected. The Canadian was saying that she was strictly at the meeting in the capacity of an observer and although Canada retained a warm and close relationship with the Arctic Nation, of course sovereignty rested with the Nation and it would be quite wrong for her to hold herself out as having any authority to make agreements.

There was a good deal more of this sort of thing.

'God, it's *boring*,' said Tom.

'No, listen,' said Noah. 'This is the bit.' His dark face was intent.

'So to wrap up,' Sanderson was saying, 'we are agreed as to the percentage. There should be no difficulty about the volume. We are agreed to work together with the able assistance of my friends, ah, in the PR department,' – an acknowledgement icon flashed – 'to minimise any adverse effects.'

'Sorry to interrupt at this late stage, Aubrey, but something has just occurred to me,' said the florid voice of the PR man.

'Please,' said Sanderson, smiling his thin smile. He was drumming his fingers on the polished desk-top in a staccato beat.

'Might we be able to get some of the Inuit actually on the miner? I'm seeing an opportunity for the people, you know, the indigenous people who live there, to demonstrate their support for a progressive approach to land use, you know, along with remediation and modernisation, of course.'

The extraction technology person immediately objected that the whole point about the Dreadnaught was that it was fully automated and roboticised so that it could operate in any environment without the need for a human presence on site.

'Well, you know, maybe a small living module? There must be some sort of task they could do? Or maybe we could say that they were being given the opportunity to bear witness for their people? Because of our respect for their, you know, tribal folkways?'

At this point waiting-to-speak icons flashed from both Heads of Security.

'I'm not saying, you know, they would have access

to any of the actual working processes. They would be purely decorative.'

'Colleagues,' said Sanderson, cutting across what was becoming a heated discussion. 'We have to wrap this up. We will need to table your suggestion, Michael, for the next meeting. I think it certainly has, ah, merit, if we can convince our friends on the Security side that the project will not be endangered by the liveware.'

Laughter icons.

'Goodbye, Cameron, a very interesting presentation. Goodbye, Taylor. Goodbye, George. Charlotte,' Aubrey held her in his pale gaze for a moment, 'I hope you're well. If you don't mind my saying, you don't seem to be quite yourself today. Good bye, Elizabeth.'

'There!' said Noah, triumphantly. 'What d'you think?'

'What was that he said,' said Tom, slowly, 'about your takealong host, about her not being herself. I'm not sure, not sure I liked that.'

'Don't be an old woman, Tom!' said Gina. She too was flushed with success. 'There's no way they could have traced us, and if they could, we would have been barred. The fact that Noah was in shows it was safe. What a stroke, what a coup!'

'Thing is,' said Noah, leaning forward, 'don't you see, there's an amazing chance here.'

Tom looked at him steadily.

'If we can get in touch with someone in the North, we may be able to influence who gets chosen for this

PR exercise. One of us must have some contacts. We could get one of our own people on the miner!'

'Thing is,' said Tom, still looking troubled, 'we don't know any Inuit. Not within Group, I mean.'

'Me, I do,' said Annie, raising her head with difficulty. 'Might know someone. Can try, anyhow.' She let her head fall back and closed her eyes.

How We Got Here

The Democratic People's Republic of Korea remains shrouded in mystery and data blocks prevent the reporting of North Korean media traffic while it is said that drones are regularly shot down over the border or in the Republic's airspace. So, how are we to assess the effects of sea-level changes in this mountainous land caught between the Yellow Sea to the west and the Sea of Japan to the east? The view here shows how the flat, fertile farmland, watered by the deep Taedong river on its journey down to the sea, is concentrated in the west of the country. This is North Korea's rice bowl where the food that sustains its people is still grown. Measurements from orbit show some degree of sea-incursion on the west coast of the Democratic People's Republic of Korea, threatening the province of Nampo and the capital Pyongyang itself. And here on archive satellite footage we can see the West Sea Barrage, built in 1986 at the mouth of the Taedong when land was being reclaimed from the Korean Gulf. Now if I put up the satellite footage from this year, you can see that the West Sea Barrage is no longer visible, and the coastline seems to have moved inland. We guess that the farmland won from the sea in 1986 has been taken back by the waves. Persistent rumours talk of fleeing populations taking up a refugee life in the forests which still cover the inland mountain ranges of this secretive realm.

So now by comparison we look at the west coast of the US …

'Amazing World' programme 7, 'The Rising Seas', 3.11.60.

Killaq

'Wake up.'

She rolled over and buried her head under her pillow.

'Killaq, wake up.'

'Wha?'

'It's the Onalik house, it's a melt slide.'

'Shit.'

Killaq sat up, fully awake. With a gesture Ma turned on the room light and Killaq leapt up and started pulling on outdoor clothes. Five minutes later she was in the kitchen.

'Ma, you know I can't eat that.'

'It's an emergency, you need the energy.'

Killaq took the seal meat and bannock without arguing. She could always give it to someone else. In the porch she found her work boots and overtrousers, and strapped a powerful head torch over her balaclava and jacket hood. Briefly she gave Ma a hug before Ma swung the inner door shut and Killaq leaned on the heavy outer door handle.

It was dark outside, and windy. She could see other lights bobbing at the far end of the street. Everyone able-bodied would be up. She leaned into the wind, her boots crunching on the snowy road, jogging as well as her bulky clothing would allow. At the junction the Fire and Rescue truck had pulled up and she held out a mittened hand and was hauled on board. No one was saying much. Killaq realised she had no idea what time it was. She checked in VR: 5.30am. The truck pulled away and she sat swaying with its rough motion, blank-minded, waking up. A melt slide, that was bad. Even where the soil wasn't deep, where there was bedrock not too far below, the melting permafrost could open up unexpected slumps and hollows. The Onaliks lived out on Qaqqamiut, on the way out of town. Maybe the truck would get there and they would find the family all lined up outside their pod cabin which had just developed a bit of a list, one of the legs had sunk, something like that. It would be all right, surely it would be all right.

The truck bumped to a stop and someone slid open the door. Immediately the fierce wail of the wind filled her ears. She got to her feet, waiting her turn to step out into the darkness. Then she was out and someone – it was Jean-Lou – was handing her a helmet and a belt. Without asking questions she struggled into the wind, fumbling with the helmet straps and then the belt buckle. Someone was fixing ropes to the towbar of the truck and someone else was hammering the support for the heavy floodlight into the ground. You had to see what you were doing, you couldn't risk anyone else in the slide. Sometimes what started as a small hole could widen suddenly, catastrophically. The light came on.

She couldn't make sense of what she was seeing, at first. Then she made out the side of the enormous swallow hole and a triangular shape sticking up – something with straight edges – my god, it was the corner of the house. A man in a harness ran a rope out past her. There were the shapes of people at the edge of the slide – someone was going down. She clipped her belt in to one of the ropes and started making her way forwards, making sure of each foot, hand over hand along the rope. Ahead and behind her other people were doing the same. She had only seen a melt slide once before and that time the guys at the front had fastened steel hawsers to hold the pod steady while the people got out, and then later on they had come with a winch and a helicopter and moved everything to safer ground. She had not had much to do except pass things when she was asked. This looked worse, much worse: it was too late for pinning the pod.

Then there was something going on at the edge, in front of her – she couldn't see, it looked like a small dark bundle was being handed up. The person in front of her took the bundle and started making their way up the rope back towards her. Killaq leaned on the rope and braced herself, and was handed a bundle of blankets and, wrapped in them, the Onalik baby, extraordinarily still asleep. Immediately she turned her back to the wind, cradling the child, and started making her way back to where the next person behind her was waiting at their clip-in point on the rope. It was difficult: she needed both hands to hold the baby, and the wind gusting behind her threatened to unsteady her. Two more steps, another one, and then she stood shoulder to shoulder with the next person back, passing the baby carefully so as not to expose her to the wind. She looked behind her. There was a person, at the edge of the collapse, lit in the sharp floodlight: it looked like

Atuqtuak, the father, with the older child in his arms. He handed the child forward to a rescuer and leaned back, holding on with one arm, reaching back with his other arm to his wife behind him.

The ground shook under her feet and someone ahead of her shouted 'Run.' The human chain broke and people came streaming past her. She turned to run herself, and suddenly the ground shifted under her feet and she stumbled and fell. There was a huge roaring, tearing sound and someone grabbed her, hauling her up, and she struggled to her knees and desperately grappled her way forwards in the sliding earth and then there was someone in front of her, pulling her, and she got herself forward onto the solid land and crawled, gasping and sobbing, and pulled herself upright, leaning on the truck bumper. She turned around.

The rescuers were standing in a semi-circle in the snow. The wind had dropped and there was no sound except for the Onalik baby, crying. The floodlight had gone in the collapse. Beams of individual torches played over the huge crater, a chaos of rocks and mud, too deep to see the bottom. There was no sign of the house at all.

Jean-Lou's voice cut into the appalled silence. 'Ok, folks, let's get these kids somewhere warm. Nothing we can do now.' And as a young man seemed to be on the point of leaning out over the drop, Jean-Lou added brusquely, 'Nothing we can do.' He clapped the young man on the shoulder and steered him back from the edge. People started to load pieces of equipment back in the truck, moving like sleepwalkers. A woman stood holding a broken rope, staring at the frayed end in the light of her head torch. Someone came through the crowd of people and pushed his way in next to Killaq. It was Amaruq. She hadn't seen him since the argument on the beach. He was covered in mud – he must have been down on the rope, at the sharp end – and his face was drawn. He put an arm around her and they stood looking over the devastation where the house had been.

'It's not right,' Killaq said. 'It's our land. This shouldn't be happening.' Amaruq tightened his arm around her shoulder but said nothing. It was very cold. She turned to look at him and realised she could see the outline of his face: it was mid-morning and dawn must be on the way. As they stood the sky was already lightening; the truck switched on its high beams and started to back onto the highway. 'I should go with them,' Killaq said.

'I can give you a lift,' said Amaruq, wearily. 'We should both be with Ma. Angela Onalik was in her sewing circle.'

Suddenly Killaq was choked with tears. She turned and buried her face in her brother's shoulder. 'It's not right,' she repeated, through her sobs. 'They can't be gone, just like that. It's horrible.' Amaruq held her and looked over her hooded head, back towards town, where a pale line showed on the horizon and a grey pre-dawn light was starting to illuminate the long snowy road, the dark shapes of neighbouring houses and the blocky outlines of the town in the distance.

The rear lights of the truck drew away down the road. 'Come on,' he said. 'Time to go home.'

After they had gone back and found Ma weeping – the news had been on the local net with realtime audio and viz – and after they had hugged her and made coffee and sat together a while, and when the short-lived daylight had gone and outside the house was night again and snow, Ma sat up and said, 'The meeting, it's tonight.'

'What meeting, Ma?' said Amaruq.

'The meeting, you know, the Arctic Council, the public meeting with the Siberian Federation, about these Koreans. We should go, we should all go.'

'Ma,' said Killaq, leaning a hand on Ma's shoulder, 'nobody would expect you to go to meetings, at a time like this.'

'Well –' said Ma, sitting up straighter and rubbing her temples.

'A good thing doesn't wait to be done at a good time,' mouthed Amaruq behind her.

'Oh, you! I know what you're doing!' And Ma laughed, a bit unsteadily.

They helped Ma install herself under the big old-fashioned VR helmet and made sure her hook-ups were all straight. Then they headed for their own consoles.

/Inter-ArcticJointCommittee/public access/join meeting/

The scenario was a steeply raked, wood-panelled lecture theatre; the audience were filing in and taking their places in curved rows of narrow benches. Just as well it was VR, Killaq found herself thinking, the seating would be uncomfortable IRL, for any length of time. She looked around. Most of the audience had treated this as a formal occasion and had come in body-normal, but there was a sprinkling of war droids, cartoon lizards and characters from film and fiction. Next to her was some sort of extinct bear, patterned in big curving black and white splodges, with dark black furry circles around its brown eyes. It wore a logo pin which said 'Unite the North!'

Down on the stage were the committee members: representatives from the Arctic Nation, the Siberian Federation, Finland, and a few special-interest groups. Standing at a lectern was an elderly woman. Her beta labelled her as Chair Elena Mikhailovna of the Yakut people, Representative to the Third Sub-Committee for Federation Affairs. She was small and white-haired, and wore a long brown felt coat, belted around the waist, thickly adorned with bands of red and blue embroidery. She had a fur cap and a far-seeing, almost truculent expression. 'It's political,' Killaq thought, 'she's wearing the old costume to make a point.'

The speaker icon lit and the old woman addressed the meeting. 'Friends,' she said, 'welcome to this seventy-second meeting of the Inter-Arctic Committee for Co-operation and Fellowship.' She was speaking in Sakha; glancing idly at Amaruq's beta, she saw that he was running a translation interface in Inuktitut. Killaq hadn't bothered: she was perfectly happy to listen in English. The translation was often less bug-ridden.

There were formal speeches of welcome and response. Then the Chair held up a hand and the lecture hall vanished. The view was from the air, a landscape at night. A string of lights picked out a road against the dark and otherwise featureless terrain. The road ended abruptly in mid-screen.

'This image has been shared with us by our colleagues in Moscow,' said the Chair's voice. 'We share it with this meeting under the same terms.' Killaq knew that the visual would be embargoed, uncopyable by anyone in the public audience. 'We are looking at the northern boundary of our Federation territory, at the shore of the Sibirskoye Morya.' A graphic traced the shoreline, intersected by the roadhead, the dark of the nighttime tundra giving way to the dark of the unlit sea.

'Now I will overlay the IR scan provided by our colleagues.'

The IR readings glowed blue, lighting up areas of hidden warmth in the sub-zero landscape. A transport travelling along the road, with an engine running and human occupants. A huddle of huts by the roadhead, with heating and again some human occupancy. A speck of blue to one side, barely big enough to register, might be a seal, or a person out on some errand at night, a fisherman or a liquor runner. The view tilted and zoomed out to sea, travelling over the empty ocean for what the beta in the corner of the screen said was 23.7 kilometres; apart from the beta the view was completely black. Killaq felt disoriented, suspended in the darkness above the dark sea. Then something started to come into view on the IR, an expanse of blue, shining indistinctly beneath her. She couldn't make sense of what she was seeing, of the scale of it.

Abruptly she was back in the lecture theatre.

'Moscow tells us,' said the Chair's deliberate voice, 'that what we are seeing is the unmistakable signal of some sort of undersea installation. They say that the information they have indicates that this may be a manufactory built by the North Koreans in furtherance of their Great Step North. They have not shared with us the source of that information. They have offered us their assistance – their military assistance – in investigating this phenomenon, as they call it. But friends,' continued the Chair, raising her voice, 'before we accept any help we must consider carefully why we are being given this information and how far we are prepared to give it credence. It is a surprising deviation from the normal protocols – I would even call it an extreme deviation – that this Committee has been given wide-access privileges and invited to share the visual with this meeting. That in itself would be a reason to tread cautiously. Furthermore, my friends, we must discuss what incentive there may be for our gracious parent nation to invite herself onto Federation territory in military strength.'

The Speaker icon light went out. Immediately request-to-speak signals blinked on from all parts of the audience. How do we know we can trust this visual? How do we know it is a manufactory? Have we not asked the North Koreans this question? Are we not being manipulated by Moscow? Why are we sharing this situation with the Arctic Nation when it concerns Federation sovereignty?

Ma had been sitting, absently watching the proceedings. She looked as though her thoughts were far away. Then, as the Chair was starting to wind up the long and inconclusive discussion, she activated her own waiting-to-speak icon.

'And we have time for one more contribution, yes, Mrs. Nanoortalik?'

'Will it be war?' Ma asked.

Annie

/skinpaint/select/menu/

She scrolled down. Jungles, mountains, no. She hesitated over a wide pale sky with seagulls flying. No, it needed to be from the North, unmistakably from the North. 'Ice Symphony', that was the one.

/IceSymphony/select/

She waited for the paint to do its work and then activated the console camera. In the small side-screen she could see herself as the camera saw her, lying in the console with her hands behind her head and a scrutinising, almost hostile expression. Over her naked body images flowed of pack ice jostling, breaking and rejoining, dark lines of running sea showing suddenly at newly made rifts and junctions.

Giving you camera view.

There was a long silence.

What, she sent, *don't you like ice.*

Oh no, sent Amaruq softly, *I like ice. I like ice a lot.*

Come surfing, then.

Killaq

In her dream, she was dealing with a question from the social media feed linked to her blog. 'You North people should be thank climate change gonna make everthing warm n sunny for YOu ☺.' Killaq was filled with anger. She swept the fringe from her face, sat up straight and activated Record.

'I am Killaq Nanoortalik and yesterday my mum's friends were killed in a melt slide that swallowed their house.' And then she was there, in the dream, teetering by the edge of the huge crater. Deep down, right at the bottom, there was an arm sticking out from the jumble of boulders and she recognised the raven's foot tattoo and the bracelet with the little blue beads – Ma, it was Ma buried in the slide. Without hesitating she crouched down in the snow and swung her legs over the broken edge, dropping down into the rocks and mud. 'Ma! Ma!' cried Killaq. 'It's all right! I'm here! It's Killaq. We'll get you out.' But the boulders shifted, rumbling, and now she could only see the fingers of the hand. 'Ma!' wept Killaq. She seized hold of the fingers. Suddenly with terrifying strength the hand wrapped itself around her wrist and pulled her down into the blackness under the boulders.

'I'm not your Ma,' said a scratchy, creaking voice.

'Angela!' said Killaq. 'I thought you were dead.'

'I am.'

Killaq woke up, sweating. She lay for a minute looking at the ceiling, disoriented, trying to shake off the evil feel of the dream. Then she padded urgently down the pod hallway.

'Ma! You're all right!' And Ma, without questioning, put her arms around her, and they stood in the pod kitchen, Killaq's cheek against Ma's soft one, holding onto each other.

Then Ma let go. 'I've got coffee on,' she said.

Killaq didn't tell Ma about the dream. It was the sort of thing Ma would have taken seriously. The spirits of the dead could do terrible harm to the living, in Inuit legend. Ma would have taken her to see that old crazy lady, out by the Eagle Rock, who would have mumbled and rocked and given her a talisman, something to wear on a thong around her neck, a bone or a feather or a soapstone carving, to keep her safe under the light of the sun. No, thought Killaq. She would exorcise the spirit of Angela Onalik in her own way.

'Look,' said Ma, handing Killaq a steaming cup. 'Nothing about our meeting.' She thumbed the control and the news filled the space over the table. War in Uganda, flooding in Bangladesh, a cyclone in the Philippines. SAPA to launch a new sub-orbital service. Football, cycling, a yacht race. Nothing about secret manufactories in the Siberian Ocean.

'Search,' said Killaq. 'Undersea factory Siberia.'

Factories, Siberian factories, undersea tourism.

'Search weird blue glow.'

That did it. The glowing blue ocean was all over sites and forums dedicated to the paranormal and the bizarre. ALIENS FOUND UNDER SIBERIAN SEA, was a fairly typical sample.

Killaq rubbed her eyes wearily. 'They do know, don't they, that it was only blue because that was the false colour chosen by the IR feed?'

'I don't like this,' said Ma. 'It's too easy to set this sort of story running, as soon as reports from our meeting started coming up. And then none of the proper news channels will touch it.' She gave Killaq a hug. 'Go and get your brother up, will you?'

Amaruq looked like someone who hadn't slept when he eventually shambled into the kitchen and took his coffee from Ma. He slumped down at the end of the table, cradling his mug. Despite everything that had happened, Killaq thought, he had a self-satisfied air, smug even. When the mug was empty he looked up at Killaq and cocked an eyebrow. 'Still got that link I gave you?'

Killaq had never gone back to the beach in VR to hear Amaruq's explanation about the Korean soldier. She had been too angry with him, and then something else had happened, and anyway she knew he wouldn't have waited for very long.

'Might have,' she said.

'See you there?'

'Might do.'

The beach was the same as before. Killaq sat on the sand, leaning back on her hands, with her legs stretched in front of her, ankles neatly together so as not to rumple the straight skirt. She looked out to the sea where Amaruq was riding the edge of a shallow breaking wave. He still didn't look much like a natural surfer. As she watched he fell and vanished in a smother of white water.

She was sure she could smell the sea, this time: she would have to ask Amaruq how he did it. He must have found a library of olfactory codings, somewhere, but accessing the receptor in the brain, that was the thing.

Then he was there, laughing, dripping on her blanket. He hadn't bothered with the paddle back to shore.

'Hey, sis.' There was something cheerful about him, at odds with the grim events in the outside world.

Killaq looked up at him from beneath her fringe. 'You're making me wet.'

'So I am!' He made himself an enormous towel, patterned with palm trees and a gaudy purple and yellow sunset, and threw himself down on it. Killaq put the conch shell he had given her carefully down in front of her, on the blanket.

'I brought your link back.'

'Thanks for coming back, sis,' he said, serious for a moment. 'Ok, so I know it looks weird, but will you listen to me?'

Killaq nodded.

'It isn't snuff gaming, I promise. But I *am* using surrendered rights.' He held up a hand to forestall her protest. 'I need access to the whole of the consciousness for what I want to do, and these guys, well, they need the money. And how is it worse, to use their mind to try and find out new stuff, compared to some snuff gamer who just wants to sell the experience of dying, someone else dying?'

'So is it takealong, is that what it is?'

'Not exactly, no, more immersive than takealong.'

Killaq thought. The soldier had spoken with Amaruq's voice.

'So you,' she said slowly, working it out as she went along, 'did you have *control* of that man?' That would have been worse than snuff gaming, a violation of the individual's self. It was supposed not to be possible.

'Not control, no. He needs to have overall control, he's fighting in a war zone. There's a protocol. Call it, guest privileges.'

Killaq struggled with her disgust. 'Can he feel you there?'

Amaruq's face lit up with interest. 'He must be able to, but I wish I could ask them more about that. Most of what you can buy is Korean, North Korean, they don't speak English.'

'Or Inuktitut.'

Amaruq smiled. 'No, not Inuktitut, that would be a bit much to expect.'

'Can you tell what he's thinking?'

'I'm working on that, on a translation interface.'

Killaq shuddered. She felt deeply uneasy, almost nauseous. Amaruq leaned over and took her hand.

'Look, sis, I know you don't like it, but I'm not doing anything these men haven't agreed to.' He looked up into her face. 'It's me, I'm not a bad guy.'

'I guess,' said Killaq, wretchedly.

'Look,' said Amaruq, 'you know you said you wanted me to tell you more stuff?'

'I don't know if I do, now.'

'Well, if you did, would you come to a meeting with me?'

'What sort of a meeting?'

'Just some guys I know. It's about SAPA. Remember, I said about SAPA?'

'Maybe, I don't know,' said Killaq. She brought up a time icon. 'Look, we have to go.'

'Oh Christ, the memorial service,' said Amaruq. 'Ok.'

Later, picking her way along the snow-stained edge of the road in the early twilight, still subdued by the memory of the Onalik boy in his dark suit, wide-eyed and uncomprehending, and the dry liturgical words which hadn't made anything easier to encompass or accept, Killaq looked over at Amaruq walking in silence by her shoulder.

'It reminds me,' she began.

'Uh huh. When Dad died.'

'I was about that age. I didn't really understand what it meant.'

'I remember.'

'They told me Dad had had an accident and wasn't coming home, but I never knew what really happened ...'

Killaq's voice trailed away. Amaruq looked across at her but said nothing.

'Thing is,' she went on, 'I am so sorry for those kids, but what I mostly am is angry.'

'Why is this happening at all?' she burst out, clenching her fists inside her heavy mittens. 'Why us? Did our people start any of this? Did we fill the air with shit, with carbon? Did we dig for oil and burn it, fuck, flying *salad greens* around the place?' She looked up at the dull cloud-covered sky, choking back tears.

'Hey, sis,' said Amaruq, reaching out to lean a gloved hand on her shoulder. 'Easy.'

'Just, fuck,' she said. 'What are we supposed to do? Are we just supposed to accept all this, all this *fucking shit,* all our land melting around us, people *dying,* for fuck's sake?' She wiped away the tears which were already freezing on her exposed cheek.

Amaruq drew her in to him and slung an arm around her shoulders, and they walked like that for a moment without saying anything.

'Sorry,' she said, after a while. 'It's just so *unfair.*'

'Listen,' said Amaruq, carefully, 'you know I was saying about that meeting?'

'Mm-hmm.'

'It's some people I know, carbon protesters.'

'Oh what,' said Killaq, startled out of her grief into irritation. 'Do they dress up as penguins and paint slogans on buildings?'

'No! Well, they might, for all I know, but that's not the point. Thing is, this group, they do some high-grade eavesdropping, they've heard some stuff that might affect us up here. If it's true.'

'What stuff?'

Amaruq looked around, then at a sensor on his wrist. 'Seems ok,' he said. 'Just turn off your VR feed, would you?'

Killaq looked at him aslant under her fringe. 'Now I know you're cracking up. On standby, there, will that do?'

'Right off.'

'Fuck, that means I have to restart everything, are you sure?'

Amaruq nodded. The dusk was thickening now and lights were coming on along the road. A few flakes of snow were beginning to settle. They stepped sideways round a pile of hardened, blackened snow, the residue of snow shovels from repeated scrapings, the whole winter long.

'Ok.'

'Sure?

'I said so, didn't I?'

'Ok, so this group, they think they have got something about SAPA, SAPA planning to do strip mining for permafrost, here in Nunavut.'

'That's it,' said Killaq, 'I'm not listening to any more of this crazy stuff. You, you know what you are, you are truly paranoid. I'm turning my feed back on.'

'Wait,' said Amaruq, catching hold of her hand, and then, maybe remembering that other time on the beach, he let go, flexing his fingers.

‘Why should I wait? All this, and now I have to listen to this crap. Permafrost mining is so illegal, it might as well not exist. The World Court would never allow it. The Council of Elders would never allow it.’

‘Are you sure?’ said Amaruq, and something about the way he spoke made her pause.

‘Why wouldn’t I be sure?’

‘Think, Killaq,’ said Amaruq, urgently. ‘That bloke from SAPA, the one you met, he was supposedly doing outreach work, community work here.’

‘Aubrey something,’ said Killaq, reluctantly. ‘He drank all Ma’s coffee.’

‘Yes, Aubrey Sanderson. Look him up, he’s management-echelon, secretary grade. Why would someone like him be coming to talk to people in Iqaluit about community facilities? Isn’t that a job for a first-year intern, or something?’

‘I *can’t* look him up because I’ve turned my feed *off*.’

‘Not now, look him up later. So then apparently SAPA have decided to build a new medical facility in Iqaluit, for no reason? Out of the kindness of their little corporate hearts?’

‘I guess,’ said Killaq. ‘They do a lot of outreach work.’

‘What these guys are saying, these guys I know, is that SAPA have done a deal with Ardsen for strip mining on a huge scale, enormous.’

‘Methane,’ said Killaq, her attention caught despite herself. ‘Methane to run personal transports, luxury living. There *has* been all that stuff in VR about turning your back on austerity, on not giving up on the carbon lifestyle. Carbon deniers, I never took it seriously.’

'Thing is – '

'What?'

'Can I – No, I know I can trust you. Thing is, are you in?'

'Am I in what?'

'Just, are you in?'

'I don't know what you're saying,' said Killaq, slowly.

'It looks like SAPA are going for buy-in in a big way. They are going to want a load of PR from the indigenous population, saying that we welcome them on our land, that kind of thing.'

Killaq raised a scornful eyebrow.

'Information we have, they want to get one of us on the miner.'

'A collaborator.'

'That's what it would look like from the outside. But we – this group I know – we want it to be one of ours.'

'What, a saboteur?' asked Killaq, and then, a heartbeat later, 'You mean *me*?'

'You met him, Sanderson, he knows you, there might be an in.'

'Would it be dangerous?'

'Li'l sis,' began Amaruq, and he sighed. 'Yes, I guess it would be dangerous. I can't ask you to do it. In fact, I don't want you to do it. But it all stacks up, it needs to be someone SAPA won't suspect, and I know you have the tech skills if it came to it.'

(*I'm not your Ma,* whispered the voice of Angela Onalik in her mind).

'I'm in.'

Annie

It was the turn of the tide, and the strong noonday light cast a blinding dazzle on the flooded street outside. The sea, washing around the stoops and doorways of abandoned houses, had a stale smell. Misha was stretched out on a shabby, patched inflatable bed, floating in the shallow wavelets which marked slack water, his naked body in the full glare of the unforgiving sunlight. Gina pinched her lips in an expression of mixed concern and irritation.

'If you want a tan, Misha, I have some skinpaint.'

'Thank you, darling Gina, but that would not be at all the same thing.'

'Leave him alone, Gina, he doesn't expect to live long enough to get cancer,' said Noah.

Tom raised an eyebrow. 'Hey,' he said, 'what happened to the caring Noah we all know and love?'

Noah shrugged. His expression was hard to read.

They were sitting on the porch, or rather, apart from Misha, dangling above it. The porch itself was under water for half of the day and the floor timbers were slimy and rotten, but the porch roof would hold an expansion bolt, and you could sling a hammock to lie in in the shade. The ferocious heat of midsummer was past but it was still too sweaty and airless to be inside at noon. Annie was lying back in a faded canvas swing, her eyes shut, frowning at something she was accessing in VR.

'What'cha got there, girl?'

Annie raised her head and looked at Tom.

'S' kinda weird, it's some files I got sent. It's to do with the North, how some Arctic rights group faced down the Canadian government. Ten years ago or more, now. Nothing I ever heard of before.'

'From your Eskimo pal?' Tom's expression was guarded.

'He's not an Eskimo, but yes, him. Anyway, have a looksee if you like.'

'Ok.'

/file transfer/

/transfer accepted/

'So,' said Tom slowly, after he had scanned the transfer, 'there's a story, a meme, about some underground army in the North, in the old days, with the programming mojo to be able to take on their government. Is that what it comes to?'

'I guess,' said Annie lightly. 'Interesting, might be interesting, anyway?'

'Your pal, is he saying that this underground setup still exists?'

'Stop calling him my pal,' said Annie with a flash of annoyance. 'I don't know. You've seen the files, you know as much as I do.'

'Oh, VR is full of crap,' said Noah. 'You could spend all day on conspiracies and monsters and secret shit, if you didn't have a life. Did you see that one about the undersea aliens in the Arctic ocean?'

Gina giggled. 'Woo-oo! I am the underwater alien! Feel my blue radiance!'

'Like,' said Noah, 'if you were an alien civilisation and you wanted to explore the Earth, a civilisation smart enough to have space travel, the first thing you would do is hole up underwater in a really inhospitable part of the planet and lurk about there making things glow blue.'

'Maybe they come from a frozen waterworld, maybe it's not inhospitable for them.'

'Yeah, right,' said Noah. 'I need a beer.'

He swung himself down from his hammock and waded into the flooded kitchen.

'Is it just me,' asked Misha, 'or is our lovely Noah a bit irritable recently?'

'Fuck off, Misha,' said Tom. 'I need a beer too.' They heard him splashing his way indoors, then he reappeared with a couple of small green bottles.

'Hey, girl, I brought you one out.'

'Don't feel like it right now, but ta.'

'I'll have it if you don't want it, Annie,' and Gina swung her hammock over and seized the bottle out of Tom's still outstretched hand. He turned away and took a long swig of his own beer, looking out over the cluttered debris washing at the base of the water-stained walls across the street. It was a depressing outlook at low tide.

'So,' said Noah, leaning on the peeling door jamb, 'never mind about aliens. Do they think they are going to be able to help, the northern boys? Can they get someone on the miner?' He beat a slow tattoo on the rotten wood with the fingers of his free hand: tap tap tap-tap, tap tap tap-tap.

'Maybe,' said Annie. 'We don't know yet.'

'Who's it gonna be? Can we trust him?'

'S' not decided, far as I know. Either someone on the PR side or a techie.'

'We gonna meet them? When the time comes?'

'Don't you think,' said Tom, without turning round, 'we can just leave them to get on with it, your "northern boys". Since when did we get involved in another group's action? It's bad security, it's a breach of the small cells rule. And what can we really do about it, from here? Can't we just let them do it and then, one day when we see some amazing stunt on the news, we can think, we had a share in that, in making it happen. What good does it do for us to be hands-on?'

'Yes, but,' said Gina, 'just this once, it was such a thing to pull off. I feel I still want to be involved.'

'It's still bad security,' said Tom, stubbornly. 'It was you taught me that, when I first joined.'

'What's the matter, Tom,' said Noah. 'Losing the fire in your belly?'

Tom clenched his fist by his side but when he replied it was in the same unconcerned drawl as always.

'I just don't see what it has to do with us. But don't let me stop you, you guys, if you want to be involved.'

He jumped off the porch and waded off up the street, heading inland.

'Is he ok, Annie?' Gina asked.

'It's Tom, he's always ok. He'll go ride some waves and then he'll feel better.'

'He didn't have his board with him,' said Misha.

Annie had said that the sun was giving her a headache and had gone back inside. She had powered up one of the consoles, meaning to see Amaruq, talk to him some more maybe about the files he had sent. She had smiled with anticipation as she fitted her body into the hollow made by many other bodies before her in the cheap padded recliner. But she hadn't been able to trace him. She had a contact link but she suspected it was just a dropbox: she still had no direct ID for him. She could only find him when he wanted to be found. Then after a while she had given up on VR and had taken the *Cleo* out, paddling aimlessly around the shoreline, keeping an eye open for a silhouette with Tom's broad shoulders, but she couldn't see him anywhere either. Now evening was falling and she was back in VR.

/Darknet/connect/TomCarver

Hey.

Tom, that you?

<not right now icon>

Ok, when you're ready.

…

I'm still here?

Want in?

Ok.

/enter/scenario/

Immediately Annie felt the rock and rise underneath her of an enormous wave. She was on her board, legs dangling in the cold sea, and above her the sky was dark and shaken by lightening. Thunder rolled in the distance. She could hear the growl of the wave beginning to break and hastily paddled backwards: a wave this size would be more than she could take on. She couldn't see Tom. Rain started to fall. 'Tom!' she yelled into the gathering storm. The swell swept her up again onto the lip of the wave. Shit, she wasn't liking this. She turned and paddled away but the wave was stronger than she was. It swept her before it, and for a moment she was poised over a black unguessable drop –

/escape/

Annie breathed out. She opened her eyes and looked up at the stained ceiling. She could hear Gina interrogating Misha about the ingredients of the stirfry.

Ok, his access was still live.

/scenario access/distance view/

And she was back in the dark storm-lashed seascape, but this time viewing it from above. She saw the towering wave start to curl and break – there on the lip, dwarfed by the curling drop beneath, there he was, poised on his board. 'Tom!' she yelled again, but he couldn't hear her. Savage lightning lit up the surface of the sea and she saw him for a moment small on the face of the wave, moving fast, before the giant wave crest came crashing over him and –

/scenario abort/

He rebooted it before she had the chance to exit. There he was on the lip of the wave, higher than a city building. Lightning lit up the dark sky. He was travelling down the face of the wave, tense, in balance. Then he fell and –

/scenario abort/

He was on the lip. Lightning struck. Then he was travelling down the wave, tense, in balance, maybe, maybe he could make it this time. Then –

/scenario abort/

Fuck this shit, thought Annie.

/exit/

She swung her legs down from the console.

'So,' she said, 'what's in this stirfry?'

Tom went out and didn't come home that evening. Later, after everyone else was asleep, Annie crept back to the console.

/connect/Amaruq/

She was paddling her board through a lazily warm sea under a blue sky. The water was turquoise clear and she could see beneath her, a long way down, where jewel-coloured fish were swimming in sparkling schools. On the surface of the water floated flowers like lilies with steel-blue leaves and silver-white blooms, and despite the warmth of the water, her way took her between ice castles, reaching above her with great arching translucent curves and filigree sprays of ice, improbably baroque and complex. Ahead the ice on either side came branching together to make an opening, almost a doorway, a gothic portico rising to a point at the top. Feeling dreamlike and content, Annie swam her board under the overreaching ice. Inside was a perfectly round lagoon, encircled by carved ice walls, engraved in a riot of frozen scrolls and whorls, tooth-white and deep transparent blue. The water was calm and the little fish swam at the surface now, emerald and ruby and topaz coloured, flashing together in the sunlight as they turned in unison. Ahead was an island, or no, a raft, and on it was a snow house, round-domed like an igloo, but in front was a porch, or a deep veranda, and lily flowers grew up the walls of the house and twined between the pillars, framing the deep shadowy doorway in white blossom.

The nose of her board touched the edge of the raft and then he was there, Amaruq, lifting her dripping out of the warm sea. She looked down at herself and found that instead of the ice paint that she had expected, her naked body was covered in curving black writing in a language she did not understand. She reached her arm around his neck and he kissed her.

After a while, he led her under the pillared doorway and into the house, where the round room inside was shining with lighted candles and there was a low bed piled high with white furs. 'I thought there should be music,' he said, smiling at her. He ran his hand the length of her side and cupped it around her breast. She felt it as sound – as the high vibrating note of a violin, pure and powerful. In reply she put her hand on the flat muscles of his stomach and felt the deep thrum of the answering cello, dark, sweet, urgent. He drew her to him.

Killaq

'Dream on dream on teenage queen, prettiest girl I ever seen.'

It was Ma, scraping a sealskin, listening to Johnny Cash in the kitchen.

'You do know,' said Killaq, 'they have machinery to do that nowadays.'

'What,' said Ma, pushing her dark hair out of her eyes with the knuckle of her greasy hand, 'for listening to the Man in Black?'

'No,' said Killaq, laughing. 'You know what I mean!'

'Nothing would surprise me,' said Ma, shaking her head, but she was laughing too. 'But listen,' she carried on, 'my Ma taught me to do this, and her Ma before her, and her Ma before, right back to when we lived out on the land, and just now,' she paused, looking into the distance, 'just now, I think it's important to keep the old ways. Everything is changing so fast.'

Killaq came round the table and put an arm around Ma's shoulders, wrinkling her nose at the pungent seal smell. 'Well, you'll have to forgive me, Ma, but this is one skill that I am not going to learn.'

'You did use to help me, when you were tiny, before you gave up eating meat.'

'Before I understood what it meant, you mean. Anyway, what's for lunch?'

'Frittata, I traded some of the seal meat for eggs, and you can have the frittata vegetables with a bit of bread.'

'Might give it a miss, Ma, I'm not really hungry.'

'Come on, you need to get your share of home cooking before you go on that miner. What will the food be, anyway? Do they know about you being vegan?'

'Apparently it's all ready-meals and there's a choice of taste-ways. Vegan is no problem. Look.'

Killaq brought up her own messages, projecting them into the space over the half-scraped sealskin. She scrolled down until she got to 'Living arrangements for Dreadnaught personnel.'

'See, you can have Mexican, Asian, all sorts.'

Ma looked carefully at the menu. 'What is a Vegetable Timbale with Echoes of the Sea Five Ways?' she asked.

'Looks like, um, I don't know. Maybe it has Japanese influences? Like, with seaweed?'

'Well, so long as they feed you properly.' Ma killed the menu and looked at Killaq searchingly. 'And you're really sure about this? You still want to go?'

'It will be fine, Ma. All I have to do is keep a blog and do a bit of PR. It'll be good experience, look good on job applications.'

'You know not everyone around here agrees with the deal, the agreement the Council made with SAPA? Permafrost mining, it's controversial. I was surprised –' Ma hesitated.

'You thought it wasn't the sort of thing your vegan daughter would get involved in?' Killaq laughed, although her heart was wrung. She hated lying to Ma. 'I guess, I guess I was persuaded by the science. I mean, they say that we are in for a certain amount of melting, whatever we do. And if we are going to have some melting, we might as well have control over the gas content, the carbon. If we can sell it, we can make some money for the Nation.

'And for SAPA.'

'And for SAPA, yes, that's how it works. But they aren't bad guys, just because they're a big corporate. They have all these social responsibility programmes. And they say the land will be remediated, you won't know the miner has been there.'

Killaq heard in her head the recording she had listened to, the scornful tone. 'Remediation! As if anyone cares if there's a fucking big hole in the tundra!' She had seen viz, too, files sent by the Australian group, land dug up, poisoned beyond repair, beyond healing in many lifetimes. She would fight that with every bone in her body. But she had to lie to Ma, it was to keep Ma safe.

'Well, I don't know,' said Ma. 'I can't say I like it. But if it's what you want to do ... You're old enough now, you can make your own decisions.'

'I wouldn't go,' said Killaq, abruptly, 'if you really didn't want.' Why had she said that? Suppose Ma did say no?

'No, no, little bird. I wouldn't stop you. There's just something about this, I have a funny feeling in my heart. Maybe it's just because you're the youngest, now you're leaving I'll be on my own.'

'Amaruq will still be here.'

'Of course he will,' said Ma, bravely, wiping her eyes. 'Of course he will.' Then she reached behind her to the lidded wicker pot on the spices shelf. Normally it had pins in it and elastic bands and kitchen bits and pieces. Ma drew out a leather thong and ran it through her fingers for a minute, considering. 'Wear this for me, will you?'

'Oh, Ma!' said Killaq, but she took the thong and held it up to the light. Threaded on it was a soapstone figure, the size of a thumbnail, a bear, it looked like.

'Let me,' said Ma, and she came round behind Killaq, fastening the thong at the back of her neck, and Killaq tucked the figurine under the neck of her t-shirt.

'There,' she said, smiling at Ma. 'Safe now.'

'So,' said Ma, making an effort to change the subject, 'what did they decide in the end, about you wearing a uniform?'

'Well, the girl from PR, I didn't like her, she kept trying to get me wearing sealskins and holding a harpoon. And then she had an argument with this guy from corporate hospitality, he wanted me wearing a uniform. And I was sitting there feeling like a fool while they squabbled over it. But in the end I think it's going to be plain t-shirts and leggings with the logos, Ardsen and SAPA. It's only for when I'm online, anyway, the rest of the time I can wear what I like.'

'Isn't that going to be most of the time, being online, I mean?'

'Kinda, yes, but there's a privacy clause, you're entitled to so many hours to yourself and apart from the core hours you can move them around, choose when you take them.'

'Hmph,' said Ma. 'I don't like the idea of all those strangers watching you while you're asleep.'

'Oh Ma! I don't suppose anybody will be interested. It's just corporate PR, nobody takes it seriously.'

'I still don't have to like it.'

'Well look at it this way, Ma, I might be able to get a job with SAPA, afterwards, or one of the other corporates, if I play my cards right. You just don't know where things will lead.'

She turned toward the door. 'Might get a breath of air, while it's daylight.'

'You do that. I'll keep your vegetables warm for you.'

Killaq pulled on her heavy outdoors gear. Even now at the end of February, at midday, the cold would be fierce. She brought up a reading of the temperature outside: -17°C. Underboots, overboots, inner gloves. She had no reason to go out, but she loved this season, when every day the light lasted a little later and it felt like there would be a time, not too far away, when you could throw off the indoors huddled life of the long dark months and stroll out in the evening under a light sky.

It wasn't that time yet, though. Killaq stepped out onto the crusted snow of the verge and took a deep breath. The cold caught the back of her throat and her nostrils, but somehow despite the dimness of the grey-brown cloud-filled sky, the air felt different, fresher. It was snowing fitfully in flurries and gusts, and along the horizon, behind her and between the houses, was a low streak of clear sky, olive-yellow underneath the clouds. Storm coming, thought Killaq. She turned down in the direction of town, snow crunching under her boots; there was a SAPA camera drone hovering at the end of the street. She gave it a cheery wave. Ever since the deal had been done with the Council, you saw the SAPA logo everywhere: not everybody liked the drones, though, they felt intrusive. Amaruq said, as far as most people were concerned, SAPA could see whatever they did in VR anyway if they were bothered to look – it didn't make too much sense to be worried about eavesdropping. Killaq noticed though that even he had started to be careful about what he said aloud. He trusted in the security he had built himself, in VR, better than in the safety of words spoken out loud to be picked up by who knew what long-range microphone or listening algorithm.

They had been back in their den, last time they had spoken about the miner. It seemed to Killaq that Amaruq had abandoned the pretence that it was still just their childhood hangout: the hollow among the brambles had been made armoured, impregnable, like a submarine or a space capsule surrounded by a hostile environment. She imagined them protected by great riveted plates of curved grey metal and swivelling laser armament, even as they sat in the round mossy den with its earth floor, just as they always had done, the warm sunshine striking down in amber shafts through the tangled undergrowth around them. There was a bow and arrows of Amaruq's hanging on the wall: Killaq remembered him making the bow in the outside world, when he was maybe eight and she would have been four or five, with a piece of bendy wood he had begged from their uncle's workshop, and kitchen string.

It had never worked very well, but Killaq thought it might have acquired other powers since then.

'So, sis, you're sure about this?' he'd asked.

Killaq had shrugged. 'Someone has to do it.' She felt less brave than the cool words implied. She realised she had sort of been hoping that she wouldn't have been chosen. There had been plenty of applicants. When she'd said something like this to Amaruq he had muttered about putting a thumb on the scales. She didn't know what he'd meant; she didn't need to know.

'The thing is,' she had added, and then stopped. What bothered her was that she hadn't been told the plan. She felt that it was all being organised over her head, or behind her back; these people in Australia (if that was really where they were) seemed to know stuff that she didn't. There was someone called Noah, and a Gina: they were the techies, and then another girl, an activist, Annie. If she knew Amaruq he would have a flirtation going with one of the girls; it was up to him, she thought, so long as it didn't mean everything was going to turn into an emotional morass at a crucial moment. And some others, Miska, or some name like that, and a Tom.

It made sense, of course, for her not to be told things. She was going in among the enemy and if she was caught, the less she knew, the better. It still made her feel uneasy, though, insecure, like when she was in junior high and Amaruq had sometimes brought her to hang out with his older high-school friends who made jokes that she didn't understand.

'The thing is,' she had said, 'I won't know what it is that I'm supposed to be doing, I might make a mess of it. Suppose you can't get through the miner security and all that happens is I spend three months living in the Dreadnaught living pod, and then I come home, and everyone hates me, and I have to work for SAPA for the rest of my life?'

Amaruq had laughed. 'That won't happen, sis. Trust me.'

She did trust him, she trusted him absolutely, but she also knew that whatever was going to happen would be on his terms – it always was – and once it was all in motion she might not have a choice, a way to back out.

He had asked her something a bit odd, then. 'D'you think,' he'd said, 'that there is stuff in VR that we didn't put there?'

'What, we, you and me?'

'No, we, us, humans.'

She gave him a long look. 'No,' she said. 'The *world* has got the stuff in it that we didn't put there. VR is 100% manmade.'

Killaq shook her head, remembering this. He spent too long in VR, without a doubt. It was all very well being a genius scenario builder, but you had to remember that it was only VR.

She had been heading downtown with no particular aim in mind, and now stopped, suddenly aware of her surroundings, opposite the Astro Hill complex. Snow was mounded in the forecourt and plastered up against the new sculpture. She could see the carved forms emerging from the high snowdrift as if from the frozen breakers of the sea: the woman, the seal and the baby. It was an old story. But it was snowing harder now and Killaq turned to walk back home. She could hear the pounding of waves in the Bay: every winter the water came higher and storm damage reached further inland. The Council were talking about building a flood wall, like so many low-lying cities had around the world, but Killaq wondered whether that could possibly be enough, if the sea kept rising. In the old days, before the city existed, when there was only an American airbase here, the Bay would have frozen clean across, all winter. But of course, that was before the Inuit lived in cities, before VR and all the paraphernalia of the modern world. If she had lived then, she would have been carrying a baby in her amauti by now, tucked securely in the back of the big coat: she wondered briefly what it would have been like, to have to grow up so early and be responsible for another human life so young. No VR scenarios, no taking time out to wield Starmaker, but maybe you didn't need adventures if there were real dangers and hardships, just getting from day to day.

Life was dangerous enough now, she thought, remembering the task she had ahead of her. She shuddered a little to think of it, closing the drawstring of her hood tight around her face, turning inland away from the wind.

SPRING

Amaruq

March 2062

He had been experimenting with sleeping in VR. He had made a flexible template to simulate brain wave pattern so that the mind could alternate in a natural fashion between deep sleep and REM sleep, dreaming sleep. The first few times it hadn't worked, or at least, the experience of 'dreaming' in VR had been no different from the experience of being in any other virtual scenario. Now he was trying again.

There were disconnected images, colour. Red. Green. His mother was leaning over him and she was angry, he knew he had done something wrong but he didn't know what it was. She was a bird, no, he was a bird, he was flying through a high white windless sky. Now the white sky was the snowy sweep of the ice-covered river and he was fishing, of course, he had been fishing all along.

He felt the coarse weave of the mat on his knees as he leaned over the hole, almost lying on the snow, peering down into the circular hole he had carved out of the ice with his long ice chisel. At the bottom ice chips clustered and circled on the rushing river water beneath. He blew gently on the chips, making a clear space, and yes, he could see a shadow there, the quick turning shape of a silver back. It would be an arctic char, eighteen inches long, good eating. Gently he tugged on the short stick that his line was tied to, holding the stick high above the ice hole, moving the line in short bursts, teasing, tempting the fish. He could see the lure bobbing, red, a red berry: in the dream the berry seemed natural to him even though there were no trees or bushes for hundreds of miles.

There it was – ah, no – the fish circled and went by. Then back it came, taking the lure, and with a smooth arching movement he pulled the fish out of the ice and held it up to inspect it. It wasn't a char, it was a small river trout, still twitching on the line. In the dream it seemed clear to him that now that he had caught the trout he didn't need to carry on fishing. He put aside his ulu, his crescent-shaped stone gutting knife, and swinging the trout over his shoulder he walked back across the ice to the hunting shelter he had built, half igloo with a roof of hides.

He laid the trout down by the entrance. It seemed to him that he should make a fire. On the earth floor there was a pile of twigs and smaller branches and he built them into a precise stack on a bed of dried moss. Then he reached for the soapstone oil lamp, holding it steady to light the moss, and blowing gently on the small red dancing flame. He bent over the fire, carefully feeding it small twigs and bark chips, until one of the larger branches took, casting leaping shadows on the hide ceiling. He turned around for his trout.

The fish wasn't by the door. In its place stood a young woman: she had beautiful, wide Inuit features and straight hair, black and smooth as a pool at midnight, falling unrestrained to her shoulders and down her back. Her arms and feet were bare and she wore a silver shift. She turned to the door, and he saw that instead of the igloo's low exit built of snow blocks, made to be crawled through, there was a hide doorway, and as she lifted up a corner a wind blew into the shelter, bringing the scent of blossom. For a second she looked over her shoulder and met his gaze, laughing. 'Amaruq!' she called him, and then she ducked under the hide doorway and was gone. In an instant he had followed her, pushing aside the hide and stepping out into a clearing in a wood, where the air had the fresh smell of spring. The trees were small, fruit trees maybe, and the sun shone glancing through the pale green of new leaves, making patches of sunshine and shadow. The girl was nowhere to be seen.

'Hey!' he called after her, running to the end of the clearing. There was a narrow trodden path, a foot's width, dark earth and leaf mould showing against the new grass. He plunged along it, brushing aside a low hanging branch. He heard her laughing, not very far ahead of him, and as the path turned a corner he caught a glimpse of her silver shift, but when he reached the bend a second later there was no sign of her. Undeterred he ran on. The fruit trees started to give way to taller woodland, oak and ash, and at first the path took him down wide forest brakes where the sun overhead filtered through in a green, leafy light. Ahead he saw a pool and a figure crouching by it – he thought it was her, stopping to cup a handful of water, but when he reached the water's edge there was only a single graceful footprint planted in the muddy earth.

Then the path began to narrow and to climb, onwards and steeply upwards in vertiginous hairpin bends. Now there was rock underfoot and pale boulders stood between the trees. He crossed a series of ledges where the white-brown granite rose in rounded steps, gritty to his bare feet, and on the rock lay pine needles: he had left the woodland behind. The gradient made his knees hurt and when the path switched direction he had to stop to catch his breath, his heart hammering in his chest.

There was a sharp scramble where he needed to use his hands – two awkward steps up in a narrow cleft – and all of a sudden the path broke out into a sort of rock balcony, full in the evening sun. He could see out above the narrow dark valley full of fir trees and across to the high peaks beyond, already purple in shadow. The air smelled cold, as if there might be snow ahead. He sat down on a boulder, resting his hands on his knees, and when he looked down he saw that his fingers were gnarled and nobbled, and the veins stood out on the backs of his hands, and the hair on his forearms was white. For a moment he frowned, wondering, and then a flash of silver caught his eye, away at the head of the valley – she must be already engaged in the long rocky climb, towards the distant unseen summit. He stood up, a little stiffly. There, there in the high hills, there he would find her.

Annie

'Quick, quick,' whispered Gina. She was filling a pack with food, clean water, a small Darknet-slaved handheld. Annie ran past her, shovelling clothes into a net bag. Misha was lying in a console, running the erase programmes in VR which would delete irrevocably the footprint of where the users had been and what programmes and contacts they had accessed. Noah had already packed his medical kit and was standing, watching, by the front window. He looked as though he was waiting for something. His face was tense and he beat a staccato rhythm with his boot toe on the floor.

'Ok,' said Misha, sitting up.

'Shh.'

He nodded, pulling a lighter out of his hip pocket. Deliberately he made a pile of burnables on the sham leather seat of the nearest console: cardboard packaging, a straw hat, some egg boxes. Reaching around under his braids he pressed at the base of his skull and pulled out his port access chip, balancing it carefully on top of the pile. 'You guys should do the same,' he said, before flicking his lighter under the cardboard.

'Hurry up, Misha!' Gina muttered, her voice hoarse with anxiety.

'Out, Gina, Annie,' said Misha, shortly. 'I'll follow as soon as this is lit.'

Noah gave up on looking out of the window. 'You do realise,' he said in a normal voice, 'that this will show whoever is looking for us, if there is anyone, that we were here.'

'They already know we are here,' said Misha, curtly, 'and I wonder why that is.' The cardboard started to burn, releasing a foul-smelling plume of dark, greasy smoke from the synthetic console cover. 'Out!' Annie swung a leg over the rear windowsill and lowered herself down a short rope, landing lightly in the Chloe. 'Ok, Gina!' she called softly. Inside the room they heard the harsh racket of a diesel outboard motor, coming closer. Noah breathed out a sigh which almost sounded like relief. Gina swung herself out of the window. The outboard motor roared louder, echoing off the house walls as the launch raced down the flooded street. 'After you,' said Misha, gesturing ironically at the windowsill. He had his semi-automatic Taurus in his hand. Noah glanced at the gun, hesitating. Misha chambered a round. Outside the launch engine slowed to an idle, reverberating off the surrounding buildings. 'They're here! Quick, man!' Noah threw himself down the rope. They heard men's shouts and the crash of feet on the stairs. Misha unhooked the rope and dropped it down into the boat. He let himself out of the window, hanging on his arms, then felt with his toe for the top of the window trim beneath him. Gina stood up, balancing in the little boat. Misha shook his head. They could hear heavy footsteps in the house. Smoke started to curl out of the window above them. Misha stuffed his gun in the back of his jeans and reached to one side with his free hand, getting a grip on the decrepit guttering. He put his weight on the downpipe. It groaned alarmingly, pulling away from the wall. 'Someone's here, boys!' came a shout from inside. Misha dropped into the boat. 'Go! Go!' he whispered. Annie pushed them off with the paddle. Gina grabbed the other paddle. They were still in full view of the window. Then there was an unendurably loud explosion and a sheet of flame erupted from the back of the house. The little boat rocked in the water. Annie and Gina bent over the paddles with all their force, taking the Chloe out through the flooded back garden and under a tangle of undergrowth where there once had been a shrub border. Behind them fire roared, but they didn't hear any more voices.

'Hell,' said Annie. 'They blew up the house.'

'Careful,' said Misha in a low voice. 'There may be more than one patrol.'

They sat in silence, appalled, listening to the roar and crackle of the burning house. Noah crouched in the bows, his dark face devoid of expression; Misha leaned on one elbow, alert, listening. Annie couldn't stop herself tensing, waiting for Tom to appear, but Tom had left the group; they hadn't seen him for weeks.

After five minutes Misha straightened up. 'There'll be a team here soon, any minute, maybe. We need to go now.' He put the gun carefully within reach on the gunwale, then shrugged out of his jacket and pulled his t-shirt over his head. He started undoing his belt. Methodically he stripped naked, then reached into the jacket pocket for a spray-tin. 'I have enough for me,' he said, bluntly.

'Wait,' said Gina. 'What are you doing?'

'Me, I will hide my heat signature and swim. There might be a small chance, that way. There is no escaping in the Chloe. They can see the boat clear as day from a satellite, and us in it, now they know what they are looking for.' He picked up the spray-tin and started covering his skin, back and front, ankles, shins, thighs, cock and balls. The oily paint spread in a clear slick over his body, locking in to the molecules of his skin. 'I don't know what you three will do.'

'You pre-programmed the paint?' said Gina. She seemed unable to take in what was happening.

'Let's just say I like to be prepared.' He picked up the gun, holding it loosely in his left hand, and twisted around with the tin of nano paint, aiming around his sides and over his shoulder.

'You can't do your own back, can you?' said Noah. He seemed to think it was funny.

'I can do it well enough not to show up as a man swimming.' He ran the spray over his head and neck, and, grimacing, eyes open, his face, then threw aside the paint tin and started going through his jacket pockets, stuffing a few items in a small drypouch which he hung around his neck. He looked regretfully at his cigarettes before leaving them. Then he sat on the gunwale and lowered himself down into the water, holding the gun high in his left hand. It was chest deep on him. 'Wait,' said Gina.

'He's right,' said Annie. She had been sitting in silence, watching Misha paint himself. 'Nano paint or not, we need to swim. And we need to split up.' She started unbuttoning her thin shirt.

'I don't think so,' said Noah. There was something hard in his voice. Misha pushed himself off, gliding low in the water without splashing, only the side of his braided scalp and his gun hand showing above the surface.

'Wait,' said Gina again, helplessly. 'Noah, stop him!'

'Gina!' said Annie, slipping out of her shorts. 'Quick!' She wound her clothes into a ball and, wearing only her halter bikini top, started looking around the boat for something to carry the dry things in.

'No,' said Noah, grabbing hold of her wrist. He stood up, balancing in the boat.

'What the fuck, Noah,' said Annie, in an angry undertone. 'Let the fuck go of my wrist.'

He didn't let go. Annie dropped her dry clothes and brought her free hand around to seize his forearm, snapping his hand away and breaking his grip. She kept hold and took a rapid step backwards down the length of the boat. Now she was behind him and with both hands she levered his arm behind his back, turning him away from her, holding his arm straight in an agonising torsion. Noah let out an incoherent yell of pain. For a moment she stood, rocking in the boat, and then she simply pushed on the straight arm. Noah fell face-first over the side, splashing heavily into the water.

There was a roar of compressed air servos. 'Annie!' Gina cried out wildly. Annie swung around. It was an armoured droid, black and gold SAPA security, riding on foot jets over the surface of the water. In an instant it had reached them and its laser cutter whined as it slashed through the tangled undergrowth. Annie threw herself over the side but Gina stood in the boat, transfixed. The droid reached out a long, jointed, armoured limb and took hold of Gina. Then too late she started to protest but the droid already had its tranquiliser needle extended. Gina went limp, her feet hanging and her head lolling to one side, looking in the droid's metal grasp like a chicken whose neck had been wrung. Desperately Annie floundered through the muddy water, struggling with interlaced branches, but the vegetation above her flashed into fire and was immediately vaporised, revealing her to a second droid. She seized a branch and tried to attack the servo jet mechanism but the droid batted her makeshift club away as if she had been a child and sent a long chain-like tendril to wrap around her, holding her arms to her sides. Still she struggled, kicking and thrashing, blood running down the side of her face, until the long tranquiliser needle loomed in her vision and at the last moment she thought she saw out of the corner of an eye a third droid carrying a person, Noah maybe. Then it went dark.

At first when she came to she thought she was in a coffin box and she had a weary sense of recognition. It wouldn't be fun but she knew how to navigate and endure this set of circumstances. Then she remembered. Hell. She opened her eyes.

She wasn't in a coffin box, but on a bed in a small containment chamber, lit by a dull strip light. The walls, floor and ceiling were all the same yellowish green. In the corner was a toilet pedestal with no seat and no paper. In the wall over the door was the glassy surface of a recessed camera eye. The door itself bore the usual Department of Correction disclaimer and a SAPA logo. It was a bit too warm. There was no VR, or no, wait. She reached around beneath her hairline and pressed her port access. Her chip was gone. There might be VR, but she couldn't reach it. Suddenly she felt very alone and defenceless.

She swung her legs down. She had been put into a grey tracksuit, a bit too big. It had a gritty feel against her skin. For a moment she felt aggrieved that she had lost her bikini top. She had liked it, it was from the pink and black set. Then she shook her head, smiling a little grimly. She had other things to worry about.

She didn't know how long she had been there or what time it was. She knew she might be kept for a long time yet, forever maybe. They could do what they liked to her, she didn't officially exist. She shuddered, slumping back onto the hard mattress and curling up in a ball. Over and over images ran in her mind: the house vanishing in flame, Misha slipping over the side of the Chloe, Gina in the grasp of the droid, Noah, Noah with that cold expression. So it had been Noah all along, or had someone got to him somehow? It had been him, she remembered, who had told them that morning that their position had been given away, that they had to move out. She couldn't work out why he had done that. If he was a SAPA plant, wouldn't it have been better not to say anything, just to let them be picked up? She wondered where everyone was now and if Misha had got away. Tom, at least Tom was safe, wherever he was. 'Babe,' she said aloud, softly. 'Where did you go?'

It had been a weird week, anyway, with Tom gone, and everything so difficult now that there had been the security clampdown. Supposedly it was to do with the threat from North Korea, but Annie and everyone she knew thought it was just an excuse to ramp up the military, SAPA uniforms everywhere in airports and public spaces, arrests for trivial things, no privacy outside the Darknet. And even the Darknet was infiltrated, they said. It had started to be hard to get food and staples without an overnet ID. They had been sending Gina, who was still clean, but then one night the breakwater cameras had been rebooted and she had had a hard time getting back home. Poor Gina, Annie thought, imagining her in a containment room like this one, in a worn grey tracksuit slightly the wrong size. It wasn't her, the activist side of it, although she was so passionate about what they did, about having a duty to speak up, to protect the natural world. She was there for her VR skills, just as Noah was the medic, and Annie and Tom were the fighters: four, there were supposed to be four in a cell. She couldn't remember how Misha had come to be part of it: come to think about it, she wondered about Misha altogether. He had always been able to get food, although sometimes what he came back with was bizarre, tins of flatki and other

Polish stuff mixed with strangely upmarket delicatessen items, expensive boxes of candied fruits and tiny pots of relish, the sort of things she guessed you might give as a present or take home from the airport. Or steal, she supposed.

And Amaruq, she wouldn't be able to contact him. She knew that they would analyse her port chip for access codes but she trusted his VR skills well enough to be confident that they wouldn't be able to trace him. Maybe she would never see him again. She started to cry a little, remembering the lily flowers and the warm ice-filled sea. Then a thought came to her. Hell, Amaruq. She opened her eyes, staring at the puke-green wall in front of her. Shit, his sister, what was her name, she was something to do with the plan to infiltrate the Ardsen miner and Noah, Noah knew about that. And she had no way of warning them. Think, Annie, she told herself. Carefully she kept an all-purpose miserable expression on her face. They would be scanning her mental state and matching it with her behaviour on the observation camera. Anything unusual might make them investigate. They could probably pick images out of her thought patterns; it would be illegal if she were a citizen, but a terror suspect was fair game. Ok, mental noise, that was what was needed. Think about the fish, the little swimming fish in the warm sea, the deep jewel colours, the swift about turns as the school moved all together. Unbelievable, she wondered how they knew to do that, real fish she meant, not programmed fish in VR.

This is good, said another part of her mind, good camouflage. She made that part shut up.

Imagine the fish, imagine being a fish, suspended in the warm turquoise ocean, imagine that you are in the middle of the school, swimming in synchrony with all the other fish. Imagine having fins. Fin, fin, *turn.* Fin, fin, *turn.*

Annie fell asleep.

Killaq

'And here we have the young woman who will be the face of the Inuit people in this exciting new venture. Ladies and gentlemen, Killaq Nanoortalik.'

Polite applause.

'Killaq, could we ask you to say a few words about your role in this project?'

She hesitated.

'Take your time.'

Killaq smiled shyly at the interviewer. She had practised this with Amaruq, in VR. It was important to seem young, naïve.

'Well,' she began, and then faltered. The interviewer smiled paternally. 'Well,' she started again. 'I am an Iqalummiut, an Inuit. I am proud of my Nation. I guess it seems right to me to develop our land, not just always to be just a minority people. So when Ardsen were looking for someone to live on the miner, I thought I would apply. I didn't think that I'd get chosen!'

She giggled. The interviewer nodded approvingly.

'So Killaq, tell our subscribers a little about what life is going to be like for you?'

'They've shown me the living quarters, high up in the miner. It's all lovely and new. So my job is to record what I see, I'm going to run a blog, and I'm going to be online for comments and questions.'

'You haven't been away from home before, is that right?'

'No! I'm going to miss everyone. I haven't been away anywhere by myself like this before.'

Except everywhere, she thought. She had worked in VR all over the world.

'You're a brave young woman. Ladies and gentlemen, a round of applause for Killaq.'

'Can I say hello to my Ma?' Killaq asked.

'Of course!'

'Hello Ma, and hello everyone from my neighbourhood!'

'Don't worry, Mrs. Nanoortalik, we'll take good care of her!' And then, 'OK, exit.'

'Did I do ok?' asked Killaq.

'Just fine, sweetheart, just fine.'

'Can I say hello to Ma?' repeated Amaruq, in a mincing, girlish manner.

'Fuck off,' said Killaq. 'You said I needed to come across as unsophisticated.'

'Unsophisticated, yes, not actually twelve years old.'

'Fuck you!' She picked up a handful of moss from the den floor and threw it at him, laughing. He froze the fragments in mid-air and then, with a slow wave of his hand, started them dancing around each other, turning in complex patterns, concentric circles of twigs and leaves breaking into three-dimensional lines and arrays.

'Very pretty,' said Killaq. 'Are we meeting the Australians?'

'Sorry, yes,' said Amaruq, and made the dancing particles vanish. 'Just one thing though.'

'What now?'

'They don't know who we're putting on the miner. Might be better to keep it that way.'

'Ok.'

'Just gonna hide your ID, wait a minute.'

He reached in the air above his head, making a twisting motion like someone unscrewing a light fitting. Killaq's persona flickered, then came back online. Now she was Randy McCormack, a plump White man with ginger hair and rumpled sweat pants.

'Randy? Really?' Killaq asked, with a lift of an eyebrow.

'Just an ID I had to hand,' said Amaruq, with one of his irritating grins. 'Ready?'

'Ready.'

The walls of the den vanished and they were in a plain meeting space, a room with wooden walls and low cushioned chairs set around a rough log table.

'Where the hell is this?' asked Killaq.

'No idea,' said Amaruq cheerfully, 'it's wherever the rendezvous link has taken us.'

The joining meeting icon chimed and a tall, black and white stork with a curved, hooked beak was sitting opposite from them. It had narrow wings, a long rising neck and head crowned with a spray of black-green feathers, and small red eyes. The beta simply said 'Noah.'

'Cool persona,' said Amaruq. 'Where's everyone else?'

'They can't make it,' said the stork.

'Ok,' said Amaruq, but Killaq, who knew him, thought there was something reserved about the way he said it. 'So you know me, and this is my colleague, Randy.'

'Randy, hi,' said the stork, 'So, ah, tell me, are we all set up?'

'Good to go,' said Amaruq, in a non-committal fashion.

'Ah,' said the stork, 'the others, they were saying we should have a bit more detail, at this stage. We need a back door, a way in into your organisation. So that, ah, if anything goes wrong, we can take over. And we can identify the person, y'know, look out for them if there was any trouble.'

'Of course,' said Amaruq. Killaq looked at him in surprise, but said nothing. She tried to keep her expression neutral.

'Ah, good,' said the stork. 'So, will you, can I have the codes now?'

'No,' said Amaruq. 'They aren't made to be handed over, just like that. I'll have to arrange it from outside VR.'

This was the first Killaq had heard of anything like this.

'Of course, of course,' said the stork. 'Security is paramount. We're all looking forward to dealing SAPA, ah, a really *killing blow.* So you'll let me have the accesses right away?'

'When I get back, yes,' said Amaruq, 'but it's not just in my hands. I have to go through a chain of authority. You remember, we talked about that before.'

'Quite right, very proper, absolutely,' said the stork. It shifted its weight in the seat, ruffling its feathers. 'So will it be later today, for the access codes? And the person's ID, of course?'

'Soon as I can,' said Amaruq smoothly. 'Straight away if I hear back soon enough. So how are the others? Gina must be excited?'

'Gina, oh yes,' said the stork. 'Terribly excited. Very, very,' and then it paused, apparently thinking better of saying 'excited' again. It tapped its talon on the floor in a nervous rhythm.

'Ok,' said Amaruq, standing up abruptly. 'We'd better leave it there. The shorter the time we spend in this space, the better. Just in case, you know.'

'Oh yes,' said the stork. 'We understand. We're all counting on you.'

'We won't let you down,' said Killaq, as warmly as she could manage.

'See you then,' said the stork, but Amaruq had already closed the meeting space before the stork could action the handshake ID burst.

'Shit,' said Amaruq.

'What was going on, back there?'

'I don't know,' said Amaruq, slowly, 'but I don't think that was Noah. Or if it was Noah, there's something wrong with him.'

'Will you give them the access codes?'

'What do you think?'

'So, what does it mean? For the action?'

'I don't know. I'm going to talk to Annie. I've a link for her outside the cell structure.'

Oh, so it was Annie that he had the thing going with, thought Killaq.

'Until I've spoken with her we shouldn't do anything. Just look as if it's all going ahead as planned.'

'The miner start-up is in five days.'

'I know, I know, and we'll have to pull the action if there's anything wrong. Just wait until I've spoken with Annie. She'll know what's going on.'

Amaruq raised his head out of his hands and looked at Killaq. 'Don't worry, sis, we won't let you get involved if there's a sniff of anything there shouldn't be.' He took her hand.

/den/exit/

Later, Killaq stuck her head around the door to Amaruq's bedroom. He was sitting in his programming space, rearranging sections of code. The green characters swam in the air like a complex three-dimensional jigsaw.

'Hey, Ma sent me to see if you wanted any coffee.'

She came in, closing the door behind her.

'Did you hear anything?' she asked in a low voice. He shook his head, absorbed in the code.

'What's that?'

'Something different. Actually, look, I can show you this much.'

He swept the code to the side of the field of view and brought up a screen view instead. It must have been recorded direct from someone's visual; it looked a bit odd. The view seemed to be from someone sitting in a transport of some kind. They were looking across at uniformed soldiers sitting on cramped metal benches. The whole view juddered and shook as if whatever vehicle they were in was traversing difficult ground. The soldiers had an Asian appearance and were wearing olive grey combats; she could see a network blazon with a red star surrounded by a golden wreath.

'Sorry,' said Amaruq. He brought up audio. Now she could hear the rumble of the transport and people speaking. She couldn't understand the language.

'Shit, sorry, shitty interface. There. Is that better?'

Now the written translation scrolled across the bottom of the view.

So why the fuck are we being recalled this time?

The sergeant said we were needed for the next operation.

Next operation, my [untranslatable]. They said that last time and we had three weeks of living in dugouts on rice and pickles.

No really, he said something is happening this time, but [pompous voice] 'It is not for the likes of you, humble soldier, to question the decisions of command.'

Not very nice rice and pickles, even.

Shut up, Ji-Hae. I want to know what else the sergeant said.

I told you, he wouldn't tell me.

Reckon it's the Great Step North, for real this time?

[Laughter]

Bugger the Great Step North, the only Great Step I want to take is [translation failed].

Pity that poor young man, friends, he doesn't know what an [untranslatable] [untranslatable] daughter of an [untranslatable] our comrade here really is.

'Fuck you too, Wu-Han.'

The recording ended. Killaq raised an eyebrow.

'Your interface needs to work on its colloquialisms. What language were they speaking?'

'Korean.'

'Ah.'

'Still, it could be for anything. That they were being recalled, I mean.'

'Yeah, maybe. But, look, did I miss something? One minute VR is full of jokes about glowing blue undersea aliens, and the next the news seems to have accepted that this thing in Korea is real, and there are security clampdowns all over the place, and the Council have gone all quiet about it.'

'Yup. I think the Siberians, the Federation is being leaned on by Mother Russia.'

'What, to allow them in? To fight Korea on Federation soil?'

'Wouldn't be pretty.'

'Christ.' And then, thinking about it, Killaq added, 'Is that why you're still messing about with this immersive stuff? Is that the same soldier?'

'No. He died.'

And seeing from Amaruq's closed face that she wasn't going to get any more on that subject, Killaq turned on her heel, saying 'Coffee.'

'Wait,' said Amaruq. 'See you later? On the beach? Still got the link?'

'Still got the link.'

Killaq closed the door and headed back down the corridor. Ma was in the kitchen.

'Ma,' said Killaq, 'why did we never hear anything more? After that Council meeting?'

Ma looked at Killaq shrewdly. 'Yes,' she said. 'I wondered that myself. To start with it was a big joke in VR, and now it has gone out of our hands, above our heads. You remember what I said, at the meeting?'

'You said it would be war, and everyone patronised you.'

'I said it would be war, and everyone patronised me,' said Ma, turning around with the coffee pot. 'And, you know, it isn't the Federation I'm worried about.

They're our brothers and sisters, even if we disagree about sea-bed rights and other things. But Russia and North Korea, they're both nuclear powers.'

'Oh, Ma!' said Killaq. 'No one is *that* crazy!'

'Maybe you're right,' said Ma. 'But it nearly happened before, in Ukraine. Anyway, I saw you on the Council news, very smart with your SAPA network blazon.'

'I've got corporate rights for the duration, ta-daa!'

'Very nice,' said Ma. 'And whatever happens here, I guess SAPA will look after you. You'll be as safe on that miner as anywhere.'

'Ma! Nothing is going to happen here.'

'Maybe so,' said Ma, 'maybe so. I hope not. Here, take your brother his coffee.'

She brought the steaming cup over to Killaq, and took her arm, looking earnestly into her face. 'Just you remember, when you go on that machine, you're just as good as all those fat white men. You don't need to let them talk down to you, or pigeon-hole you, or dress you up as a cute indigenous girl. I know it's all corporate PR, but don't let them make you talk babytalk. You're better than that, twice the programmer any of them probably are. You're a strong young woman and I'm proud of you.'

'Ma,' said Killaq, embarrassed. She hadn't thought how her naïve act would look to people that she knew.

'Ok,' said Ma. 'I've said my piece. Take him his coffee, now.' She gave Killaq a gentle push.

When Killaq looked around Amaruq's door again, he wasn't in the programming space, and the console lid was closed and silvered, the privacy icon shining. She sighed, and put down the coffee, heading for her own console.

/scenario/enter/

It was the beach, but it had a desolate, uncared for air. The sky was grey and the incoming waves swept in with an unreal regularity, as if no one had bothered to add any cyclicity to the programme. Killaq looked out to sea, but she couldn't see her brother on his surfboard. She shivered. She could almost believe that she felt cold. She looked down at the conch shell in her hand, feeling its roughened spirals, turning it over to reveal the smooth pink interior. Then she stooped and, standing on one foot at a time, took off the little kitten heels and lined them up on the sand. She rolled down the stockings and left them neatly folded, one inside each shoe. Barefoot, taking a direction at random, she walked along the water's edge. One after another the too-regular waves arrived with a shushing sound, the last of the foam spreading hissing up the beach, splashing her toes, and then there was the gravelly sound of the wave withdrawing, the newly wetted foreshore glistened, and her feet sank in, leaving neatly printed footmarks behind her. No one was here.

She came to a tangle of washed-up seaweed, dark olive coloured, greasy-looking, and stopped, frowning. It seemed to be too detailed a thing to have a place in this sketchy environment. If someone had bothered to dot the beach with flotsam, then she would have thought they would have done a better job with the waves, and the repetitive pattern of the sand ripples, which was always the same, like wallpaper. She walked on under a grey sky, stepping over more seaweed, snarls of blue twine, broken plastic junk.

After some time, a long time for VR, the indistinct boundary ahead of her, where the pale beach met the dark sea, developed a rugged outline. Rocks, black rocks, running down to the water. As she came nearer she saw their jagged shapes barring her way; it was a long black stripe of stone, a volcanic dyke. Careful-footed she climbed up among the rocks, balancing on the slippery surfaces, keeping her bare toes from the small sharp shells and the glossy pods of bladder wrack draped over the geometric faces of the basalt. She got to the high point: she could look down on the far side where the rock ended and the sand began again. There was a hunched figure sitting on the sand, arms around his knees, looking out to sea.

'Hey,' Killaq called to him, and then, receiving no answer, started picking her way down towards him. 'Amaruq!'

He turned a bleak face up to her.

'You gave me the link.' She hesitated. 'So I came.'

'I can't find her,' he said, staring at the repeating waves. 'I can't find her anywhere. There can't be anyone online I can't find. So they must have caught her, she must be offline. She must be in danger.'

'Annie?'

'Yes, of course Annie, who did you think I was talking about?'

Killaq squatted down next to him, awkward in her pencil skirt, and put a hand on his shoulder.

'You don't think –'

'I don't know, how could I know?'

He paused. 'I thought we could talk to her, find out what was going on. Now it's obvious there's something wrong. We'll have to get you out of it somehow.'

'I can just say I changed my mind,' said Killaq, but even as she said it she felt doubtful. 'Look,' she went on, 'have you tried any of the others?'

'Noah must have been corrupted. Maybe they all are too. Maybe they always were.'

This wasn't like him. She sat down properly on the hard sand, folding her legs under her, still resting her hand on his shoulder. 'You can find them, though, the others? Without them tracing you? So that might be a way to go, first?'

Amaruq sank his head in his hands, clutching his hair. Then he shook himself.

'Yes, I can do that. In fact, I have to do that. We have to find out what's going on. And there might be – other resources I can call on.'

He sprang to his feet.

'Come on, sis. I need to talk to some people. And this sand is cold.'

He pulled her to her feet, and hugged her. 'Thanks for coming to get me.'

/beach/exit/

Tom

He had wound up in a place called Nindaroo, some ways out of Mackay in Queensland. There wasn't much there.

To start with he had wandered angrily, at random. He hadn't meant to go for good, if he had he would have taken some stuff, his board. It was just more than he could handle, his Annie, so distant, and he was almost sure there was something going on, something with the northerner, in VR. He found himself travelling recklessly beneath the sea wall, in the full view of whatever camera or drone eye might see him, and when the tide was in he waded, and when he was hungry he climbed the wall and stole something to eat, going into houses, right into the kitchens, eating leftovers by the blue light of the open fridge door while the family slept.

After about a week of this he got a scare, a light coming on at the top of the stairs, someone awake. He'd bolted out of the back and hid in the garden. He had just enough sense of self-preservation not to go running down the street. If the resident had a security contract they would dial it in and he would be shot by the guard drone before he could get very far. He had stayed under the porch decking the rest of the night and all through the next day. Then he had gone back in when the family were out, doing it properly this time, hacking the house access and neutralising the cameras. Fortunately the guy in the house had stuff he could wear: a bit big but he helped himself to clean shorts and a t-shirt. He couldn't find any shoes that fitted him. He picked up a canvas bag and packed some bread, ham, a tin of skin depilatory that he found in a bathroom cabinet. He stripped out of his filthy clothes and put them straight in the disposal. Then he left by the front door, taking care to look purposeful. He found a quiet corner and ran the depilatory over his face and head. The dirty blond hair fell away in clumps. Somehow he felt better for it, his mind felt clearer. He looked about him. There was a pedestrian sign on a pole above his head. It said 'To the beach.'

It turned out to be a small family beach, just the other side of the tide wall. There were a few people about, kids on the sand, a middle-aged couple walking a fat Shi Tzu that huffed and waddled after them. He left the bag on the sand – if someone took it, too bad – and stripped down to his stolen boxers. Then he walked down to the water's edge and waded out. The salt sea felt good on his body, on his naked head, on his back and shoulders. He kept swimming.

He had got a long way out, further than he had been before without his board, when he turned round to look back at the land. For a moment he thought he would turn to the open sea, just keep swimming until the strength ran out of his arms and the current took him, but then he shook his head. That wasn't him. He started to swim back to the land, aware now of starting to be tired, of being hungry.

So, he thought, when at long last he had reached the beach again, and had ravenously downed most of the bread and ham. What now? Was he going back to the group? He realised that the answer to that was no. It wasn't just Annie, there was something the matter, something bad about the way things were going. The image of Noah drumming his fingers on the verandah post came to his mind. Noah, Noah was a good guy, no doubt about it, but he had been acting weird, jumpy. Tom shook his head again. He, Tom, he had always deferred to Gina and Noah, they had been in the group longer, they understood how things worked. He and Annie were just muscle, he knew that. But there was something wrong about the decisions the group had been making, this whole northern thing, it didn't seem right. It didn't seem worth risking security for.

Ok, so he wasn't going back. What was he going to do, in that case? But that was as far as his thoughts would take him. He tucked the canvas bag under his head and slept.

The tide came in overnight, and Tom woke up to the dawn over the damp sand and the sea murmuring not very far away. He still didn't have a plan. He pushed himself up and went looking for breakfast. Over the days that followed he worked his way north, sometimes walking, sometimes catching a rail runner. Carbon controls meant that security was tight on the old road network: you couldn't hitch a lift on a fuel vehicle without ID, and anyone driving a hydrogen car would be a corporate, likely to turn you in straight away. But the train network was still there, and they couldn't police every inch of it. If you knew who to talk to you could buy some miles on one of the illegal, solar-powered rail runners: small makeshift cabs, big enough for three or four passengers at the most, hugging a single rail, making the most of the low friction. There were horrible accidents every now and again, and then the rail companies got prosecuted, and would swear to up security, and the rails would be inaccessible for a time, but after a while the rail runners always came back.

This was how he had wound up in Nindaroo. It wasn't that he chose it, it was just the place he was when the travelling came to seem even more pointless than just staying put. He slept a night in a ditch in Mackay, then two, then he called in some contacts from the Darknet and got put in touch with the emergency safehouse system. No one back in the group would be able to trace him; contact with the safehouse network erased itself after you had used it. It was designed for when a cell had been corrupted, or something had gone wrong, not for nameless drifters whose girlfriends might be having an affair, but no one would know or ask him his reasons.

The safehouse was a dilapidated trailer in the corner of a field, half-hidden by a stand of gumtrees. He walked down the dusty track from the road and found the physical key where the Darknet avatar had said it would be, under the rotted seat of a crop sprayer leaning up against the fence. Whoever had lived here last had been into astrology: the walls were covered with faded star charts and zodiac symbols, and a faint persistent scent of patchouli competed with the smell of mould. Tom sat down heavily on the narrow bed, ignoring the dust that rose up, and gazed out of the open door. The view was of the yellow field and some fence posts. He let himself fall back on the bed, staring instead at the stained ceiling.

He had been living like this for a couple of weeks, numbly going through the motions of keeping out of sight, of venturing out at night to find food, of shitting in a corner of the field behind the gum trees, when his message waiting icon flashed. He frowned. He was disconnected from everything, he had turned off all his alerts. There should be no way anyone could trace him. He cancelled the icon and turned over in the dusty bed. The icon flashed again. Tom sat up. He didn't like this. It could be Annie, or one of the others, Gina maybe would have the skill to override his disconnect. Or it could be a trap. The safe way, the only safe way was to take the port chip right out. He hesitated, one hand reaching behind his neck. Then the view of the yellow field vanished and all around him was white. He yelled out incoherently: this was VR, but somewhere he hadn't chosen to be. It was impossible, no one could be pulled into VR without their permission. He looked around him wildly.

A door opened in front of him and a figure stepped through. He was short, much shorter than Tom, and stockily built, with wide Inuit features and dark hair. He was wearing sealskin leggings and a sealskin jerkin, a bear's tooth necklace making a broad half-circle over his bare chest. It was the fucking Eskimo.

'Sorry about that, mate,' the Eskimo said, 'but I really needed to talk to you.'

Tom hit him.

He knew of course that he was in the other man's scenario, that the Eskimo could just neutralise the blow, but despite that he felt his fist connect. Then abruptly they were in deep water and he was grappled with some dark strangling tentacled thing. He sent all his willpower into his own strength, wrapping his long suckered limb around the other's bulbous head, avoiding the razor beak, he would choke him until he /

he was a flying reptile, a pterosaur, riding a windy sky with huge leathery wings outspread, and from above him came diving the other reptile, colliding with him in the full force of his descent and gouging /

and the bell rang, it was the beginning of the next round. Woozily he forced himself up from the ropes and pushed aside the sponge his second was offering. 'Fucking stand still!' he shouted. 'Fucking stand still and fight!'

'You choose,' said the other boxer.

Lightning crackled in the dark sky overhead. The two men sat their boards, riding the swell and uplift of the enormous wave. Rain was falling in sheets. 'Shit,' said the other surfer. He turned and grinned at Tom. Then he let the wave take him over the lip.

That was him gone. Tom didn't think about him any further. He gathered all his focus and sent the board into the crest of the wave, swinging his feet under him, standing up in one muscular movement. Lightning struck the sea, very near, but he barely heard it. All his concentration was in the board, in his balance, as he sped down the towering side of the wave and ahead he heard it start to curl and break with a deafening sound like an avalanche, like a landslide, and now he was in the barrel, but like no barrel that he had ever surfed before, a huge long hall of moving black water, the curving ceiling far above him. He kept going, barely aware of his surroundings, his mind empty of everything except his poised stance on the board, one trailing hand in the wall of water beside him. It couldn't last, he knew it couldn't last. Now the barrel was closing and the huge hall became a narrow tube, the crashing water just above his head, and without making any conscious decision he put his weight on the nose of the board and turned sharply into the face of the wave. For a moment the weight of water was all around him and then he punched through the back of the wave and he was out, and the wave was travelling away from him, and the air was clear. A gull came shearing past him through the blue sky.

'Ok,' he said out loud. 'What you got?'

In a heartbeat he was back in the white space. The Eskimo, the northerner, whatever, was there too. Tom saw that he was nursing a split lip and blood was running down the side of his head. Maybe he got a knock from his board when he wiped out, thought Tom, with a sense of satisfaction. He stood looking at the northerner, arms folded, smiling an unfriendly smile. This was his shit, whatever it was, let him start.

Maybe Annie had sent him, but he would have thought more of her than that. If she was leaving, she could tell him herself.

'That was some wave,' said the other man, ruefully shaking his head. 'I fell through the air for like, forever.'

'Yeah,' said Tom. 'Some wave.' He wasn't going to be drawn into this fucking buddy stuff.

The northerner held out his hand. 'Amaruq,' he said.

Tom found himself shaking the hand without having meant to.

'Look,' said Amaruq, gesturing around the white space, 'I'm sorry about all this. I know you're offline, and I don't need to know why, I just really needed to talk to you, you and Annie, if she's there. I'm hoping she's there with you.'

Tom stared at him. 'What the fucking hell,' he said, speaking softly although rage was rising up in him, 'what the fucking hell business have you got, bringing me here to ask about Annie.'

Amaruq held his hands up, palm out, placating. 'Ok, ok, I get it. I wouldn't have interrupted you both. I just need to ask you about Noah, something about Noah. Then I'll leave you alone.' He paused a moment, looking at the floor. 'I'm glad she's safe.'

Tom took two rapid steps towards Amaruq. '*Safe?*' he yelled. 'You fucking piece of shit, why wouldn't she be *safe?*'

'Ah,' said Amaruq. He looked suddenly sad and weary. 'I'm sorry.'

Then he was gone. Tom was sitting on the dusty bed, looking at the yellow field. What the fucking hell was that all about? He lay back down, feeling seriously unsettled. That Eskimo, that Amaruq, had he thought that Annie was here? And what was that about being safe?

/connect/AnnieLing/

Nothing.

/connect/AnnieLing/

Still nothing.

/message/AnnieLing/

No message facility even. She really was completely offline. Gina, Gina would know what was going on.

/connect/AleiginaGabor/

Nothing.

/message/AleiginaGabor/

Nothing.

/connect/AnnieLing/ /connect/AnnieLing/ / connect/ AnnieLing/

Nothing.

Killaq

Amaruq came to sit on the end of her bed. 'Sis, wake up.'

Killaq opened her eyes. She hadn't really been asleep.

'I need to talk to you. Before it all starts.'

Killaq knew what he meant. After she had been set up for access to the SAPA blog, it would be much more difficult to communicate privately. Everything she did in VR would be monitored – of course, that was the idea. Amaruq had said he would build her a back door and she had every confidence that he could outwit SAPA security, but it might not be the kind of door that you could use on a regular basis.

'Ok.'

/den/enter/

She was there before him. For a few minutes she played with the puppy Ila, and then she started to worry. He hadn't looked good, when she saw him on the beach, and since then she had been busy with SAPA induction and participation in what seemed like endless PR. And there was the whole business with Noah, she didn't know what he had found out, what it all meant.

'Hey, sis.' He was sitting behind her, leaning on the withied wall of the den. She leant back on his shoulder, relieved, and he slung an arm around her.

‘So.’

‘So, look, I don’t think you should go ahead with this.’

‘What?’

She turned around to look at him fully, seeing how drawn and anxious he was.

‘I don’t know what’s going on.’ It seemed to be an effort for him to admit it.

‘Why didn’t you say something earlier? The miner launch is tomorrow. How am I going to make any sort of reasonable excuse now? It’s too late, whatever it is, I can’t get out of it.’ And then, when he didn’t reply, ‘Tell me!’

‘Ok.’ But he still didn’t reply straight away. She shook his arm, gently.

‘Ok, ok.’

‘Did you find Annie?’

‘No, at least, I haven’t spoken to her. I spoke to Tom. I don’t think they’re involved in the miner thing anymore, they both seem to be offline. So maybe they thought they needed to get out as well, I don’t know. Tom wasn’t really happy to talk with me.’

No shit, thought Killaq.

‘I can’t get hold of Gina at all, there’s no trace of her. I tried the other one, Misha, but he was shooting up, I couldn’t get any sense out of him.’ Killaq grimaced. ‘And meantime this Noah keeps pestering me for the accesses that I promised him. I’ve been putting him off, telling him it isn’t authorised yet, but he’s getting insistent.’ He paused. ‘If there was nothing else, that would tell me there was something wrong.’ He took

Killaq by the elbows. 'I can't let you do it, the whole thing smells. Ma would never forgive me.'

Killaq looked up at the round brambled ceiling, thinking. 'Look,' she said, after a while, 'if I pull out now, it will look really weird, everyone will know that there's something the matter.'

'Can't be helped.'

'No, look. I don't know what the plan was, I never have known.'

'We couldn't make that data secure, if you knew it.'

'Right, I know. But if I just go ahead with it, if I go on the miner, and do all the blog, and the publicity, and stuff, it gives you more time to find out what's going on. What's the worst that can happen?'

'It could be bad, sis, really bad. They know we have someone on the miner. They don't know it's you, but they'll be watching constantly.'

'So if they do suspect? Why would it be bad? Nothing's going to happen unless you let the Ozzies do it. You aren't going to let them unless things start making a bit more sense. Worst is, I do my three months and I look like a total corporate fangirl from the outside.'

'Perils of being a double agent,' said Amaruq, with the beginnings of a smile. 'But it's still way too unpredictable. I just can't let you. And what about Noah?'

'Couldn't you, I don't know, build him a fake door?'

'Right, a fake door, leading to what, a fake universe? In twenty-four hours?'

'Ok, no, bad idea.'

'Actually,' said Amaruq, this time with more like a proper smile, 'as it happens I do have a spare universe. One I made earlier.'

'That's not a universe,' said Killaq, looking over his shoulder. 'It's barely a small town.'

'Well hey, it's not bad for short notice.'

He was in his programming space, moving code around with sweeping gestures.

'See, I've been trying to make somewhere a person could live in, temporarily, a sort of emergency hideout.'

'If they were in trouble of some kind?'

'Yeah, or if their body, if they couldn't get back to their body. Temporarily.'

'Why wouldn't they be able to get back to their body?'

'Well, ah, for whatever reason. It's only a little hideout, you wouldn't want to stay there for long. This one, it's insulated from the rest of VR. You can't get in or out. For safety. It's just a little box, really.'

Killaq looked at him dubiously. 'But you're still linked through the portal, linked back to your body, aren't you? So how is that safe?'

'Well, no, you don't have to be. You can take the whole of your consciousness inside and, you know, just close the lid.'

'This is beyond insane, you know that. I don't believe that it's even possible.'

'Want to give it a try?'

'No!' She looked more closely at the code swimming in front of her. 'And what are you writing in? I don't recognise any of this stuff.'

'Ah,' said Amaruq, his face lighting up, 'that's the clever part. See, you couldn't replicate the whole world in code, the way we code VR now.'

'The information density,' said Killaq, shaking her head.

'Right, you have to describe the thing, then you have to describe how the thing behaves in the environment, piece by piece, all algorithm-based. Completely impossible.'

'Right. So what's all this?'

'I'm using the data to make up the fabric of the world. It's built out of data gradients. So if you drop a piece of paper, in VR, it flutters down because someone's written an algorithm explaining how a piece of paper behaves in air, under gravity.'

Killaq smiled. It was a standard high school exercise.

'In my box, here, if you drop a piece of paper, it flutters down because that's the only possible outcome of the data gradients which make up the paper and the world. I'm using the data itself, to build the shapes of the forces.'

'Cool,' said Killaq. 'Does it have a name?'

'The world, when it's done, it'll be like a pocket kingdom. I'm calling it the Real.'

'Show me sometime?' asked Killaq, and then, 'So right now, is it finished enough to hold someone? Are we going to trap Noah, or whoever is running Noah?'

'A stork trap, yeah. But you, sis, aren't going to do anything. I've already told you more than I should for now.'

'Coffee?'

'Coffee.'

Next morning Killaq got up and put on her SAPA-logoed leggings and top. She had a last look around her usual VR desktops and platforms. She had tidied and deleted ruthlessly, and most of the everyday clutter of her life was gone. The link to the Ambra character she had hidden, under the subtlest security she knew how to code. She might need her. Everything else, SAPA was welcome to.

/SAPA employee portal/login/

/ID accepted/

This was it.

Ready, Killaq?

It was the PR lady, Consuela Wincanton. Killaq couldn't stand her.

Now, remember, you're on live blog, but we've got a 3-second delay built in for security. If you say something you think might not have come out just quite right, just use the erase icon and the oversight algorithm will pick it up and stitch across. We'll have a human controller on standby too for the launch. Feeling nervous?

Fool, thought Killaq.

A little nervous!

That's natural, but remember, you're going to do just fine. Ok, ready for the pre-record?

I think so!

Ok, counting you in. And live.

Killaq took a breath.

Well hi, hello everyone, I guess. I'm Killaq Nanoortalik and this is the first post of my blog for SAPA. So, I guess you all know that I'm going to be part of the new mineral development programme here in the Arctic Nation, I'm going to be bearing witness for the Inuit people. I'm actually going to be living on the huge Dreadnaught mining machine! They showed me around it last week, it's awesome! So this is me packing, saying goodbye to my bedroom for the time being. See, this is my bedroom, I've tidied it all up. It feels like being properly grownup at last, leaving home, although of course I'll be back soon enough, it's not for very long. But I still feel a bit teary! So this is my little bag, I don't need to take very much because the living quarters, on the miner, it's all climate controlled and SAPA are giving me everything I need, clothes, everything.

So it's going to be a long day, I guess, there's a ceremony with the Council here in Iqaluit and then they're flying me out to the miner in a personal transport. So I'll tell you how it all went in my next post. Just for now I just need to say thanks to SAPA for giving me this amazing opportunity, I can't believe it, the team prepping me for the miner have been awesome, and thanks especially to Consuela, couldn't have done it without you. And love too to everyone here, I love you Ma, and Ma, I'm going to remember the advice you gave me, you know the advice I mean.

/exit/

Was I ok?

Lovely, lovely, you're a natural, Killaq. Go and get some breakfast, and the transport will be there for you at 11.00.

It was many hours later, after the speeches and the reception, the handshaking, the photographs, the canapés and the small glass of fizzy wine, that Killaq found herself looking out of the window of the SAPA VTOL transport, watching the brown land unroll beneath her. There was still snow, lying in long white tiger streaks across the landscape, but the thaw was well set in. Every year the snow came later and thawed sooner, and the loosening grip of the permafrost meant that the thaw revealed a treacherous terrain, full of uncharted bogs and sinkholes.

Killaq leaned her head against the window. She was exhausted with all the ceremonial stuff, and even now she wasn't alone: her full viz and audio was being streamed straight to her blog, so that anyone who wanted could watch the brown thawing landscape with her. To start with a drone eye had kept pace with them, recording an image from outside: Killaq waving good bye, Killaq looking pensively out of the window, but Killaq suspected that there was only so much footage anyone wanted to watch of someone looking out of a transport window. Anyway, the eye was gone, now, leaving her with only the scrolling messages from the blog feed in her heads-up, interspersed with advertising and infotorials and sponsored links. Most of the messages were variants of 'You go girl, you are awesome, good luck,' although there were also the other messages, the ones saying that she was a traitor to her people, that she was complicit in an illegal carbon release. 'YOU are suppose to be representing the INUIT PEOPLE but YOU are not REPRESENTING me because I DON AGREE to the MINER,' was a typical example, although there were more creative posts, and one contributor had put up a clip of someone setting themselves on fire, a Schedule II protest from the old days, over and over again on repeat.

Consuela said that they could edit out the hostile messages, but it was better to leave them, it would give an impression of openness, and anyway (she said) nobody cared, and once the miner was up and operating the message density would die down and people would forget about it. Killaq wasn't supposed to turn off the message feed because people liked to see the scrolling messages in her heads-up, when they logged in to her visual – apparently it heightened the sense of immediacy, according to Consuela. It made them feel as if they really were sitting in Killaq's seat in an executive lounger in a personal transport, flying over the Nunavut landscape, north and west into the heart of the Arctic Nation. Killaq was weary of it already.

It was later that afternoon and the Arctic dusk was falling when Consuela's voice cut in on private message.

Nearly there, Killaq, are you awake?

There was still a glowing green strip of sky on the horizon, and you could see the shadows of the landscape passing beneath the transport's harsh lights. There seemed to be more snow and less brown land here. They must be a long way North of Iqaluit by now. Killaq shook herself: she hadn't been asleep really, just watching the view roll by in a sort of drowse.

Hi Consuela, I'm here!

We're going to give you a 15 minute privacy break, you can go and freshen up, and then we're getting ready for Miner Arrival.

Ok, I'll be ready!

/blogfeed off/privacy setting/

It was a relief to clear her heads-up of the blog messages. Even though she had long ago stopped reading them, the constant words felt like a pressure in her head. She unclicked her seat restraint and walked down the plushly carpeted corridor to the comfort station. The room acknowledged her and she went straight to the shower, throwing off her logoed clothing and stuffing it in the chute. A new, identical outfit was already laid out on the side. She didn't bother to marvel over the waste, the carbon cost; she was getting used to how SAPA did things.

She let the warm water run over her face and neck. It was worse than she had thought, being on full-time viz and audio. She was going to need all the solitude she could get. Of course, SAPA were still monitoring her: it wasn't true privacy, but at least it was freedom from the intrusive blog messages.

She pulled on the new top and leggings, exactly the same as the old ones, and looked at herself in the mirror. Killaq Nanoortalik, SAPA corporate. She pulled her hair back from her face and held her fringe back from her forehead, exposing the double-dipping tattoo, the long parallel lines coming to a point over the bridge of her nose, like a bird's wings across her face, she thought. She looked older with her hair back, more competent: it wouldn't do. She let the fringe fall and turned to the door.

/blogfeed on/

So hi again, it's Killaq Nanoortalik from the joint SAPA/Ardsen mineral project here in the heart of the Arctic Nation. So I've been watching the landscape go by, you can see out the window, it's kind of all the same. Makes you realise what a great unexplored land this is. They're telling me that we're going to be landing on the miner soon, so I'm going to swap you to the VTOL camera and we can watch together.

/transport camera view/activate/

Not a lot to see just now, but wait, we're going to see the miner in all her glory any minute now.

The transport's nose camera showed a blurry dusk. A dark looming outline could be made out bulking against the sky. Then white light splashed out and the massive shape of the miner sprang into view, lit up by hundreds of floodlights, its yellow walls towering over the transport now coming in at speed. The pilot took the transport low around the miner, making one full circuit; Killaq caught only a glimpse of the heavy laser ablation machinery at the business end, before the transport swooped sharply upwards, landing on the docking station with a fanfare of engine noise.

Woo! We're here!

It was synthetic enthusiasm for the blog followers, but despite herself Killaq felt excited, almost moved. There was something elemental about the sheer size of the machine, despite everything she knew about what it was going to be used for. Killaq stood up and her SAPA minder steered her to the transport exit.

Gotta get wrapped up, it's gonna be cold out there!

She was handed an enormous hooded jacket and overtrousers, full all-weather gear, bright yellow with the Ardsen dark blue logo. It would of course have been perfectly possible to dock the transport direct to the living quarters, but the SAPA co-ordinators had wanted the retro drama of the disembarkation into the snowy night, the girl's slight figure muffled by the bulky clothing, the contrast between the comfortable tedium of the journey and the windswept landing platform under a sky of stars. Killaq walked down the gangway and stepped onto the metal plates of the deck, breathing the bitingly cold air. This was it.

An unfamiliar icon flashed in her heads-up. A conch shell. Killaq smiled into the harsh camera lights, comforted.

3rd March 2062

Welcome to this week's edition of the Live World Programme, and here to bring you all the issues of the week is your host, Aidan Macito!

[applause]

Welcome to the Live World, subscribers! This week we're going to look at the threatened North Korean incursion and the controversial topic of the environmental cost of war. Here to help me get to the bottom of these thorny issues is environmental scientist Josie Sigurdsdottir –

Hi, everyone!

– and expert military observer Karl Rauchenberg.

Hello.

I'll start with you if I may, Karl – we're hearing a lot about war in the North these days, but how likely is it that we will actually see shots fired in anger, in Siberia?

Well Aidan, that is a difficult question to be sure. It seems clear that the North Koreans are building something, up there in the Sibirskoye Morye, but how serious a threat it is we cannot know. It has happened in other years, that the North Koreans have claimed capabilities which have not, it turns out, been fully verified. What may be happening is, that they want to make a bargaining platform, to be allowed to extend their boundaries.

But Karl, everyone is saying that surely the North Koreans

don't really want the land that they are threatening, the land in the far north – it isn't useable for living, for human habitation.

That's right, Aidan. What some analysts think the most likely outcome is, is that Korea will hold out for a land bridge into the southern part of the Siberian Federation. Maybe Russia would back a deal, if the threat of war seemed real enough.

And compensate the Federation with land elsewhere?

Or mineral rights, Aidan. It has always been a sore point with the Federation, that Russia maintains title to the mineral rights under Federation land.

So a deal maybe, peace with honour?

Maybe, Aidan, but at the moment we cannot say.

So turning to you, Rosie, your specialist subject is, I believe, the environmental cost of global conflict?

That's right, Aidan, my research is about the environmental impact of conflict and the way that we as a global society attribute value to that, negative value of course. But before I start, Aidan, I just want to say that it's all very well for people like Karl to talk about Siberian land being given to the Koreans, but there are people living there! There is a human cost. You can't just parcel out the world in response to whoever has the biggest guns at the time.

Aidan, you will perhaps allow me to respond. Rosie, these are complex issues, but can we not say that we have a duty, a global duty, to respond to the human need of the Korean people whose own land will be inevitably lost to rising sea-level. There is a human cost here too, is there not?

Yes, Karl, but there is a protocol, the World Court Resettlement Protocol, and we should be encouraging people to follow it, not just come out shooting when their land is inundated. This is going to happen more and more, we have to control it, it has to be dealt with by policy means.

Flawed, deeply flawed, of course, the Protocol. But in any case these theoretical considerations have to be put aside when the real situation demands it.

The Protocol is not a *theoretical consideration!*

Karl, Rosie, I see that we have strongly held views here. But perhaps I can bring you back, Rosie, to the topic of your research. Can you tell our subscribers a little about what the consequences of this conflict in the North might be, the environmental consequences?

Yes, of course Aidan, got a bit carried away there! My research looks in detail at the cost of war, conflict. In many cases we are looking at the value of infrastructure, farmland, solar installations, industry, and things like water purity and accessibility. These considerations are different depending on whether you run the analysis for the North of Siberia or as Karl suggests for areas on the southern boundary. In the North the land isn't useable for much more than subsistence hunting, you know, people who are living traditional lifestyles, and of course that has a value in itself, what we call an amenity value, but the real killer, Aidan, is permafrost.

Methane release?

That's right, Aidan. My research shows the melt component that might be generated by escalating levels of conflict. You start with the sort of running guerrilla war, where the carbon cost is comparatively low, and then this graph shows the escalation of carbon release depending on the intensity of the conflict. For example, this part of the graph here is based on work modelling the effect of a conventional land war followed by an exchange of intercontinental warheads.

It makes grim viewing, doesn't it, subscribers? And this part of the graph here, right at the end, you've modelled a nuclear exchange. Do we really need to be frightened of that?

Well, Aidan, that degree of escalation isn't predicted in any of the forecasting, so it's just an intellectual exercise, it gives us an end-point, a maximum for the data. But you can see, yes, that would involve pretty much 100% permafrost melting over the impact area.

From Live World Weekly, 3.5.62

Tom

It was maybe three in the morning. Neon light flickered at the end of the alley, throwing the piles of refuse and the ancient mattress leaning against one wall into intermittent harsh focus. Orange/dark. Orange/dark. There was vomit splashed on the cracked paving where Misha's boots were planted. He leaned forward, putting his weight on the smaller person, pinning them face first against the wall, gripping their wrist in an uncomfortable hold over their head. 'Hey,' the person said. 'You're hurting me.' The person trod backwards onto Misha's foot, skewering his toe with their spangled stiletto, and in the same moment slid around, freeing their wrist, so that now they faced Misha, looking up into his face, as he leaned over them, both his hands on the wall. They had dark malicious eyes, outlined in peacock colours, and their trimmed stubble, too short to be a beard, framed exaggerated pink lips. They wore a dress made of narrow metal chains, which barely concealed the jutting, enhanced breasts, the defined abs, and the bulge under the skin-tight shorts. They leaned back, raising their thickly muscled arms languidly above their head, and laughed. 'Like it better this way.' Misha reached for his belt buckle.

Then the person's eyes unfocussed. 'Misha,' they said, their voice sounding somehow different, flat. The malicious look was gone. 'Misha. Tom needs to talk to you. Tom is in the street. Tom needs to talk to you.' Then the person closed their eyes and slumped, unconscious. Misha caught them as they fell and lay them down, gently, in the vomit.

'Whoever you are, motherfucker,' he said, 'you have my attention.' He left the person unconscious and walked to the end of the alley, doing up his belt. There was no one there. He flattened himself against one wall, waiting, one hand on the Taurus in his waistband. Nothing happened. Carefully he looked around the corner. It was dark, but motion-activated streetlights showed a figure at some distance, pacing backwards and forwards, facing away from him. It had Tom's build but not his long hair. It did look like Tom, like Tom might look if he were bald. Misha drew the Taurus and walked soundlessly up to the figure, stopping behind him. The man looked around.

'Tom, darling,' said Misha. 'Have you not heard of the Darknet? Apparently there is a message facility.'

'Shit, man,' said Tom. 'I'm sorry. It wasn't my idea. Is your, uh, your partner, are they ok?'

'I have no idea.' He stuffed the Taurus back under his jacket and put a hand on Tom's shoulder, steering him across the street to where a little bar was still open. 'Marcus! We need vodka.'

Marcus had known Misha too long to be surprised that he had left the bar with a small gender-enhanced person and had come back in an hour later with a large raw-boned bald bloke. He served them without comment. Misha knocked back the shot and looked thoughtfully at Tom. He was thin and haggard, wearing ill-fitting shorts and a t-shirt, and green flip-flops which might have been stolen from a market stall. Tom took a gulp of his vodka, but didn't say anything.

'You look terrible,' Misha said. 'What is so important that you had to interrupt me for it?'

'It wasn't me,' said Tom. 'It was him, the northerner. He thought Annie was with me, but I didn't know, I didn't know what was going on, I had to try to trace him again, I couldn't find him. I never would have found him, it was him that found me, the second time, I thought Annie was with him. But if Annie isn't with him, then where is she, Misha?'

Misha put the vodka bottle in front of him. 'Drink,' he said. 'There is no good news.'

'Fucking shit,' said Tom, but he drank.

'You were offline,' said Misha. 'But even if you had been online, I would not have contacted you. One of us has betrayed the cell. And even now, how do I know that I can trust you?'

'Man, I don't know. It's me, Tom. I can't prove anything to you. What's happened? Where's Annie? I just want to find her.'

'Give me your portal chip.'

Tom paused a moment. He was either entering the access and release codes, or calling for help, Misha thought. Then Tom reached round to the base of his neck and pressed. He handed Misha the small port access capsule, still warm from his body.

'I will keep this for now, I think.'

'Whatever, man, just tell me what's going on.'

'What the hell,' said Misha, and smiled, although it was a grim smile. He topped up both of their glasses.

'So, it turned out there was a traitor in the group.' Deliberately, watching Tom's expression, he drummed his knuckles on the sticky bar counter. Tap, tap, tap tap. Tap, tap, tap tap.

'Noah?' asked Tom. 'Ah, shit. He was always such a good bloke, you know. But before I left, I thought there was something weird going on. 'S why I didn't come back. One of the reasons.'

Misha studied Tom's gaunt face with something like compassion. 'There was a raid,' he said. 'They took Annie and Gina. Noah too.'

'But you got away,' said Tom.

Misha nodded.

'And then you did nothing about it.'

Misha nodded again.

'You always were a cunt, Misha, you know that?' said Tom, almost dispassionately.

Misha spread his hands in an unrepentant gesture. He kept his eyes fixed on Tom's face.

'So, look,' Tom said, 'I don't care about any of that. I'm going to find Annie and you're going to help me. You have to tell me, tell me everything about the raid.'

Misha leaned back on his elbow, shaking his head. 'Tom, my dear,' he said, 'it was SAPA armour. They will be at a correctional facility somewhere. There is nothing we can do about it. I am sorry.' He poured from the vodka bottle again but Tom pushed the shot glass away.

'No, listen,' he said, 'there may be a way.' He paused, looking at Misha with narrowed eyes. 'Give me *your* port chip.'

'You are growing up,' Misha said, with a tone half-way between approval and condescension. He reached behind the narrow braids. 'Here.'

Tom palmed the small warm capsule. 'Don't suppose it's your real ID, anyway, is it?' he said.

Misha shrugged. 'Whether it is or not, at least you know that there is no one in takealong hearing our conversation.'

'And what about –' Tom gestured towards Marcus, who was watching some sort of subscriber porn at the other end of the bar.

'You don't need to worry about him.'

'I guess I have to take your word for that. Well, this is the thing. This northerner, Amaruq, he can't find Annie. I guess,' Tom swallowed, painfully, 'I guess he and Annie, they had a thing going on. Enough for him to want to find her. But anyway, he has serious VR skills. He showed me some stuff.'

'Like that trick in the alley?'

'Yeah, stuff like that. I've never seen that before. He doesn't seem to mind too much about privacy protocols. Anyway, I don't trust him, but I can see he knows what he's about, on the tech side, I mean.'

'He got my attention,' said Misha.

'Right, though I could have just messaged you once I was back online, you would have got back to me, right?'

'I might have. Or I might not.'

'So thing is, I have to find Annie. And then when she's safe, we can sort out, stuff between us, I don't know.'

'So you have made a truce with him, with your rival.'

'Kinda,' said Tom, uncomfortably. 'He has, he says he has, other people behind him, people with VR capability. He calls it an army. He says, what we could do, is his group, his *army*, whatever, they could take down the SAPA security, or fix it somehow. Long enough for someone to get in. But I couldn't do it by myself.'

'We would have to know what facility she was in.'

'No, what he says is, he says if he gives us an in, they could have stuff going on at *all* the facilities. Different facilities, anyway. He says he can boobytrap it, it would take SAPA security a while to work out where the intruders were.

'Even if they can do that, which I doubt, we would still have to know which fence we would be waiting by with our wire-cutters when the lights went out. Or whatever was going to happen.'

'Right, so he says, if you can give him access to your memory of the raid, he might be able to tell where the droids were tasked from.'

'Firstly, there is no way I will allow that, even for you, Tom darling, and second, in any case I wasn't there.'

'Right. You weren't there. Why the fuck weren't you there, Misha?'

'It turns out I was right, not to be there. Or would it be better, now, if I was in a SAPA facility too, hooked up to a truth machine?'

Tom flinched. 'They wouldn't do that, it'd be illegal.'

'It would be illegal,' Misha agreed, his expression opaque.

'Ah, shit, Misha, you gotta help me. Whatever's going on in that place, wherever they are, it's not gonna be good. I can't bear it, I can't stand to think of Annie, locked up like that. And Gina too, of course.'

'Well,' said Misha, looking at his fingernails. 'I was bored, anyway.'

It turned out Misha had an apartment overlooking Middle Harbour. Or it wasn't his apartment, exactly. Tom wasn't really clear about that. The door recognition module called him a different name. 'Welcome,' it said, in its beautifully modulated voice, 'Mr. Ambrosius and guest. Would you like to tell me your guest's name so that I can be of better service to you?'

'Fuckwit,' said Misha with a nasty smile. 'You can call him Fuckwit.'

'Now, Mr. Ambrosius,' the module said, managing to sound just very slightly shocked while still keeping its mellifluous cadences, 'you know I can't call him a name like that.'

'Tom,' Tom interrupted hastily, 'I'm called Tom.'

'Tom,' said the beautiful voice.

'Full privacy,' said Misha. 'Silent mode. Bottle of Zubrovka and two glasses.' He turned to Tom. 'I can't stand that Barbie doll voice.'

'You could reprogramme it,' Tom started to say, but then caught his breath as Misha pushed open the door to the main living area. Hidden lighting illuminated a long sweep of polished floorboards, ending in wall-to-wall windows looking out over Middle Harbour. The furnishing was sparse and clearly expensive, although as Tom looked around he thought that it looked somehow mismatched, the enormous mirror with its rococo guilding at odds with the retro teak sideboard. Misha strolled the length of the room and stood looking out over the dark harbour front where patterns of street illumination rippled, following the movements of the few pedestrians still out at this time in the morning. Over the windows a message scrolled in red letters:

CARBON BREACH – PLEASE ACTIVATE WINDOW SHUTTERING.

Misha ignored the message.

'Shit, Misha,' Tom said, 'how did you get a place like this?'

'It is not exactly mine. It is convenient for now. Sit.' Misha gestured at the deep black squashy leather chairs. In the provision aperture stood the vodka bottle, frosted with cold, arranged on a silver tray with two shot glasses, small bowls of olives and nuts, wooden toothpicks, and two white linen napkins. Tom sat down on the edge of one of the squashy chairs, feeling out of place in his grimy shorts. 'Fuck,' he said, 'talk about the carbon lifestyle. S' not your flat, this, is it? Who d'you get the accesses off?'

'Never mind,' said Misha, reaching fastidiously for a single almond. 'Business. We need to see what is the range of possible facilities, so that we can work out where Annie and Gina are most likely to be.'

Tom started to say that this was SAPA classified and you would never get hold of it, at least not without paying handsomely, and even then the data would be stolen, unreliable. Then he looked at the schematic Misha had brought up. 'Man,' he began, and then the anger mounted up in him again. 'You could've found them all along.'

'Maybe. But I could not have broken in, not without this plan that your rival has conceived. Even now it is far from a certain thing.' As always when action was impending Misha had abandoned his languid manner and he spoke crisply. 'Your northerner, can he help? We need intake records for the afternoon of April 25th.'

'He's not my northerner. But anyway I doubt they'll show up as intakes, in that case they'd have had to be logged and have access to legal counsel, all that shit.'

'So intakes *and* cell occupancy. If we have more cells occupied than prisoners logged, then we will know we are on the right lines.'

'I dunno,' said Tom. He was immensely tired all of a sudden. 'D' have to ask him. If you give me back my port chip, I'll try. But I can't contact him, I have to wait for him to message me.' He lay back on the soft leather, looking up at the tastefully underlit ceiling, and closed his eyes.

'Contact him first, then sleep,' said Misha. 'You can post an alert even if you can't message him. Here.'

Tom sat up groggily. 'I wish there was a way we could do this, without him,' he said.

'It is for Annie.'

'You're a manipulative shit, y'know that?' Tom growled, but he took the port chip.

/alert/contact request/Amaruq/

'Ok,' said Misha, steering Tom to an unobtrusive door at the side of the tall windows. There were two steps down to a guest sleeping area, slung in a glass pod on the outside of the building. The floor was covered in tatami matting, hiding the vertiginous drop, and all around shone the lights of Sydney; before him was the dark expanse of the sea. The sky had just started to lighten but directly overhead there were still stars. Tom ignored the geometrically folded kimono with its motif of storks, and let himself fall onto the fluffy white futon, his filthy feet trailing on the floor. He closed his eyes and was instantly asleep. On the far horizon a streak of pale sky suddenly intensified and a pre-dawn glow filled the capsule. Misha closed the door behind him.

6th May 2062

The State Department advises against all travel to the area affected by the potential Korean conflict and including:

- All areas of the Siberian Federation east of and including Tomsk. Travel to Novosibirsk is not restricted but essential travel only is advised.
- Mongolia.
- The Chinese provinces of Heilongjiang; Jilin; Liaoning; and the Autonomous Region of Nei Mongol, east of Hohot.

UPLOAD ADVISORY ON ESSENTIAL TRAVEL

UPLOAD MAP

We are monitoring the situation in the Siberian Federation closely and further assessments of threat level will be posted as soon as they are available.

REGISTER FOR THREAT ASSESSMENT UPDATES

govadvice/foreign-travel-advice/koreanconflict

Killaq

So hey, everyone, this is Killaq here bearing witness for the Inuit people from the SAPA / Ardsen mining operation here in the Arctic Nation. So this is day 5, the mining hasn't started yet, what's going on down there is they are prepping the slave fleet, see if I show you, here, each of those little tankers, look like your little brother's toy trucks, don't they? Well if I was standing next to them, let me overlay my image on the visual to scale, see how big just one of those little trucks is? So the idea is, the acquisition end of the miner, what we call the business end – see, I'm learning miner-speak! – when it's working will just be digging up huge amounts of frozen earth. Then the whole processing is done in the body of the miner, when we're up and running I'll show you each of the processes one by one, so what those tankers are going to be taking away is market-ready methane.

So I know some of you are saying that the landscape is going to be ruined, and the carbon cost of the methane is too much. So I'm not a scientist, all I can tell you is what SAPA are telling me, that the land is going to be completely remediated, back to pristine wilderness in ten years' time, maybe just with the ground surface at a slightly lower level. And on the carbon, guys, the warming rate we are looking at means all this permafrost is going to melt sometime anyway, we are just doing it in a controlled way. At least that's what the scientists here, that's what they're telling me.

Killaq felt sick to be saying all this, even though if all went well this would be an action which would put a stop to permafrost mining for a generation. She had no faith in SAPA's promises of remediation, and she also knew that significant amounts of methane, released all at once, could cause a carbon spike which would send the atmosphere into runaway warming. But that wasn't going to happen, she told herself, that was what she was there to stop.

So guys, love talking to you, but it's time for me to have my own downtime. So I'm going to leave you with this, look at this panning shot, right over this amazing scenery.

She sent the blog camera slowly circling, describing a full circle around the miner. It was a featureless, barren terrain: dull rocky slopes, roughened with boulders, alternated with bright flashes where innumerable small pools and wetland patches reflected the noonday sun. On the horizon, to the west, was a low range of hills rising from the matte, flattened landscape. Then she swapped to the view from above, pulled from the daily satellite oversight. Gradually she drew the camera's view upward until the gaudy blue and yellow of the miner's livery became a dot in the vast brown expanse of land; nothing else manmade could be seen in the whole field of view, and the miner itself vanished into insignificance in the wild tundra.

If that doesn't show them the grandeur of this country, Killaq thought, what a terrible awe-inspiring wilderness it is, I give up, nothing will.

/blogfeed off/privacy setting/

Killaq took a deep breath. It wasn't true privacy, she knew that SAPA would be keeping an eye on her via the blog link even if it was closed to the public, but it was freedom at least from the synthetic Killaq persona. If any young person really was that naïve and that relentlessly enthusiastic, Killaq thought, they should be strangled. She took her mandated daily exercise during her public time, grimly jogging on the fitness suite's treadmill and working joylessly through the toning programme, so that she would have her real personal time to herself.

She reached up, stretching, filling her lungs with the flavourless conditioned air, then headed for her console. So far she had not gone anywhere in VR that would give a SAPA minder any concern. She wanted them to get the idea that she liked to go for a swim when she was off duty, and she had taken to using a scenario from the SAPA recreational suite that came with the miner VR programme.

/Mediterranean Morning/select/

She had the beach to herself and the sun was rising over the rumpled sand. Last night's footprints, and the deep scuffed indentations where people had been lying, showed up clearly in the low light. Apparently there wasn't enough tide, here on the shore of the simulated Mediterranean, to wash away the traces from the night's revelry. Every time she had visited it looked a bit different: you had to hand it to them, the scenario builder's attention to detail was impressive.

This was what you got for your executive subscription, Killaq thought.

She went down to the water's edge and waded out. Her beach librarian persona would have been far too whimsical for the part she was playing now: she was wearing a plain blue one-piece with red piping, a sort of school-swimming-gala type of swimsuit. She kept walking out till the rippling wavelets were at thigh level, then waist deep. She shivered even though in truth there was no hot or cold to be felt. If this had been Amaruq's scenario, she thought, she would have been able to feel the cold sea lapping around her, and smell its sharp briny smell. The smell of the sea: she wondered how he did that. She plunged in. The water buoyed her up and she struck out, the rising sun in front of her forging the water into gold droplets every time her hand broke the glassy surface. The light caught the bracelet she wore and the blue beads shone in the dawn.

She settled into a steady crawl, letting her mind rest in the rhythm of the stroke, the breath, the kick. It was like a drink of fresh water to be alone, or at least to feel alone; it was like clean air in a stuffy room, like silence and space after noise and argument. She kept swimming, thinking of nothing. Breathe, kick. Breathe, kick.

After a while she stopped, treading water, and looked back at the distant beach. The sun was higher now and she could see the small figures of early morning joggers and dog walkers. She selected Mermaid and swam back underwater, undulating along the unremarkable seaweed-covered sea floor with powerful strokes of her finned tail. Once she was back in shallow water she reselected Human Basic and walked back up the beach. There was no one there – it was only from a distance that the illusion of there being other beach users was maintained.

/exit/

There, she thought, a harmless routine, hopefully nothing that the SAPA minders would look at too closely. In a couple of days she thought she might be safe to use the cloaking function Amaruq had given her and build a simulacrum of her swimming out and back. It would give her a little time to escape unseen elsewhere in VR if she needed to. She sat up in the console, checking her time-away stats from long habit, and yawned. She had time to shower, check in with Ma and have a bit of a prowl around before she was due back for the evening blog post.

She had taken to wandering the corridors and living areas of the little habitat, taking care to look aimless and a little bored, but in fact assessing the spaces with the fighter's awareness she had gained from being Ambra. Where was defensible? Where was a hiding place? She took care to do no more than glance incuriously at the exit port and its pressurised antechamber, but she looked for other ways out: the ventilation was all through small ceiling level vents, though, and she thought the toughened viewing windows in the observation platform would probably turn out to be unbreakable, military grade even. Perhaps if there was a fire, the emergency fire protocol would give her an escape route, although since this involved her being enclosed in a fire-resistant capsule, sedated and processed to a slaved external vehicle, it was hard to see how that would help if she really needed to get away. She had no equipment or clothes with her that would allow her to survive outside the climate-controlled living quarters; even the working areas of the miner would be bitterly cold. If the action went ahead, whatever it was. She couldn't stop herself nagging at the thought, wondering what it was she was going to be needed for, if she was going to be needed at all.

She would have help, she reminded herself: if the action went ahead, she would have help on the outside. No one would abandon her to the mercies of SAPA Oversight. She shook herself. Don't think like that.

/blogfeed on/

Hey, it's Killaq back again, just been talking to my family back in Iqaluit. Have to say it is kinda lonely here on the miner all by myself. Of course I stay in touch with all my friends back home and keep up with all the gossip, and of course all you lovely people are there for me, so that helps a lot. Keep those messages coming!

So they tell me, let's see, I've got the miner prep schedule here, today is the test day for the automated slave fleet. So the daylight test went fine, and now they're doing the darktime test. So outside the sun is setting, look, it's getting dusk, but the slave fleet just carries on working, they don't need the light to carry on. See out there, see all those little lights? Just think, the technology those trucks use to navigate by themselves is the same as was invented for the early Mars rovers, and now the lunar base constructor machinery. Crazy, eh? Just crazy, the things we humans can do.

The next day rolled by, then another. She dutifully reported the first test of the miner's laser cutting machinery, exercised in the fitness suite, worked her way through the module's repertoire of vegan cuisine. She kept an eye on the outside world, but she felt she should keep clear of the proper news reporting which she would usually access, and the magazine-style gossip blogs which seemed to fit better with her gosh-golly persona were stultifyingly boring. It was very difficult to pick out what was actually going on in between the blizzard of emo-pieces, all opinion and sound bites. The World Court seemed to be setting up some sort of intervention in Korea, at least that was what she gathered from what passed for world news on the blogs. 'If *your* land was flooded would *you* move to Siberia (select YES or NO),' was more the kind of thing.

After a few more swims she had dared to use the conch shell icon which Amaruq had installed, and which gave access to a heavily shielded editing suite. The suite slotted in a cover image repeating whatever it was you had been doing when you accessed it, but it wouldn't pass more than a casual inspection: the first job was to build a more convincing simulacrum. Strangely enough, she found she missed the swimming, or not so much the swimming itself, but the morning beach, the sunrise. She couldn't go swimming twice in a day, though, it might look weird. And it felt good to be doing proper work in VR, something real at last.

After about a week she had the simulacrum to her satisfaction. The first run, she just stayed in the editing suite, watching herself swim, monitoring the VR feed of the synthetic Killaq. No alarm bells rang. She couldn't attach too much security to the simulacrum's VR feed – that in itself might be suspicious. But she could mimic the normal response to a message alert. What she hoped she had built was that a probe by SAPA Oversight, testing the consciousness of the Killaq simulacrum, would trigger a trapdoor, replacing the simulacrum instantaneously with her true self. Time would tell if she ever needed to use it.

Next time, she set up the swimming Killaq. Then she messaged Amaruq from the safety of the shielded suite.

Hey, sis.

Hey. Can't stay long.

My access work ok?

Seems to. So, any news?

No, we're working on stuff, but you sit tight for now.

You are incredibly irritating, you know that?

<grin>

I'm going to need to know sometime, what I'm actually doing here.

Yes and no.

Ok, I'm off, tell me when there's something I can actually do.

Wait, look. This is what I'm working on. One thing, anyway.

A view opened up in front of her, first Amaruq in his editing space, at home. Then an image of tundra. There was more snow than where she was, but otherwise it was very alike. There was something moving, tracking from left to right across the field of view. Amaruq narrowed in on the moving object. It looked like a bear; it was a bear, huge, grey-white, gaunt, ragged, pacing across the empty landscape.

Old bear footage?

Nope, real-time image, sis.

My god, a real surviving bear. I don't believe it.

And get this.

The field of view jumped and now she could see the tundra from eye level, the view shifting rhythmically, right to left, moving relentlessly forward, taking in the snow-covered rocks, the patches of marshy ground. Then there was water in front and suddenly the view rocked and then continued, right at the water level now, advancing over the lake, apparently a few inches above the surface.

You've made an eye-level view sim, as if you were the bear?

Nope.

So … So what, what is that, what are we looking at?

Some fucker has fitted the bear with a portal. Believe it or not. We're in takealong.

I don't believe you. It's another of your setups.

Can't help your cynical nature, sis. But hey, you need to get back.

Wait!

But she was back in the editing suite, alone. Mentally she shook her head. Shit. What was all that about. It was impossible, wasn't it, there weren't any bears left, and if there were you couldn't fit a bear with a portal, the technology didn't work with non-human input, that was what everyone had always been told. It must be one of Amaruq's little inventions, had to be.

/exit/

And she was swimming, just at the point where she usually turned back towards shore. She selected Mermaid and set off back, weaving between the weeds of the sea-bottom, her mind still filled with the wide light of the tundra landscape and the rhythmic pacing footfall of the bear.

18th June 2062

Mr. Sanderson, I know you must hear this all the time, but before we begin may I just say how much I love *You can get there if you think you can*, it has been my constant companion since I started in business school.

Why, thank you Amelia, that's very kind.

Everyone knows of course that *YCGT* is Mr. Sanderson's motivational blog in which he shares insights gleaned from his business life in SAPA. And Mr. Sanderson is here today taking time out of his busy corporate schedule to answer *your* questions. We've got everyone's questions mixed in this data set and the randomiser will choose a question for you. Here goes – let's hope it's a good one!

[Text starts to scroll across the screen: HOW DOES SAPA EXPLAIN THE DISAPPEARANCE OF PRISONERS HELD AT SAPA FACILITIES? The student interviewer frowns.]

Well that's, that's not the right question, I think, perhaps we can choose another one.

That's quite all right, Amelia, freedom of speech is what our great educational establishments are all about. I'm happy to answer that question. Now the trouble with our VR-intensive world is that these sort of rumours do gain currency, and it is almost impossible to prove them wrong, once one of these ideas starts running. But I can certainly say that there are no prisoners who are not accounted for. If you're a business major I'm sure you know how strict our laws are protecting the integrity of the person. The algorithms we use to control admissions into our facilities are subject to very careful oversight. SAPA is honoured to hold the contract for first-stage prisoner processing here in New South Wales, but you can be sure we wouldn't hold it for very long if there was any doubt whether our operation was scrupulous in upholding the laws of the land!

Well, thank you for that frank and open answer, Mr. Sanderson, and let's look at the next question.

WHAT DO YOU HAVE TO SAY TO THE RELATIVES OF

Ok, I'm going to stop that question there, I think there must be something the matter with our randomiser today. Perhaps I can ask you a question of my own, Mr. Sanderson. What advice would you give to a young person hoping to set out in a career with one of the great corporates, SAPA for example?

From UNSW Business School Student Weekly

Tom

'You can get there if you think you can! You can get there if you think you can!' The image of a line of high-kicking dancers sashayed across the shuttered floor-to-ceiling windows of Misha's apartment. 'You can do it! You can get there!' They wore pink and silver body paint and were adorned with white feathery ruffles across the bum, around the thighs and hugging the line of the nipples. More white feathers stood up in a stiff plume from each dancer's forehead. Now the lead singer leaned into the camera, licking her lips and shimmying her whole body, running her clawed pink and silver fingers suggestively over her torso. 'Ooh you can do it! You can do it! But only if you think you ca-aa-an!'

'Hm-hm hm-hm if you think you can,' Tom hummed, reaching for a soldering iron.

'Turn that shit off.'

'What?' Tom asked, looking innocent. 'I like her arse. Don't you like arses?'

Misha clicked his fingers and the dancers vanished. The room filled with the processional, deliberate music of clarinets, then strings. Across the shutters rolled a panorama of dark conifer forest. Tchaikovsky Symphony no. 5, said the red lettering in the corner. It was a little louder than Tom would have chosen.

Misha and Tom were building explosive devices, completely manual, controlled only by an internal timer. Unstoppable, except by a bomb disposal bot on the ground; unhackable. The floor was littered with wiring and tools. Tom was sitting cross-legged on the floor, back to one of the squashy sofas, concentrating on soldering. He was less haggard and destitute than when he had arrived, but Misha thought he still had a tense, unhappy look. A tin of beer was open by his elbow.

'There,' said Misha, putting aside his completed device. 'Nine.'

'Gettin' there.'

'I need to talk to the northerner, sometime soon. We need to be certain that his side of things is going to hold up.'

'No worries. I'll ask him. But I don't care, you know, Misha, I just want to get there, to find Annie, find Gina. And then, boom. You know, it was always you that said it was all pointless, you couldn't fight SAPA, and I guess you were right. Or, you can, but it's not worth it, it costs too much. When this is all done, that's it for me.'

Misha looked at him consideringly. 'It is not just Annie and Gina.'

'I know, I know, the fate of the fucking world. I don't give a shit. Everyone can drown.'

'Tom, my dear, I have very little interest in the fate of the fucking world. What I wonder is, what your northerner is doing about the mining exercise?'

'Is that still even happening?'

'I don't know,' said Misha. 'Look at this.' He raised a finger, and the scrolling woods and the Tchaikovsky were replaced by a blogfeed. An earnest young woman in a blue and yellow uniform seemed to be explaining some sort of manufacturing process. She was solidly built and had a dark fringe falling over her eyes; Tom couldn't quite place her look, somehow she was familiar. She was leaning on the railing on a high walkway, pointing out features of whatever it was that was going on.

So this is the bottling end, see the methane, it's been driven off from the slurry, I showed you that yesterday. They're telling me the melting generates this enormous pressure, see this here, that's the manual alarm, that'll shut down the miner if the pressure got too high, if the proper control processes failed for some reason. So you've got safety and double safety, first level controlled by the miner itself, back-up safety with the human operators back at base. Safe as houses, has to be, when you think about it, otherwise if you put a match to this lot – well, it's basically a giant bomb. Just as well it's controlled by the good guys!

'Some sort of corporate girlie. So what?'

'She's his sister.'

'Whose sister?'

'Your northerner, his sister. Listen again.'

It's basically a giant bomb. Just as well it's controlled by the good guys!

'Fuck,' said Tom. 'Is that her, is she on that Ardsen miner?'

It's basically a giant bomb. Just as well it's controlled by the good guys!

'Yes,' said Misha, as Tom stared at the image, his soldering iron forgotten in his hand. 'I think it is likely that she is saying exactly what you think she is saying.'

'My god,' said Tom, 'so the action is going ahead?'

'It would not be rational to think so. Annie and Gina knew, well, they knew quite a lot. And so did Noah. And the status of Noah is – uncertain.'

'Shit.'

'I hope,' said Misha, choosing his words carefully, 'that your northerner has not over-reached himself.'

You could only meet Amaruq at a place of his choosing. This time, Misha and Tom followed the link to a white space. It wasn't an undesigned white space, though: your feet sank into the white, as if it was cloud, or low ground-hugging tendrils of mist. Wind buffeted them and they could feel the cold, actual bodily cold. And from somewhere seemingly beneath them came the crashing, booming sounds of waves beating on a sea-cliff. If Tom hadn't known that there was no smell in VR he would have sworn he could smell the salt spray, and something else, something like a herb. He couldn't place the smell, but he was imagining a creeping plant, growing in crevices, with aromatic leaves and small brilliant flowers. It was a far northern sea, Tom was sure, nothing like his beloved Australian surf.

They were in body-normal, although Tom had had to argue with Misha to get him to leave off the persona he had originally chosen, giant, bearded, turbaned, muscled, as much like the genie out of the Arabian Nights as anything else. For a moment they stood, looking at each other. Misha shrugged. 'It is impressive,' he said, 'but I am cold.'

'Hey!' Tom shouted. 'Hey! You!' His words were taken away by the wind. He started walking along where he thought the line of the cliff ought to be. Suddenly the sea-sound was louder and he had the vertiginous feeling that he was standing at the edge, right on the edge of the drop. The breeze blew a packet of spray into his face. He stepped backwards, carefully, in the direction he thought was away from the drop. Then he took another step back. Moisture ran down into the side of his mouth. It tasted salt, by god, it *was* salt.

He walked back to Misha, cautiously.

'Where the fuck is this?'

'I cannot tell you, but I think it is time to leave.'

/exit/

They were still there. Tom was wearing his board shorts and his knees were cold.

'Shit! Misha, did that happen to you too?'

Misha nodded. Even he looked afraid.

/protocol emergency abort/

The wind blew around Tom's feet. His thongs were invisible in the wreathing ankle-deep mist.

/protocol emergency abort/

Nothing. Tom threw his head back, yelling at the sky. 'LET US OUT OF HERE, YOU FUCKER! LET US OUT! LET US OUT RIGHT NOW!'

'Tom!' Misha grabbed his forearm. 'Tom! Think!'

'What?' Tom asked him angrily. 'The fucker has brought us here for some fucked-up reason of his own and now he's laughing at us. What is there to fucking think about?'

'Delete your accesses. Do it now. Everything, delete it.'

'How the shitting hell will that get us out of here?'

'Just do it, talk later.'

'Ok, ok.' Reluctantly he brought up the accesses, one by one, deleting the addresses, the heads-up icons, everything that he used to navigate online. He could reinstate it all from his console when he got back. If he got back.

'Are you done?'

'Yup, done.' He shivered.

'Now delete the portal ID.'

Tom stared at him. 'But that's, I don't even know if I can do that.' Your portal ID was the connection to your portal chip, sitting in your bloodstream at the back of your head. Tom's head, lying in its console, in Misha's flat, in faraway Sydney, Australia. The ID wasn't made to be uninstalled. It was your only way home.

'You need to take down the portal security and firewall. There is no choice. Do it now.'

'Are you – are you going to?'

Misha vanished.

Tom stood for a while in the mist, looking out into the featureless sky. It seemed to be getting darker. He tried the protocol abort, one more time. Nothing happened. Shit, he thought.

/uninstall firewall/uninstall personal safety/uninstall ID protect/uninstall ID failsafe/uninstall portal alert/

His field of view was full of urgent flashing warnings.

/confirm/

He was in a high-ceilinged room, lying on a bed on clean, pressed linen, looking up at the ornate moulding that ran around the top of the walls. He rolled over. White voile curtains framed open French windows, and through the windows he saw a paved terrace bounded by a white marble balustrade, decorated at measured intervals with elaborately carved marble urns. Ornamental lemon trees stood in pots on the terrace and a fresh, scented breeze fluttered the curtains. Ok. Where the fuck was this now? Wherever it was, he wasn't interested. He checked his accesses.

Everything was back, the emergency alert, the portal protocol; his icons were green; his security was on. Time to bugger off, Tom, old son, he thought. In a minute. Maybe he would have a look-see, first. Drawn by an unwilling curiosity he got to his feet and stepped outside. Beyond the terrace was a blue-green sea under a brilliant sky; over to the left, leaning on the balustrade, were two figures. One was blue-skinned and rippling with muscle: Misha in his Arabian Nights persona. The other was the northerner. Well, hell, he thought, and winced. He could hear Annie's voice in his head. Go for it, babe. He walked over to join them.

Amaruq turned to him with an apparently guileless smile. 'Hey, Tom,' he said, easily. 'Thanks for being part of my experiment.'

He wants you to lose your temper. He wants you to go off on one. Tom ignored him. 'You know, Misha, blue doesn't suit you,' he said.

'You don't think?' said Misha, putting his clenched fists together and making his corded biceps bulge.

'Guys,' said Amaruq. 'You're allowed to be pissed with me. But really, it was in a good cause. I'm building something, I needed to try it out. And it worked, you realised the only way out was to go completely naked, without even your upload links. And then, if you had been an enemy – .' He clenched his fist, as if he was squeezing something.

Misha turned to him, towering over the stocky Inuit. 'One,' he said, evenly. 'We cannot verify who you are. Two, if you are who we believe, you may yourself be an enemy.'

Amaruq put his hand on Misha's broad forearm. 'If I was SAPA Oversight, you would already be lost.' There was a moment of horrible silence. Then Amaruq leaned back on the balustrade, smiling at them as they stood over him. 'But,' he said, 'I'm not.'

'We cannot know that,' said Misha.

'I know, I know. And the way I brought you here hasn't made you think well of me. I guess I was showing off, it's a weakness of mine.' He glanced up at them, a look of appeal in his dark eyes. 'But we're on the same side. Listen. I know you've had a traitor in your group already, you're right to be careful.'

'Noah,' said Tom.

'Yes, Noah. I met him. At least, it was his persona, but I think he was being run by someone else.'

'No shit,' said Tom, his attention drawn despite himself. He stared intently at the northerner. 'You didn't think you should tell us?'

'I wasn't sure. And then I thought you and Annie, you know, I thought you had pulled out of it. I thought you weren't in danger.'

'You didn't think *I* had pulled out,' Misha said.

Amaruq laughed a short laugh. 'I thought you, Misha, could look after yourself.'

'All right,' said Misha. He shook himself, the blue-skinned persona fell away and he reappeared as Misha, body-normal, in his jeans and leather jacket. 'We are here on your terms. Talk.'

For a moment Amaruq was silent, looking out over the blue-green sea. He ran his finger around the moulded edge of one of the stone urns. 'There's two things,' he said, at length.

'We, at least I, I only care about getting Annie out of wherever they've taken her. Whatever other shit you have going on, I don't care.' Tom looked at Amaruq defiantly.

'You might need to know about the other shit, though, some of it. I'll tell you what I can, without endangering anyone else.'

'Like your sister?' Misha asked.

Amaruq looked at Misha appraisingly. 'Yeah,' he said. 'Like my sister.'

'Go on.'

'There are lots of strands to this,' Amaruq began. 'SAPA, I've been keeping an eye on SAPA for a long time now.'

'Pardon me,' said Misha, dryly. 'You must be older than your persona looks.'

Amaruq grinned at him. 'No, you're right. This is the age I am. It's not just me, it's work other people have carried on.' He watched his own finger tracing the line of the urn. 'My father, for one. When he was alive.'

'Ok.'

'You're going to have to take my word for some of this. SAPA, they have fingers in more pies than most people know about. More power than governments. Same as a lot of the other corporates, I know. But SAPA, they get into people's lives, right inside. They control what people access in VR. What people want, what people save for, who people meet, what people dream about. Who gets the top jobs, what decisions get made, right up the ladder, right the way up. And it's all about money, about carbon. The execs, the SAPA high-ups, they shape the world to benefit them, their children, their families, without regard to anyone else, without regard to the future, to the earth.'

'I know you know all this. You're not innocents. But what can we do? Any one of us? The days of revolutions are over. The way the world has evolved, the way we've chosen it to evolve, we're all data, each of us, we're all categorised, we live in little boxes and an algorithm knows our innermost desires. So a group like yours, you can write slogans on buildings, but you can't change the massive power of SAPA, the data control, the statistical predictive control. Everything about you is known, is recorded. You, Tom, when you go shopping, the shop knows your shoe size.'

'Yeah, when I had an Overnet ID.'

'It's handy, isn't it, the shop knows what you like. It knows your budget. It knows your purchasing history. Well what SAPA, any big data agency, what it knows, is much much wider than that. It knows your amniotic environment, from when you were in the womb. It can tell what your health profile is likely to be, your economic profile, your genetic markers. It knows how you vote, how you live, how you fuck.'

'Don't you see? I'll fight SAPA with you, of course I will. But in the end the only way we can take back the world, take back our freedom, take back our own selves, it's in here. It's in VR itself. The outside world, it's already broken.' He cocked an eyebrow at Misha. 'Don't you think?'

Misha met his gaze but said nothing.

'Here, in here, this is the world we can shape to our own liking. We can create our own environments, forge our own lives; we can seize our own risks and face our own dangers. This is our frontier. Out there –' he gestured – 'out there it's only boxes. Locked, cramped boxes. It's safety, but a tepid kind of safety. But now we have a chance to choose a different life. Now, right now, this moment, today, is the fork in the road, the turning of the ways. We can spend our days, our whole existence, restricted, surveilled, only able to grow to the shape that the cage allows, like suckler veal in a pen. Or we can turn our back on that life, that constricted, stunted, mutilated life, and walk away. Here are our new oceans, new prairies, new mountains, here in VR. Here is unimaginable freedom, unimaginable choice. This is where the true heart of humankind will evolve in the years to come.'

'Nice speech,' said Misha, half-ironically. But Tom pushed himself up from where he had been leaning on the balustrade. 'All right, Captain,' he said. 'If this, this crusade of yours, if it fits in with what I want to do, that's good enough for me. When do we start?

SUMMER

24th June 2062

[The figure appears to be standing on a rocky slope, although he is wearing light office clothing. There are thin drifts of snow on the stony, ridged ground, and behind him is a pine forest. He gesticulates back towards the trees, where a column of smoke is rising.]

'I'm here on the frontline of the NKS advance, and behind those trees you can see signs of the battle beginning over this disputed land. We're here looking north over the territory of the Siberian Federation, and about 75 miles in that direction is the coastline of the East Siberian Sea. If I show you in the satellite view –'

[The reporter moves his hand and the aerial view is overlaid.]

'Here you can clearly see the North Korean automated forces, which experts are saying have been assembled offshore in the shallow Sibirskoe Morye, and opposing them, *here*, the armoured vehicles of Russia herself, protecting her mineral interests in the Federation. It seems this is the long-awaited first attack in the NKS's claim for land here in the far North-East of Siberia. If I zoom out a little –'

[The map now shows the whole of eastern Siberia and the political boundaries to its south.]

'you can see how North Korea is blocked from trying to expand its territory, by the vast military complex of Vladivostock to its north. The eastern border – *here* – is with China and although China is committed to defend

North Korea under the Treaty readopted in 2032, it seems that Beijing has little appetite for its former ally's military adventures here in the far North. North Korea is of course not a member of SAPA, whose marine strength is a force to be reckoned with in the East Pacific. And since international mediation under the Resettlement Protocol has failed, although I understand that urgent efforts are still underway in Delhi, the North Koreans are really buttoned down in that little enclave, unless they can break out and establish their Northern Homeland as they are attempting to do here today.'

From Newseast.com

Li Ji-Hae

His leg, there was pain in his leg. He tried to move it and the pain shot up into his spine. For a moment there was nothing but the pain, white hot, and then his head started to clear, although the leg still throbbed like a deep drumbeat. He opened his eyes. It was dusk, as near to dark as it would get at this time of year, and his cheek was resting on something cold and muddy. Now that the pain had eased he could feel the deep seeping chill of the ground beneath him.

He must be hurt. Cautiously he reached a hand down to his leg. There was blood. He couldn't tell how bad it was. He would just rest a minute, then he would try again to move it. He closed his eyes.

When he came to again it was full daylight. It was still very cold. There was frost on his battle jacket. He peeled his face from the mud and, gasping, heaved himself onto one elbow. As far as his view stretched was the flat expanse of the tundra, churned to mud by the great battle machinery that had passed over it, and there were the charred misshapen outlines of destroyed armoured vehicles, and other smaller, huddled shapes too. Far away there were pinpoints of light flaring. The battle must have moved over him in the night. Briefly he wondered who was winning; then he steeled himself to inspect the wounded leg.

From the knee down was a disaster of blood and flesh. That was it then. That was the end of him. He was never going to leave this patch of mud. He let his head fall back and watched the yellowish pale clouds moving above him. Time went by. He wondered how long it would take to die and whether the cold would finish him before infection set in in the leg. Would it hurt very badly? Perhaps the cold would take him gently before the pain got unendurable.

After a while he began to feel that there was someone standing above him, looking down on him. What was that? He must have been dreaming. He had thought it was his sergeant. Shouting at him again. Duty, duty. He was tired of duty. A tear ran down his muddy face. Still, perhaps the old fucker had a point. He struggled up again onto one elbow. The good leg was trapped under the bad one. Grabbing a handful of trouser he hauled at the bad leg so as to free the other one. The pain was tremendous, like a skewer in his knee. He screamed. The good leg was numb. He couldn't move it. It was still under the bad leg. Still maybe now he could get his weight – he could get his weight on his other hip. He screamed again.

There, now at least he could sit up properly. He felt a stab of happiness at the progress he had made. That would show the old fucker. Now who was doing his duty to the Homeland? Suddenly the blood returned to the good leg and it was seized with violent tingling, so unpleasant it made him retch. He groaned and rocked, pummelling the thigh with his hands, until the sensation died down and he could feel instead the deep throb of the injured leg again. He needed water, he had some water somewhere. Then what? Maybe, if he took it slow, he would be able to shuffle himself over to the burnt-out ruins of armour he could see over his shoulder. It might give him some shelter. Maybe someone would come looking for them, a med-team in a hover, maybe if he could just hang on, stay alive for long enough, help would arrive. And they would lift him so, so carefully onto the stretcher, because after all he was a Hero of the Homeland, and there would be a beautiful army nurse whose gentle hands would bely her stern expression, and, yes, there would be music playing, and as the tailgate of the hover raised up they would see in the viewscreen the flag being raised over the new territory, and morning would shine on the land, and he would have been part of it. And before they sedated him they would give him something sweet to drink, just to moisten his lips.

Water, he had some water somewhere. The pouch was on his belt, it had twisted round under his back. He couldn't reach it. No, it must be possible to reach it. He tried again. He shifted his weight onto the bad leg and suddenly it was agony. He couldn't do it. Try again. One, two, three, go. Screaming, he leaned over onto the injured side and grabbed behind his back for the container. Got it, no, can't reach it. Got it *now*.

He fell back, dizzy with effort, clutching the neck of the pouch. For a minute he slipped back into his daydream of victory. The beautiful nurse would have eyes like clear dark water and in the urgency of rescuing the wounded heroes her medical tunic would have come unzipped, just a bit, just enough to let him see the curve at the top of the breast, and she would lean over him and praise him for his bravery, and give him something sweet to drink.

Water, he needed water. He struggled with the spout of the container.

Once his immediate thirst was satisfied he leant back again and there was a time of watching the pale sky. The project of hauling himself to some shelter seemed less urgent now and the idea of moving, of the pain of moving the leg, too forbidding. If the med-hover was going to come for him, it could find him just as well here, as over there. It would pick him up, and there would be the beautiful nurse with her cool touch, and then he would be able to sleep, and the next thing he knew the stretcher would be being carried down the ramp from the hover, and there would be crowds, and people cheering, and a band. He would be famous – that was what they had said to them, before they were embarked into the transports, that everyone who had been in the first battle would be famous forever and their names would be known and remembered and theirs would have been the first hands that had been lifted for the Korean Homeland. From the loyal heart, to the fighting hand, that's what they told them. It was their proud slogan. He had repeated it to himself under his breath, after the great transports had risen out of the sea, and he had been shuffling in a line, waiting to disembark. The fighting machinery that had been assembled in secret offshore was going to clear everything before it, and he and all his mates would follow, and mop up any pockets of resistance. That's what they had been told. He had imagined marching proudly across a grassy plain. He hadn't thought it would be so cold. It was too cold, and they had been stumbling in a sort of marshy, icy terrain, and you couldn't march properly, and then there had been running in the dusky twilight, and there was light in the sky, huge explosions, the Russian artillery, and then, Pak, Pak Yo-Han, had fallen over, right in front of him, and he didn't get up, and then, then he couldn't remember.

There would be a band, there would certainly be a band, and his mother would be there, she would run to the stretcher with her waddling run. He wondered whether his mother would approve of the beautiful nurse, or whether she would be jealous of her. His mother – she had been so proud of him, when he went away in his uniform. She used to sing to him, what was it? The song about the bridge of birds. The girl in it – the girl had a blue apron, and there was a kiss and a parting, by the river. From one shore to the other, there flew a bridge of birds, and I met my love there – something, without many words. How did it go? His mother used to sing to him, when he was a small boy, a very small boy, when he was going to sleep. If she was here now, she would sing to him, like in the old days.

Blue was her knotted apron,

Blue as the sky,

Dark rolled the river past us,

Dark as her eyes.

Li Ji-Hae dozed, and above him the clouds passed and the pale sun dipped towards the horizon, and nothing else moved on the tundra.

25th June 2062

Overnight, fighting has intensified around the isolated hamlet of Ambar-Dyelyaria in Yakutia. From our drone view it seems as though the North Korean invasion initially struck hard into this treacherous territory of swamp and tundra, but now they are being strongly repulsed by Russia's land forces and it appears that the North Korean advance has stalled. In the meantime the people of the Siberian Federation can only look on as war rages across their land.

Viewers are warned that the following footage contains scenes of a distressing nature. There is no audio.

[The ornate wooden building would have been three storeys high, with single-storey wings on either side. The left-hand wing has nearly burned to the ground and charred remains stand in a precarious skeleton. A jagged hole gapes in what remains of the corrugated metal roof.

A picket fence has been uprooted and lies across the trodden earth of the road. A few cattle wander disconsolately.

An armoured vehicle lies half-submerged in a swamp where hummocky pale sedges are interspersed with occasional birch trees. As we watch the hatch opens and a soldier climbs out. He perches on the sloping deck of the vehicle, looking dubiously at the deep water around him. He swats his face: there are stinging insects in the swamp.

At the base of a shabby building lies what looks like a bundle of colourful rags. The drone eye moves closer. There is a naked foot protruding from the rags. The bundle doesn't move.

A young man in a blue tracksuit runs along a dirt track, casting frightened glances over his shoulder. Suddenly he pitches forward onto his face. Behind him the trees are red with fire.]

Newsdirect.com

Killaq

The day had been spent practising evacuation protocols. Consuela said that it was *very* unlikely that the North Korean conflict – she called it a 'local difficulty' – would come anywhere near the Arctic Nation and she had been *assured* on *very good authority* that SAPA were keeping a *very* careful eye on the northern coastline, but their Duty of Care meant that they had to run the evacuation and miner shut-down drill, just in case. They ran it in VR, of course: no point incurring any loss of production days, but it ate into Killaq's private time since the security provisions on the miner weren't for the eyes of the blog followers.

When they were done she took her meal tray up to the observation suite and sat looking out. The big windows faced the miner's direction of travel: you couldn't see the devastation it left behind it, although even looking this way the tundra was rutted by tyre tracks, and scarred with conical mounds of mining spoil.

Hey guys, today I've been in VR doing a lot of admin stuff, so I'm a bit wiped. Just sitting up here looking at the view and having my dinner. It's, ah, looks like Mexican, some sort of chilli beans. Tastes good. Tell you what, I don't have any complaints about the food here, no complaints at all. When I've done my three months here, I won't know how to cook for myself anymore!

Mm, that was good. In a bit I might go and get some dessert. First I'm going to look at some messages. You know I can't answer all your messages, right, but I do my best!

The messages were one of the most tedious parts of the whole thing. Killaq wondered whether these folk really had nothing better to do, with the whole of VR at their disposal, than to message an unknown Inuit girl employed in a mining PR exercise.

Hey K-girl, whatcha think of this viz of me and my buddies in the pool at Las Rochas? SuperBoy.

Hi SuperBoy, for sure looks like you're all having a good time. Killaq.

The answer was supplied by an algorithm, in fact she didn't need to be involved at all, except that she felt she should keep an eye on what was going out in her name. It was very boring. The messages were harvested for SAPA's statistical analysis of public attitudes to the mining operation: it all counted as 'support', no matter how inane or off-topic the response. The programme was tuned to focus on the less sophisticated members of the blog responders, so that messages identified as positive could be preferentially gathered. The whole process stank.

Hey Killaq, fancy getting together [private link] Noah.

That was weird, normally private invitations were weeded out and sent a bland corporate answer before they ever got to her. She hesitated. If SAPA were testing her, what she should do was report the link immediately. But if it was really Noah, or SAPA in the guise of Noah, still hunting for a back door, she should lead him on.

/message quarantine/dump/

She was playing it safe. Maybe Amaruq would be able to retrieve the link from the quarantine dump. She would ask him later, quite a bit later. If it was a test, they would be watching what she did next.

Guys, great to talk to you all, but I've been in VR all day, I need to stretch my legs. So I'm going to stop it there, go for a stroll about. Looking forward to getting more of your fantastic messages, keep them coming, it's great to know you're all out there.

She put the meal tray in the disposal chute and wandered away, exiting the blog, feeling the release of pressure as the messages and advertising scrolling in her heads-up came to an abrupt end. Never again, she would never do something like this again, she didn't know how professional bloggers stood it, even with really efficient spam-stripping algorithms. What she really wanted was a swim, just for the sake of the swimming, for the clean movement and the sunrise over the ocean, but she had no VR time-away left.

Sourly she headed for the gym: some treadmill work and then a long shower would have to do instead.

In the end she decided to leave Amaruq out of it. It was too risky, getting him involved. So she swam, without going near the shielded suite, and left Noah's message in quarantine for two days. Then she quarantined a message from Ma without reading it, as an excuse for when her access to quarantined messages showed up on someone's alerts. She wrote a clumsy cover programme – she didn't want them to see what her true programming abilities were. If anyone asked she would say she had been too embarrassed to ask for access through the proper authorisation channels.

/Noah/direct link/

Hello?

She was running this from the outside, message only. There was no way she was going to put herself in link space in VR with an unknown person, either SAPA Oversight, or some creep who had enough programming strength to overwrite the blog firewall.

Thank you for following this link. The person you have messaged knows you have responded.

That was it. With some relief she exited quarantine and deleted her cover programme. Now she would wait to see whether Consuela said anything to her about it. That might give her an idea of what level of suspicion she was subject to.

Two more days went by. There seemed to be work being carried out deep in the body of the miner, heavy-duty work. One night, she had woken from a dream in which she was being pursued by Noah's stork persona down endlessly branching corridors. She gave up on trying to sleep and had climbed up to the observation deck to watch the miner's grinding progress through the undarkened night – the blog followers thought it was strange, to have daylight at 03.00, but for her it was natural, it was the sign of summer – when she saw transports landing. You couldn't see what was being disembarked but it must have been something substantial, to have come in VTOLs that size. The miner could make most of what it needed: it didn't have to be resupplied. And then, when Killaq tried to access the methane bottling bay, where she had been before, to report on the processes for the blog followers, she found her access was denied. A bug, said Consuela, it would be reinstated if she wanted it to be. Killaq smiled to herself. Her guess was, they were building blast containment doors: her comment about the miner being a giant bomb had not gone unremarked. A piece of misdirection, she had agreed it with Amaruq. As if it would do anyone any good, as an act of protest, to blow up the miner in the middle of the tundra, hundreds of miles from anywhere. She still knew nothing about the original plan, or even if it was still live, but she guessed that if it was explosions that were wanted, the slave trucks would make better targets: fast, mobile, filled with methane, shuttling between the miner and distribution roadheads. Or maybe trapping Noah was the aim now, and it was only necessary to make it look as though there was an action brewing, to get him to take the bait. She didn't know.

That evening, there was another message.

Need to talk now your family in danger Noah.

So, she'd been right not to contact Amaruq, it would have led them straight to his Darknet ID. She had to respond, or else report it to Consuela. First she messaged Ma, it was what anyone would expect her to do, if Ma was threatened.

Hi Ma, how's everything?

Same as it always is. We miss you. Half-way through now, before you're home.

Oh Ma! It isn't long really.

I just worry that you're ok, all by yourself there on that machine.

We all worry about each other. Are you ok, Ma, really ok?

Why wouldn't I be, little bird. I'm fine.

Love you, Ma.

Love you, my girl.

That didn't tell her much. She paused a minute, seeing Ma in her mind's eye, sitting outside in her comfortable pink tracksuit. Unconsciously she ran a finger over the soapstone bear she wore around her neck. Then she took a deep breath. Time to contact Noah.

/direct link/message only/

/message refused/

Shit. She could follow the link into VR, but she had resolved she wouldn't do that.

/direct link/message/

/message refused/

Now who was trapping who? She would have to try the link, to see if it was still operational at least. She knew the rational thing was to exit and put it to one side, wait for Noah to contact her again. She couldn't get the thought of Ma out of her mind, Ma in danger.

/direct link/enter/

To start with there was nothing, but her exit sigil still shone reassuringly live. Then the meeting joining icon flashed and at the same time her surroundings resolved themselves into the corporate room where she and Amaruq had met Noah before: low leather chairs, glass coffee table, subdued lighting. The stork was sitting behind the table, drumming one clawed foot on the table edge. She looked at him warily.

'Ah, Killaq, good. I thought you wouldn't come. I, ah, I needed to talk to you. Urgently.'

'I should report this,' she said slowly, 'to Oversight.'

'Quite right, ah, of course. Killaq, I can't explain now, you have to trust me.'

'I'm not sure that I do.'

So far she hadn't said anything that would give herself away. Except that she shouldn't be here at all.

'Killaq!' the stork hissed. 'Don't fuck about! You know what I mean. I need the door now.'

The stork image rippled and shifted, as if some internal conflict was shaking it. Now was the time, if there ever was a time. She still held out.

'What about my family? That's the only reason I'm here. Can you promise me, can you *guarantee* me their safety?'

'Ah, shit, Killaq, yes, yes, just give me the door, give me the door now.' The stork image shuddered, one wing going out of focus. It looked like there was something else there, something else with scales, talons. Killaq held out her hand to it and something grasped her hand in a strangling grip.

'Quick, Killaq, quick, now.' The voice was agonised. Killaq reached behind the conch icon in her heads-up and selected the door. Together they fell into darkness.

'Killaq? Killaq?'

She couldn't see anything, but she could hear Noah's voice. She didn't know what she had brought with her, here into Amaruq's locked room. She knew there was only one way out for her. She needed to follow it fast. She didn't know what capabilities the Noah creature had. She fumbled with the start of the commands. Quick, quick.

/uninstall firewall/uninstall personal safety/uninstall ID protect/uninstall ID failsafe/uninstall portal alert/

'Killaq? Where have you brought me?' Suddenly the voice was right next to her.

Shit, hurry, hurry.

These actions are not recommended. These actions will prejudice your personal security. It is necessary to reconfigure your ID before these actions may proceed.

'Killaq?' There was a cold talon on her arm.

/profile/ID/reconfigure ID/

'Here you are.' The talon gripped her wrist painfully. Shit, the reconfigure wasn't coming through. Oh, Christ, what now?

/confirmed/

It was the den, and she was lying on moss, looking up at the interwoven leafy ceiling. The sun shone through the gaps between the branches and made a mosaic of sharp-edged pieces of light on the earth floor. She checked her ID, her accesses, her protocols. Everything was fine. She rolled over onto her elbow and he was there, Amaruq, working with a small knife at a carving, something wooden, or maybe bone. He looked up and smiled at her.

'Hey, sis. Well done.'

She was in her five-year-old persona and it seemed the most natural thing to run across the mossy floor and bury herself in his shoulder, pressing her face into his sealskin jerkin. Then after a moment she drew away and shook herself, becoming Ambra, and sat down opposite him, one leg straight, hugging the knee of the other leg.

'Did we get him?'

'We got someone. I'm not going in there to take a look, just yet.'

'It was horrible. His persona wasn't stable, it kept on rippling and changing. There was something underneath, a different ID. Some kind of monster.'

'Yeah, I think Noah, the real Noah, might be resisting the control he's under. But I don't know whether the monster, whether that's the real Noah, what there is left of him, or whether the real Noah is the overlay.'

Killaq shuddered. 'I don't know how they can do that to another human being.'

'Yeah, well. Anyway, you got out.'

'Only just! I tried to strip my ID, like you showed me, and that was scary enough, but then at the last minute it wouldn't let me and it made me reconfigure everything and that, that thing had its hand, its claws right on my arm.' Killaq rubbed her forearm under the sleeve of her wine-red robe.

'Yeah, that might have been my fault. I tried to give you an extra layer of security, a failsafe to keep your sense of self together, but that might be what triggered the reconfigure, I don't know.'

'What d'you mean, an extra layer?'

Amaruq gestured with his whittling knife and Killaq realised that, incongruously for her Ambra persona, she was still wearing her soapstone bear around her neck on its narrow leather thong. She looked at it closely: there was a flicker about it, a hint that it was more than a piece of jewellery. Code, densely written code.

'Oh, ok, I see. I'll have a look at that later.'

'You won't have it later,' said Amaruq, with his irritating look of someone who has secrets. 'Just the one Ma gave you.'

'Yeah,' said Killaq, determined not to ask him about it. 'But I need to change the thong, I don't wear leather.'

Amaruq rolled his eyes. Then he adopted a more businesslike tone. 'Look, you need to get back. I don't know what's going to happen, but we have to expect some sort of counterattack, if what we've got in the stork trap is actually him, Sanderson.'

'Sanderson? I thought it was Noah.'

A flicker of disgust passed over Amaruq's face. 'Yeah, it's Noah, part of him at least, but I think he's been slaved to Sanderson. His ID, in VR. He doesn't have a separate self, anymore.'

'Oh god. Horrible. So that was the other person, the monster?'

'Maybe.'

'But really, Sanderson, himself? Don't they have people to do that stuff?'

'I know,' said Amaruq. 'But somehow I have the feeling it had got personal, for him. And if he's slaved Noah to him, then he's the only one that can use the Noah ID.'

'Are you saying,' Killaq said slowly, 'that we have actually trapped a SAPA executive in VR?'

'Who can say?' said Amaruq, evasively. 'Point is, if it is Sanderson, SAPA may be open to a hostage exchange.'

'Sanderson for Annie?'

'And the other girl, too, Gina. But I'm sure they won't offer until they know they can't do it any other way.'

'Are Annie and Gina, are they *safe*? While all this is going on?'

Amaruq looked grim. 'We don't know for sure. But there's a plan B.'

'Don't tell me.'

'I wasn't going to.'

'And is that it? Or is the action still going ahead?' And then, when Amaruq didn't answer, 'You *are* going to have to tell me sometime. If it's something that involves me.'

Amaruq was slow to reply. 'It does involve you,' he said, at length. 'You might not like it much. It would be up to you, you'd have to agree.'

'Just tell me, then I can decide.'

'Maybe. Right now we need to get Annie and Gina back, before anything else.'

'Right.' She paused. 'Are *you* going to be ok?'

He grinned. 'Never worry about me, li'l sis. Now, go.'

He drew a circle in the air with the point of his knife and the den vanished. For a moment she thought she could see through the circle, back into the den, and then she realised that it was the rising sun she was looking at, as it cast its long dazzling path over the quiet expanse of the Mediterranean. She ducked her head underwater, washing away the fear, and suddenly she laughed aloud. Salt, it tasted salt.

Li Ji-Hae

In the capital of willows

By the broad riverside,

In the capital of willows

A skein of birds flew by.

It was bedtime and his mother was singing to him. On the wall the shadow of the maple tree nodded. He was so warm, tucked under his blue and white quilt, he was so cozy, and his mother was there, and everything was safe.

From one shore to the other

There flew a bridge of birds.

I met my love there walking

Without many words.

He curled in closer to hear her singing. His leg hurt when he moved it. He must have fallen and hurt it, but she would kiss it better. He opened his eyes, but instead of the bedroom wall there was light, a pale sky with high clouds. He had been dreaming, or no, he had dozed off and this was the dream, it was a dream of lying on cold ground, under a cloud-streaked sky. He didn't like the dream; he would wake up, and then his mother would tuck him in, and he would go to sleep again in the warm, and everything would be all right. There, there she was singing.

Blue was her knotted apron

Blue as the sky.

Dark rolled the river past us

Dark as her eyes.

He came to a little. He had thought his mother had been singing to him, but now he remembered. No one had come to find him, then. He struggled up onto his elbows. At least the leg didn't hurt so badly anymore. Maybe it would be all right. He looked around. Everything was quiet. There was some bird piping, but far away, at the edge of his hearing. The burned-out vehicles were still in the same places. A tuft of yellow grasses swayed in the light wind. He watched it intently, his whole concentration caught up in the motion of the seeded grass heads as they bent to the breeze, sprang back, bent again. Then he looked up into the moving cirrus. He felt as though his whole consciousness was being dispersed over the wide sky, spread out, breaking up into the wind and the running clouds.

There was someone there, someone behind him. No, nothing, there was nobody. The thought had been enough to bring him back to his body. His elbow was leaning on something sharp. It was uncomfortable. He shifted the arm and wondered what day it was and how long he had been lying there. For a moment a weight of despair fell on him and he knew that he was injured, badly injured, that if no one came he would die here. Then he shut his eyes, refusing the understanding. He would just rest for a moment, he would just get his strength back, then he would be able to work out what to do next.

And as the birds flew over

And the river rolled by

I held my love and kissed her

By the dark riverside.

There, that was better, his mother had been there all along, she was stroking the side of his cheek, the way she always used to. He sighed with happiness, abandoning himself to the dream, to the warmth of the blue quilt, to the sunshine on the wall.

Now I must go and leave her

Without many words

In the capital of willows

Across the bridge of birds.

Killaq

They were in VR, but the VR space was engineered to look like Amaruq's programming suite at home. She even wondered if he had overlaid her VR experience onto the programming suite where he was in the body, she couldn't be sure. More and more now he did stuff with VR that she wouldn't have said was possible. She wasn't even sure where VR started and where it left off, for him.

'IF YOU WANT HIM BACK, DO AS WE SAY.' He was going to paint the slogan on the heads-up of each of the SAPA inner command. Killaq shivered, looking over his shoulder. 'Don't you think – .' She hesitated.

'What? Too bold?' He looked back at her with his trademark grin. 'Gotta show these fuckers we can play their game.'

'I worry,' she began, absently running a finger over her soapstone bear. 'It's just like, I don't know.' Then she asked abruptly, 'Is this what Dad did? How he died?'

'What, you think I'm a little boy cub, following in daddy's footsteps? You don't think I can fight my own battles?' The grin was gone.

'I lost Dad. I don't want to lose you.'

'I've gotta be better, is all.' He smiled, but there was no warmth in it. 'I can do programming no one else knows is even possible.'

'I know. I know you can. That's what scares me, really. I think one day you're going to go too far.'

'And how far, li'l sis, exactly, precisely how far is too far? Tell me?' Now he had his remote, cold look.

'I don't know. Just promise me …' Her voice tailed away.

But he had already turned back to his code. 'Send,' he said, aloud. Killaq covered her face with her hands.

'Look,' he said, after a long moment, 'it's done now. We'll know soon enough. But it's not just for me, there's those girls down in Oz, I want to find them if I can.'

'Annie.'

'Annie, yes, and the other one. Gina. But Annie, I think I, I miss her, y'know. Even if, if,'

Killaq put her hand on his shoulder. 'Hey,' she began, but just then a chime sounded on his console.

'Shit, gotta deal with this. Stay if you want.'

As before a view of tundra opened up before her, but this time she was also aware of Amaruq, still in his programming suite, overlaid or superimposed or somehow there at the same time. It was a desolate scene, the aftermath of a battle: great armoured vehicles lay burned-out, scattered across a pale flat expanse of rocky ground interspersed with harsh, dry grasses. Patches of snow had been churned and darkened by the passage of heavy machinery and long charred lines showed the strike tracks of laser cannon. A uniformed body lay sprawled on its back, looking sightlessly at the sky; on the upward-pointing chin perched a bird, a crow, its plumage glossy and darkly green. As they watched it pecked swiftly and –

'No,' said Killaq, hiding her eyes. 'What is this, news footage?'

'Nope. Hush. There's something I need to do.'

The view tracked onwards, moving across the battlefield, a metre above the ground, maybe, but moving fast. It was the image feed from a low-flying drone, Killaq realised. Now ahead there was another shape moving, grey in the flat light. Not a droid, not battle armour. A shaggy outline, something on all fours, padding purposefully away from the image as the drone came up behind it. It was the bear. The drone slowed, keeping a distance from the great pacing beast, as the bear stopped at one of the broken uniformed figures, sniffing the body, placing a clawed foot on the dead chest. The view swung around and now Killaq could see the soldier's face: he was lying on his back, propped against a rounded rock, and one hand had fallen away, still clutching a water carrier. He was only a boy, she thought. The bear bent over the soldier, nosing the contours of his face, delicately, gently.

'Ah no!' Killaq cried. 'Is the bear going to eat him? I don't want to see it.'

'Not now, sis.' Amaruq was creating code at a ferocious rate, the symbols forming in mid-air around him, re-ordering and reforming themselves.

'Even if he is dead. I can't stand it.'

'He's not dead,' Amaruq said briefly.

Killaq let out a cry of anguish. She brought up her own exit commands.

'I won't do it, I won't watch.'

'Sis, just shut up, will you?'

The bear leant down again, showing its huge incisors, and opened its jaws. Amaruq was coding now like a symphony conductor, sweeping his arms wide in a series of all-encompassing gestures. Code flew and dazzled with his movements. Then he drew himself in, and now it was as if he was shaping a rounded space, a ball; he made it smaller and smaller, modelling it, smoothing it, until the code spun shining and balanced on the palm of his hand and the bear's teeth met in the man's neck. 'Transfer,' Amaruq said, aloud.

Tears ran down Killaq's face and she turned away. 'It's all right, sis, at least I think it's all right, give me a moment.' He brought up a different set of code. 'You might not want to watch this bit.'

It was a view of something close up, it was red and stringy, it looked like meat. For a moment Killaq couldn't understand what she was seeing. Then the view swung nauseatingly towards the horizon. It was the bear, they were seeing again through the bear's eyes. Killaq cried out wildly with sorrow and disgust. Amaruq circled his hand around in a closing gesture and the tundra, the dead man and the pale overarching sky all vanished.

He leaned back in his console chair. 'Got him!'

'Fuck you!' Killaq shouted at him, between spasms of tears.

'It's ok, sis.' And he came over and put his arms around her, rocking her, until her sobs had died down and she was crying steadily against his shoulder.

Eventually she drew away, looking at him with mistrust. 'How is it ok? And, why did you want to watch the bear eat him? It was horrible, horrible. I never want to see anything like that, ever again.'

'Don't you see?'

'No, I don't fucking see, I don't see at all.'

'Look. This is what it's thinking.' He spread the fingers of his left hand with a gesture of a flower opening, and suddenly there was audio. It was a song, a woman singing. Something about a river, and birds.

'That's what the *bear* is thinking?'

'No!' He gripped her shoulder, smiling. 'It's not a bear anymore. That's what the man is thinking.' He looked at her in triumph. 'He was fitted with a portal, he'd probably sold the viz to one of these games companies. That's what the drone was probably doing there.'

'It wasn't your drone?'

'Like I own drones. I just piggybacked on the one that was there. So the guy, the Korean, he had a portal, it meant I could get in. I got him, I held him safe, and now I've put him in the bear. Remember, I showed you, the bear had a portal fitted too.'

Killaq looked away, shaking her head. 'Got there just in time, too,' Amaruq added.

'Look,' he said, when Killaq still said nothing. 'Which would you rather, if it was you. Be dead on the tundra, or be alive, have your consciousness in the bear? I've saved him. He was going to die, otherwise. He was wounded, badly wounded, and he was going to be eaten, whatever I did.'

'I can't,' began Killaq in a low voice. 'I don't really believe it. You can't move someone's mind like that, away from their body.' But as she said it she remembered the diagram on the sand, Amaruq picking up the black cord, replacing it. *You aren't moving the consciousness, you're moving the interface.* It couldn't be true, she refused to accept it. 'And anyway,' she said, 'you didn't ask him. You didn't ask if he wanted to live on in a bear. Maybe it was the right time for him to die. And what about the bear, what about its life, its awareness. You can't just go about, making decisions like that. It can't be right.' She looked at him pleadingly, but then a further thought came to her. 'And *anyway,* that voice, it was in English, wasn't it. So you're not telling me a Korean soldier is thinking, remembering, whatever, in English?'

She relaxed: it must have been one of his hoaxes, more elaborate and grisly than usual, but just one of his scenarios. But he looked at her gravely, rubbing his jaw. 'Ah, that's the easy question, I'm running him in a translation interface.'

All of a sudden Killaq lost her temper. 'You know I *said,*' she started, her voice rising. 'You know I *said* you were going to go too far. Well this, this is it, this is too far, either it's a joke, in which case it's a very fucking unfunny joke, or if it's real, it's disgusting, it's playing with someone's life, that poor man!'

Amaruq sighed. 'Sis,' he said, 'I didn't make him a soldier.' He paused. 'I thought you might see how exciting it is. No one has ever done anything like this before. And it proves it, you know, it proves you can move consciousness, you don't need to be linked back through the portal all the time. It's massive, it's going to change everything.'

Killaq looked at him in dismay. But then Amaruq raised his head as if a new scent had come to him on the wind. 'Gotta go,' he said, and vanished.

Killaq stayed in the programming suite for a while, looking at her hands. The place seemed empty now there was no one there to call swirling code from the banks of input terminals. Maybe, she thought, maybe it was time to go home, keep an eye on her brother. There was no one she could talk to about stuff like this. There was Ma – but Amaruq would never forgive her. They had a long-standing pact. But what if he was in danger? She didn't like any of this. The fear that had risen when he had sent that taunting message to SAPA High Command had stayed with her, underlying the whole episode with the bear. Craziness, all craziness, even if it was real. And what if he was in actual fact losing touch with reality? She was profoundly sceptical about anyone, even him, having the ability to put a man's consciousness into a bear's portal. Arrogance, madness. What if it wasn't a hoax, what if he somehow really believed he could do stuff, stuff that was impossible. Either he really had taught himself near godlike skills – in which case SAPA would hunt him down and end him – or else he thought he had. In which case he was insane, he needed help.

She clutched the soapstone bear, running her thumb over the long back, the stylised head. Here in VR, it buzzed with code. It was the proof of real coding knowledge, made by Amaruq, to keep her safe. Maybe he could do the things he said he could.

/exit/

She surfaced in her swimming routine to find what should have been the moving sea frozen into a 2-D visual and RETURN TO BASE signals plastered across the scenario. Shit. She hadn't allowed for this. How long had she been gone? Quick, time to get back.

/exit/

YOU ARE CONFINED TO YOUR CONSOLE FOR SECURITY REASONS. THERE IS A STATE OF GENERAL ALERT. PLEASE DO NOT ATTEMPT TO EXIT THE CONSOLE. FURTHER INFORMATION WILL BE PROVIDED. THERE IS A STATE OF GENERAL ALERT. PLEASE DO NOT ATTEMPT TO EXIT THE CONSOLE.

Killaq tried the console lid but the latch was locked. She tried the emergency release routine, mandatory since the early days when scenario users, away from their bodies, had burned in house fires or been murdered by burglars. The emergency release had been disabled. She was imprisoned in the narrow space under the curved console lid. She felt her heartbeat thudding and her breath caught in her throat. Wait, wait, breathe. Breathe. She forced herself to think. What did they teach them at school, when they had been old enough to have portal implants for the first time? The emergency routines which no one ever used because no one was ever trapped in their console. First, keep your body moving. Dutifully she tensed and relaxed the muscles of her arms, her back, her sides, her legs. Suddenly her left calf contracted in agonising cramp. She couldn't reach it, she couldn't bend over far enough to knead the muscle. She pressed her toes against the plastic end of the console, willing the cramp to go away.

Ok, that was better. What now? At school, they taught them to bring up some soothing wallpaper, to help to keep them calm. She wasn't going to bother with that, calm wasn't appropriate. Or no, wait, maybe they would expect her to run through the emergency routines. Ok, ok. *Woodland fantasia,* there, that would do. A vista of sweeping glades, sunlight shining through the branches of oak trees, played across the inside of the console lid. She ignored it. What next?

Probably she was under surveillance, she should avoid going anywhere near any of her secret accesses. Amaruq had said there was a plan B, hadn't he. She would have to trust to the plan B, whatever it was. Anyway, she expected her VR access would be disabled now. She checked anyway. Yes, disabled. But hang on, there were new messages. Her inbox must have been functioning up to the time the alert was imposed. Something from Consuela, about the publicity catchment for next week's blog. Blog participation and sign-on stats. Next week's menu. A SAPA junior personnel social function. Health and safety for blog workers. Ah, one from Ma.

It was Ma's face, full viz, not a message in words. Ma must have gone to the lengths of putting her bulky VR helmet on, attaching the sensors, running the accesses. It wasn't hardwired for her, she didn't have a portal. It looked like she had been crying.

Killaq, I can't get hold of you, I left a message, I haven't heard back. I don't know what's happening. There are soldiers here, SAPA soldiers, they're searching the house, they've turned everything upside down, they say they're looking for your brother. I don't know what to do. Message me as soon as you get this. I hope you're safe, little bird.

Immediately Killaq hit reply.

Your access to VR messaging is suspended momentarily at the present time. Please try again later.

Killaq screamed in frustration, hammering the unyielding plastic lid with her fists. 'Ma! Ma!' she shouted. Then after a while the futility of this came to her and she stopped, turning her face aside, and wept. 'Ma!' she sobbed, and then, falling back into Inuktitut, 'Ana, Ana.'

Tom

'You realise, of course, that we still don't know if that was him. Or if he really exists, at all.'

Misha was screwing together dark, gleaming sections of metal tubing: the long barrel of a laser rifle. An Alienator. Tom had no idea where he had got it from.

'Yeah. What he showed us was he could control us totally, in VR. So you tell me, Misha, what choice did we have?'

'The same choice we always have. Go forward, into the unknown. Or don't.' Misha smiled a slightly unnerving smile. 'I thought he was cute.'

Tom let himself fall himself backwards on the beige carpet. 'Fuck,' he said. 'That takes the cake. You think he's fucking cute. You think he's cute. Motherfucker. He's just about the most scary person I've ever met and you just said you don't even know if he really exists and you think he's *cute*.'

'You called him Captain,' said Misha, slyly.

'Yeah. Yeah, I did. He's, I dunno, when he talks you want to follow him. But I don't *trust* him. If I could think of any way of getting in there without him, I would.'

'If it was really him, if he can do what he says he can do, then we stand a chance. A small chance. If it was not him, then we are dead men walking.'

'Know what I like about you, Misha, you're so fucking comforting.'

They were in the shabby upstairs bedroom of a safehouse. The room was empty apart from a stained mattress, and the wallpaper was torn away in a large square where sometime in the past an old-fashioned screen for viz and audio would have been fixed to the wall. Tom didn't know what Misha had told the network about why they needed the safehouse. He had a feeling that he might have pulled in a favour, told someone he needed a rendezvous for sex. Tom smiled to himself humourlessly. He didn't think he was Misha's type somehow.

From the upstairs window he could see the other side of the street: small bungalows with sagging chain-link fences around dusty yards; plastic bins overspilling with rubbish; large dogs lying in the sun. They were two blocks away from the cleared area surrounding the high wire fences and searchlights of the correctional institute. This was probably the right facility: at least, this was one of the two where the prisoner occupancy records didn't match the cell occupancy. Prisoner occupancy was published on VR; cell occupancy came from data Amaruq had stolen; there were two more cells occupied than prisoners declared. Didn't have to mean Annie and Gina were there. Could mean anything. Annie and Gina could be out of the country, or kept at different places from each other. Or dead. Tom's lips set in a thin line. Or Amaruq could be a SAPA agent, or if he was genuine, he could have been fed made-up data, it could be a trap. They would know tonight. Tom reached for a warm beer from the shopping basket over the door handle. He made to pass one to Misha but Misha shook his head. Pretty much the only time Misha didn't drink or do drugs, the day before an action.

Misha finished assembling the Alienator and ran a hand sensually along the long black barrel. Then he put it aside, within reach. 'Now, we wait,' he said. He leaned back against the wall and closed his eyes. Tom looked at him in disbelief. How could he fucking sleep, a day like this? Tom levered off the top of the lukewarm stubbie and took a mouthful. It tasted of nothing. He sighed and put the beer down, looking up at the ceiling. There was a crack wandering across the middle, maybe where a light fitting used to be. There was a fat fly buzzing in the corner. Shit, man, how many hours of this? Patience, patience, Tom told himself. He'd waited empty-minded for actions many times. This was no different. But it *was* different: the thought of Annie tugged at him painfully, like an old injury, like a memory of something shameful. They were so near; maybe she wouldn't be there; he had to school himself. He imagined opening a door on an empty cell. Opening a door on a cell where some unknown prisoner, someone he didn't give a shit about, turned gladly towards him. Opening a door and it would be Gina, not Annie, and he would have to put a happy face on it. Maybe they wouldn't get in at all. Maybe he would be shot and die in the dust outside the compound. Maybe they would find her and she would have chosen *him,* him, Amaruq. Ah, shit. Think about something else. Tom watched the fly buzzing angrily against the edge of the ceiling.

In the end he dozed a bit, dreaming disjointedly of being late, he was running behind, but he needed to find something before he went, he was hunting distractedly through his canvas back pack. He couldn't remember what it was he was looking for. Misha shone a torch in his face.

'Fuck, man, you woke me up.'

'Thirty minutes to go.'

Tom rubbed his face, surfacing groggily from the dream. 'What time is it?'

'Oh one thirty.'

'Ok, right. Gimme a minute.'

He stumbled to the dark bathroom and took a piss in the sink. The house had no water or power. Back to the upstairs room. He pulled on the ochre SAPA tunic and pants that they had downloaded and run off on the printer: might as well look right on a casual inspection. There was nothing to drink except flat beer. He took a swig anyway, grimacing at the stale taste. Boots, pack. Weapon.

'Misha?'

'There's no answer.'

Amaruq was supposed to have set up a face-recognition overlay for them, inserting Tom's and Misha's face scans and biometrics into the system so that the compound's security would register them as legitimate staff members. He was going to confirm, last thing before they set off. Now they couldn't contact him.

'Are we still on?'

Misha shrugged. 'At least if it is not working, we will know straight away.'

'And then what?'

'Shoot. Run.' Misha's eyes shone.

'You know what you are, you are one insane son of a bitch,' Tom told him, punching his shoulder. Misha drove him crazy with his mannerisms and his secrets, but now they were about to go in, he felt a wave of affection for him.

'Ok?'

'Ok.'

/staffmember/login/

/login accepted/

As easy as that. Too easy, maybe. Tom's mouth was dry. He picked up his kit and without saying anything more Misha and he let themselves out of the safehouse, deleting the access code on their exit, and walked down to the end of the street. It was a cloudy night, a bit cool; it seemed surreal to be strolling along between the lines of shabby bungalows, on their way to break into a SAPA compound. They could see the floodlights shining over the tops of the houses. Now they were at the street corner and crossing the wide stretch of cleared gravel that separated the facility from the surrounding housing. Tom knew that their images would have already been scanned and checked on the database. Sweat crawled between his shoulder blades. He found he was holding his breath. He made an effort to breathe.

Misha was humming to himself. The bastard, Tom thought, he could at least pretend to be frightened.

Now they were at the entry lock. A steel door shutter barred the entrance. Once they were through, Tom knew, that would be when there would be trouble if the face-recognition didn't work. If it was never going to. If Amaruq had set them up. If he had tried but made an arse of it. Tom tried to keep his face neutral. The entry system would monitor his biometrics; if he was too sweaty or looked shifty or nervous, that would be enough to trigger an alert.

Misha sauntered up to the eye-height reader. He looked bored. He held himself where the reader could scan him. Right profile. Left profile.

'State purpose of your request for admission,' said the automated voice.

'Misha Simonovsky, shift 17B, reporting.'

'Entry authorised.'

With a metallic groan the shutter rolled back and Misha stepped into the claustrophobic scan room inside.

Suddenly Tom laughed aloud. Misha, that cunt, he had used his real name! Still laughing, he stepped in front of the reader.

'Mike Walker, shift 17B, reporting.'

'Entry authorised.'

It was an uncompromising small room with steel shutters front and rear, lit by a harsh white light. There was room for maybe ten people standing. The walls were covered in admonitory signs.

It is an offence to introduce registered psycho-active substances into this facility.

It is an offence to attempt to enter this facility while carrying a prohibited device or weapon.

Legal Counsel must submit their papers for inspection if a request is made.

Next of kin must produce completed identity documentation.

The result of security scans will not be made available unless a formal request is made pursuant to 315.1 (b) of the Criminal Code.

The door they had entered by shut behind them with a grating, scraping noise. They were being scanned again now, Tom knew. If the face-recognition wasn't solid, if the overlay Amaruq had written didn't effectively conceal their identities, tagging their visuals as existing employees and the weaponry they carried as authorised equipment, this was where it would end. Sedative-gas nozzles loomed out of the walls. Misha was leaning on one shoulder, concealing part of the signage ('If you have failed to declare something which,' was the part which could be read). He was still humming.

Nothing happened. The light over the exit door stayed red. Tom shifted his weight from foot to foot.

'Shit, man,' he muttered. Misha shot him a warning look but remained silent.

Then the communication panel by the outgoing door lit up. 'Scan complete,' a voice said. 'Complete entrance ID.' Without hesitating Misha stepped forward and lay the palm of his hand against the panel. How had he known to do that?

'Misha Simonovsky, ID accepted. Next.'

His heart in his mouth, Tom stepped forward and laid his hand palm-forward on the panel. It was greasy to the touch. He felt as though the silence went on too long. It had accepted Misha but it wouldn't accept him. Maybe it was Misha who was the traitor. Maybe Misha would go through to congratulations and back-slapping from his colleagues, and he would be left here to await the pleasure of SAPA Oversight.

'Mike Walker, ID accepted. No further individuals identified in scan room. Prepare for exit.'

Tom hadn't realised he had been holding his breath. He breathed out. The shutter door rolled slowly aside and he and Misha stepped through. He set off purposefully across the gravelled inner compound. He was determined not to play the weak sister in front of Misha. His boots crunched on the gravel and each stride was outlined by multiple shadows cast by searchlights on either side. In front the correctional building rose up in front of them, windowless, grey, squat. Most of the facility would be underground. The concrete façade was broken only by the outline of the pedestrian entry port, and the dark recesses on either side where defence armament swivelled, tracking them. They do that for all incomers, Tom told himself. It doesn't mean anything.

The entry port opened to a palm print. There was a dingy reception area. Behind a screen of shatter-proof plastic was a human operator. He was an obese, balding White man, barely fitting into the ochre uniform, watching something on a small screen while one hand reached into an outsize packet of Twisties. He looked at them incuriously.

'All right, guys?'

'All right,' Tom said, in what he hoped was the right unemphatic tone.

'Mid-shift replacement,' said Misha, sounding businesslike.

'Go on through.'

They stepped past him, into the corridor beyond. 'Now what?' said Tom. Amaruq had the schematics of the building.

'Just keep walking,' said Misha. The corridor stretched in front of them. It smelled of antiseptic. This was never going to work. And if they were on their own in here, how would they ever find Annie? And Gina, of course.

Then their heads-ups lit up with Amaruq's ID.

Fuck sake, man, you left it long enough.

Guys, this isn't the Captain. This is Jean-Louis. Been a bit of a change of plan at this end, still working on a few things.

Tom and Misha exchanged glances. Who the hell was Jean-Louis?

Can you give us ID? That was Misha.

I've got this ID, haven't I? I know how it looks. There isn't time to explain. If you want to back out, we can probably get you out safely from here.

'We'd never get in again,' said Tom, aloud.

Wall microphones, sent Misha.

Sorry.

There was a silence. Without realising it they had stopped walking, staring at each other in the deserted corridor. It was Misha who made up his mind first.

Well, Jean-Louis, if that is your name, I am not ready to leave this fascinating building without seeing some more of the sights.

Tom felt as though he was falling out of control down the side of a wave that would break his body and spit out the pieces.

Yeah, ok, whatever. Do it.

Immediately their heads-ups gave them the schematic: a geometric maze of luminous green with their route outlined in a thicker green line. Without any further discussion they set off, following the flashing green circle marking their position. End of the corridor; left; right; lift bays. Tom hit the lift call and a door opened immediately. The lift smelled of confined bodies and there was some sort of smear on the floor, rusty-brown, imperfectly cleaned. Floor -5, said the schematic. Tom punched the numbers and the lift set off with a perceptible rocking motion. Minus five. He wondered how deep the facility went down. The lift settled and the door opened. Down at this level the corridors were dark, only illuminated where sensors detected movement. They stood in a small pool of dim light. The walls were concrete, unpainted. The schematic lit up again. Left, right, right, small flight of steps, double doors. The dim light followed them, coming on just ahead, going out behind them. Another long corridor. A T-junction at the end.

Wait, sent Jean-Louis. They stood in the pool of light, waiting. Across the end of the corridor they heard a clattering noise, something wheeled going by. Of course, the automated prisoner conveyance systems didn't need light.

Ok.

Left at the end. Another corridor.

Before the end of the corridor, a step sideways.

AUTHORISED PERSONNEL ONLY.

A door. A room full of cleaning materials. Someone's stash of private stuff, a zippered bag, some vaping kit. Another door. A stairwell. Up now, two flights. A landing, a door at the top.

Ok, we're on the edge of the inner system. The security clearance for your overlays won't work beyond this point.

Tom looked up, startled, but Misha was nodding. Chrissakes, what else did he know that Tom didn't?

I think the Captain had a plan, but. Well anyway, you should be able to manage from now on. We've brought you to behind the wall of the prisoner detoxification facility.

Again Tom had that feeling of falling out of control, but Misha had already knelt down by the base of the wall and had his pack open. The charges, right. They had planned to use them if they had needed a diversion on the way out, but a shaped charge would take out a wall. Tom swung his own pack down as Misha busied himself with the intricate wiring.

Last thing, guys. The minute you set that device off, Oversight antivirus will be all over us. We'll try to keep up with you, but we may have our hands full ourselves.

'Tom!' hissed Misha. 'Pliers!'

'Right.' He reached in his pack, thinking.

Your Captain, is he ok?

'Tom! If it is not too inconvenient!'

Tell you the truth, we don't know. You just do the job you came to do and we'll give you backup the best way we know how.

Tom found the pliers. Quickly he knelt down next to Misha, taking two sets of respirators from his pack. Oversight's first response would be to flood the facility with sedative gas. He pulled his over his head and handed the other to Misha. If nothing else this would breach the overlay: there was no way a person wearing a respirator was legitimate staff.

'Ready?'

Misha settled the strap of his respirator, running his finger around the face seal.

'Ok.'

The timer was manual, unhackable. Misha set it to 10 seconds. Walk, don't run. Shut the door behind you. Far corner of the stairs. Crouching down, hands over head.

Good luck, guys.

Unendurable noise filled the stairwell.

Killaq

She had run out of tears and protests and had been lying in a despairing stupor, when the emergency comms light came on and a voice spoke in the confined console space. It was a woman's voice, sweetly reasonable and calm.

'Hello occupant, can you hear me?'

'Yes,' said Killaq out loud, her voice sounding scratchy in her ears.

'Occupant, this is SAPA Oversight automated Care and Security. You may call me Alicia. I am tasked to look after you during this unforeseen exception event. Do you understand me?'

'Yes,' said Killaq. 'Can you tell me what's going on?'

'Occupant, our first priority is for your care and security. Since your console has been in emergency mode for over two hours, I must first evaluate your health and state of well-being and morale. Do you consent to this?'

'Yes,' said Killaq. There was no point refusing. 'Can you tell me what the emergency is?'

'There will be an opportunity to ask questions once I am satisfied of your state of well-being and morale. Scan commencing now.'

Killaq could hear the light hum of the scan machinery. She forced herself to relax and then thought no, some degree of tension would be expected. She scrunched up her toes and fists, but this only brought back the cramp in her calf.

'Please remain still while the scan is completed.'

'I've got cramp in my calf,' Killaq gasped, trying to press her feet on the end of the console lid.

'You are complaining of cramp. This is verified by scan. Would you like an injection of muscle relaxant?'

'No! No, it's ok now, it's better.'

'Scan is still showing muscle tension. An injectable relaxant is recommended. Would you like an injection of muscle relaxant?'

'Injection refused,' said Killaq, firmly.

'It is noted that you have refused the recommended prophylaxis. This is your right unless this programme determines that your care and security will be prejudiced by your refusal. If you change your mind, please tell me. The injection is ready for your use.'

Killaq kept quiet.

'Your scan is completed. May I tell you the results?'

'Please tell me the results.'

'This biometric data will be shared by SAPA Oversight with such of its partner organisations as may request it for purposes of research and analysis.'

'Get on with it.'

'Your scan reveals no acute or life-threatening conditions. You have mild to moderate anxiety. You have muscle tension for which a relaxant has been recommended. You have 15% dehydration. You have not eaten recently. Other conditions and biometrics detected are assumed to be known to you and a summary is available for download. Please reply yes or no to the following suggested therapies:

FOR YOUR ANXIETY choose as many options as you like from the following list: sedative by gas; sedative by injection; sedative by oral administration; calming music; calming poetry.'

Killaq, thinking that she had better accept something, chose the calming music. Immediately the console was filled with the tinkly sound of synthetic piano music. She did her best to ignore it. Working through the menus she again refused the muscle relaxant, accepted oral rehydration therapy, and refused the sedative that was again suggested as part of the oral rehydration. A small tube was released from near the hinge of the console lid and she took hold of it and sucked: it was a syrupy gel. She didn't trust the algorithm not to add the sedative anyway but she needed liquid.

'You may now ask me questions which I will answer to the best of my ability. My priority is your Care and Security. I am therefore authorised to restrict the answers to questions if testing shows that this is likely to cause you harm or distress. Do you have any questions for me?'

'Can I message my Ma?' Killaq immediately asked. She figured that the answer would be no, but it would look odd if she didn't ask.

'VR connectivity is suspended for the duration of this exception event. We apologise for any inconvenience.'

'Can I message my manager, Consuela?'

'For internal correspondence you may record a message for collection at a later date. Would you like to do this?'

'This is a message for Consuela,' said Killaq carefully, thinking hard. There was really no point in messaging her manager except that they would expect it. 'Consuela, I don't know what's going on, but there's some sort of exception event and I'm in my console for Care and Security. I'm just messaging you in case there's a problem you didn't know about. Looks like I'll miss the blog post this evening but I guess you can post one of the pre-records? Ok, talk soon.'

'I have recorded your message for transmission at a later time.'

'Ok, thanks, um, Alicia. Is there any news you can tell me? What's going on? How long am I going to have to stay in here?'

'I am authorised to grant you access to selected infotainment sources.'

That was better than nothing. Killaq eagerly ran through the menu. As she suspected it was all internal SAPA channels: light VR subscription stuff, blogs and whatever. Right at the bottom there was what called itself a news programme ('SAPA brings you the latest from around the globe'). She selected that one and scrolled down through celebrity lifestyle updates and Fact of the Day pieces until she came to 'What's happening in our Marvellous World.' Amazingly enough there was an item labelled 'Korean Local Difficulty.'

The images started with men and women in dark suits slowly climbing a flight of shallow steps before an imposing pillared edifice. The figures in suits crossed a formal forecourt, where geometric lawns were bounded by low box hedges, and filed between the tall colonnades into the building. It was tagged as the seat of the Russian Government. Peace talks were being held in Moscow, the voice-over said, to establish the terms of Korean withdrawal from the territory of Russia's beloved sister territory, the Siberian Federation. It was anticipated that a treaty would be concluded within 7 days. The image of the building was replaced by one of Russian automated armour rolling across the tundra, against a background of birch trees swaying in the sunshine. When it passed a small village of prefabricated pod houses not unlike Killaq's own at home, women in headscarves and scampering children ran alongside, waving and cheering. The Russian tricolour flew tautly in a blue sky alongside the diagonal white and green of the Federation.

Enough, thought Killaq. She paused the item. Now she was afraid. She realised that she had assumed that the security alert, if that was what this was, was to do with the blossoming of war in Siberia. Consuela had talked to her about the evacuation processes which would come into play in the unlikely event of hostilities crossing the Arctic Ocean. But it looked like there was a ceasefire at least, if you could believe the news. That meant that she was confined in her console for some other reason. Maybe her cover, thin at the best of times, was blown; maybe Amaruq was under attack. Killaq remembered Ma's tearful message and her heart went out to her. Maybe this time Amaruq had gone too far. Maybe SAPA would go to any lengths to retrieve Sanderson.

'Alicia?' she said out loud. 'How long do I have to be in here?'

'The situation is under evaluation at the present time. You are restrained for your care and security. I will let you know as soon as any update is available.'

Killaq felt her heart beating faster despite all her efforts to remain calm. The golden oak woods scrolling across the inside of the console lid seemed to have taken on a sinister air and the empty glades looked dangerously expectant. She felt as if she was starting to whirl around to the beat of the tinny music, like a marionette dancing on a circus ride. She fixed her eyes on one of the oak trees. She thought there were faces looking out of the bark, faces with seeing eyes and long pointed incisors. Maybe this was the beginning of the questioning, maybe they had added a psychotropic drug to the rehydration gel. She felt the console spin around her and without knowing she was doing it gripped her soapstone bear, still on its leather thong around her neck, holding it tightly in her curled fingers. The stone was cool and the feel of the stylised curves of the carving soothed her a little. It reminded her of the kitchen at home, Ma fishing among the pins and string in the little woven box to find the bear. Suddenly she felt terribly lonely.

A message flashed in her heads-up.

Biometric accepted.

Part of the scan process, probably. She felt her heart thudding again. Then, improbably, her message icon shone. Maybe they had reconnected internal messages. It might be Consuela. Warily she selected it.

Hey Killaq, that you?

Who is this?

It's Jean-Lou, you know, from the Shack?

What the ...

Listen, your brother gave me this access, he said there might be a time you needed help. Said you were wearing a beacon, some sort of personal jewellery.

What?

Look, Killaq, things are a bit hairy here, if you don't need my help, I gotta go.

What do you mean, hairy?

Did you use a calling beacon, yes or no? Something you're wearing?

Her bear? Killaq uncurled her fingers and held the bear on its thong up to her eye. Immediately the message feed cut off. Shit. Would she be able to get it back again? She wrapped her hand around the bear, holding it hard against her heart. Immediately a musical tone sounded.

Jean-Lou?

'This is Alicia from automated Care and Security. Biometric data show that your anxiety levels have increased. I am authorised to offer you a sedative. You may find that use of a sedative decreases your immediate anxiety levels at a time of particular stress although use over a longer period is to be discouraged.'

'No, thank you.'

'Are you sure?' asked the programme, sounding suddenly disconcertingly human.

'I'm sure, thanks.'

'I am disconnecting now but please be reassured that we will continue to monitor you and your care and security are our utmost priority.'

Jean-Lou?

She's back on line. Hey, Killaq. JL's busy right now. Tell us quick, is that a legit beacon alert.

Who are you?

You can call me DogGirl.

Where's Jean-Lou?

Shit, woman, you need us or not? This is the Nuna army, not a babysitting service.

Sorry. It's just, I didn't know this, my bear, had a beacon facility. Yes, I need help.

Can I access your location data?

Go ahead.

Location determined. Right in the heart of SAPA territory, girlie. You need an out?

They won't let me. I'm in lockdown in my console. I don't know what's going on. I don't have any VR.

Reckon we can deal with that. Ok, what's your skill level like at ingress and control? If we get you to a slave vehicle, can you hack it?

Yes. Yes, I probably could.

Ok, we'll fix it. Next time they offer you the sedative, take it.

What? Why?

Just take the sedative. I've gotta go. We've got a full scale –'

The message feed went dead. Slowly Killaq uncurled her fingers from the bear, staring up at the golden woods processing across the concave inner surface of the console lid. Jean-Lou, what was all that about? She remembered him calling Amaruq 'Captain', back at the shack. And the Nuna army, chrissakes, that was just a joke, an old meme. Surely.

Then she took a deep breath. She had no way of telling what was really going on, if those messages were for real, or if it was a SAPA test. If she was in SAPA-controlled VR, right now. No way of knowing. If there was any chance of getting out, however unlikely, she had to take it. The risk was, that if her cover wasn't already blown, probably this would blow it. Chances were, her cover was already blown. Ok, that decided it.

'Alicia?'

Killaq was breathing fast, hyperventilating to bring her anxiety index up for the scan.

'Hello, occupant. I see that your anxiety is increasing. Can I help?'

'I really don't like being in here, how much longer is it going to be? What's going on outside? I'm beginning to feel really stressed!'

'Would you like me to offer you a sedative or calming therapies?'

'I guess I need something, if this is going to go on like this, I feel really uncomfortable in this little space.'

'The menu is –'

'I don't need the menu, I remember from last time. You can give me an oral sedative, right?'

'You have requested a sedative administered orally. You are assessed as having the legal capacity to make the request. Beta of the drug or drugs administered together with summaries of contra-indications and side effects are available for upload. Do you consent?'

'I consent.'

Once again the small plastic tube came down from the corner of the lid. Killaq took the soft rubberised mouthpiece between her lips. If this was SAPA trying to get her to sedate herself without them having to impose it compulsorily, she had walked into their trap. If it was SAPA they could sedate her anyway on any number of pretexts. She clenched the mouthpiece in her teeth and sucked.

It was a sugary gel, the same as last time. It had a synthetic fruit flavour, strawberry, maybe. Killaq had never tasted a real strawberry. They could grow them hydroponically in the co-operative greenhouse, back at home, but the Council had always chosen to grow more calorie-efficient crops. A bead of sweat ran down her temple. It was hot, here in the greenhouse, hot and humid. She thought she was standing on one of the narrow gravel paths, and all around her a tall leafy crop reached its yellow-green shoots above her head, and vines dangled from growing trays hanging from the transparent panels of the ceiling. There was a rich earthy smell from the mulch that the plants were rooted in. She spread her arms wide and turned her face up to the sunlight filtering through the fronds. Pale-green tendrils, velveted like a stag's antlers, were twining around her legs and unfurling glossily immaculate new leaves, and espaliered along her outstretched arms grapes and tomatoes and nectarines were ripening. Foliage curled through her hair and framed her upturned face, and round her feet squashes opened their yellow trumpet flowers. Away in a distant part of her consciousness she could hear the shrill sound of an emergency alarm sounding, but it didn't seem very important, and here she was in the full morning sunshine drinking in the warm vaporous air and it seemed that she was the greenhouse, and she could feel the light shining through the clear roof panels, and the roots of plants extending into the dark soil, and the drip of cool water running, and she was a part of everything growing and climbing and fruiting in between.

Tom

His ears were ringing despite the ear defenders. He opened his eyes. The air was full of choking grey smoke. There was a crack running across the concrete of the landing floor. He saw it in sharp focus: the zig-zag shape of the crack, the way it narrowed towards the wall and widened darkly towards the stairs, the crumbs of debris on its lip. He went to stand up and the floor shifted under him. Shit, shit. Carefully, trying to take his weight on the wall next to him, he got to his feet. He balanced for a minute before the slab he was standing on groaned and abruptly shifted downwards, maybe two centimetres. Wildly he lunged across the crack, desperately stretching for the safety of the far side, and at that moment the floor where he had been gave way and fell loudly crashing in blocks down the height of the stairs, sending up fresh clouds of grey dust. Tom leaned against the wall, facing the drop, trembling. A red light came on and a siren started to wail.

Misha?

The half of the landing he was on seemed solid enough. A jagged hole gaped in front of him, between him and the corridor where they had laid the charge. The door that had been at the head of the stairs was nowhere to be seen. It was too far to jump, without a run up, and the corridor floor was at a higher level.

Misha?

Never let it be said that I don't deliver a good bang.

Tom grinned with relief. *Fuck off, man! Are you all right?*

More or less.

Where are you?

Up here.

Misha, I'm not going to be able to get across, the top of the stairs is gone. Is there anything there you can chuck me, a rope or something?

Wait.

Tom waited. His breath hissed in his respirator. He was tempted to pull it off, to wipe the grey dust from his forehead and around the respirator seal. It didn't look as though there was gas released in the stairwell, not yet anyway. Easy, man, he thought. Careful. He put his hands behind his back to remove temptation, and closed his eyes. Even behind his closed eyelids he could see the red emergency lighting strobing on and off.

Misha?

Wait.

Then an urgent message icon shone in his heads-up.

Guys from DogGirl.

Who the fuck was DogGirl?

Yeah?

Oversight have your thermal signature, gonna burn you out. You two gotta move now.

Misha!

I heard.

Suddenly air started to blow up the stairs, taking the thick smoke with it. A yellow light burst into life at the bottom of the stairwell.

Misha!

I'm here.

A shape appeared on the other side of the drop. It was Misha, crawling. Tom was expecting a rope, but what Misha was manhandling over the edge was something angular, an office chair, two office chairs lashed together, one above the other, dangling from the broken corridor lip.

You have got to be kidding me.

Best I could do.

Will they hold?

Suck it and see.

Tom shook his head. It couldn't be possible. A waft of fiercely hot air blew past his face.

Jump or burn, brother.

He thought of Annie, waiting for him in some cell somewhere. 'Well hell, babe,' said her voice in his mind, 'are you a surfer or what are you?' He bent his knees and sprang, an enormous standing leap, reaching out over the drop for the rickety contraption Misha had lowered to him. His hand closed around the back strut of the lower chair and without a pause he swung the other hand up to the upper chair, pulling himself up on his arms, his feet kicking uselessly above the stairwell. Another pull, and now Misha had him, and he was lying on his stomach on the corridor floor, and scrabbling his hips and legs up behind him, and behind him the stairwell space was suddenly filled with yellow flame, roaring like a blowtorch.

'Fuck, fuck, my feet, fuck,' Tom yelled. Misha hauled him the last half-metre and together they lay in a heap on the floor, watching the sheet of fire cutting off the end of the corridor.

'We have to keep moving,' Misha said. Tom turned his head to look at him. All down one side of his face was caked in blood.

'Man, you ok?'

'For now. We must keep going.'

Tom raised a hand towards Misha's temple but Misha flinched away.

'Looks like you took a knock.'

'You think?'

Tom shook his head. Without discussing it any more he started to disentangle himself from Misha, hauling himself onto hands and knees, and then onto his feet. The soles of his boots were melted and his feet felt tender. Later, he would think about it later. He held a hand out to Misha and hauled him up. Behind them was a pile of rubble, the wall that Misha's charge had disposed of. A girder hung at a reckless angle from the ceiling. Misha's pack was nowhere to be seen. He shouldered the Alienator and together they ducked under the girder and clambered over the remains of the wall.

It was a long hall, lit only by the red emergency light. Along each wall were ranged rows of consoles. They stepped cautiously down the empty space in the middle. Above each console was a number in black outsize lettering, and a bar code. Tom peered into the console on his left. It was empty.

A hospital facility?

Or an interrogation ward.

What now?

Start looking.

Didn't we have a schema showing where the girls might be?

We don't have it now.

They took a side each, Tom left and Misha right, and worked along, peering through the transparent face cover, moving on. The first three on Tom's side were empty. Then he looked through the next face plate straight into the open blue eyes of the man inside. The man was staring sightlessly outward and his head and shoulders were shaken by unending tremors. His face was drawn in a fixed grimace of pain or shock. Tom leapt back.

Shit, Misha, take a look at this.

Is it one of them?

No, no it isn't, but Christ, shit, what's happening with this guy?

Misha stepped briefly over and inspected the blue, staring gaze and the shuddering body. Then he put a hand gently on Tom's shoulder.

Tom. We cannot save everybody.

I know. Keep going, right? But still.

He wrenched himself away from the man and steeled himself to look in the next console. It was empty.

In this way they worked their way down the ward. Tom passed two more occupied consoles, one containing a plump middle-aged Black lady who looked as if she was simply asleep. He looked down on her for a moment, promising her silently to remember her. The second contained a young boy of maybe nine with ginger hair and pale, peaky features: over his head and face livid cords stood out from under the skin, pulsing in blue and purple, making him look as if living writhing snakes encircled his head. Tom made himself look at him for a moment too. Poor little sod, there was no hope for him. Then he met Misha at the end of the ward. He didn't ask him what he had seen on the right-hand side.

The way on was barred by steel doors, with a security scanner at eye height.

We gonna blow this one too?

Not if we can find another way.

Reckon we can risk contacting, you know, them? Whoever they are?

The intriguingly named DogGirl? Misha was smiling underneath the slick of blood covering the side of his face.

I don't know if, y'know, if we risk corrupting the link.

Best if only one of us does it.

I don't mind.

No, you disconnect. I want to ask her if she is free on Tuesday.

Crazy bugger, Tom thought as he disconnected. There was no way of telling, with Misha, whether it was just bravado or whether he was really setting up a VR meet in the middle of chaos and destruction. He leaned on the wall, to the side of the door eye. Oversight would pick up their signature again soon enough, but there was no point making it easy for them. He rested one foot on the other knee and inspected the sole of the boot. It was a mess. The laces were welded together at the ankle; he guessed he could cut them through. Not now.

He looked across at Misha who had the abstract expression of someone messaging in VR. Tom sighed and rolled his shoulders. He looked back down the line of consoles. Might there be time to do something for some of the occupants? It needed a tech's skills, Noah or Gina should be here, he thought wryly. Of course, if they were here, he and Misha wouldn't need to be. His message icon lit.

Three-second ID gap in scanner Go

Tom spun to show his face to the scanner and slapped his palm on the palm print register.

'ID accepted,' said the scanner. 'For your comfort and security, before exiting please ensure that you have used the disinfectant spray provided.' The metal doors started to hiss open and Misha immediately pushed through into the corridor beyond, Tom following on his heels.

'So,' Tom said aloud, 'did you get your date?'

He couldn't see Misha's expression through his respirator.

Guys, two floors down is prisoner containment, we're still workin on getting the schema for you.

They looked around. There were no signs or directions: of course, this part of the facility wasn't open to the public. Anyone with authority to be here would have the schema on their heads-up. Misha shrugged and set off down the corridor under the red light. One way was as good as another. They needed to find a way down, stairs by preference. They passed more sets of the grey doors and an alcove where body-length trolleys were stacked. Then there was a whirring sound in the distance. A prisoner transport, moving on the corridor. The whirring got louder. Tom ducked back into the alcove. Misha already had his Taurus in his hand and was swinging the Alienator down from his shoulder. Tom reached for the rifle. He had had a hand weapon, at the start of all this. He didn't know what had happened to it. Lost in the explosion, along with his pack. The transport vehicle was nearly level with them now. It might not have thermal scanning abilities. It might just go past. With a clatter and a hiss of brakes it stopped.

Hey Tom and Misha, you can take the transport, we have it slaved.

DogGirl, we owe you one.

They stepped cautiously into the corridor. The transport was waiting for them. It was a low-slung metal oblong on squat tyres. All the corners were rounded – there would be nowhere you could get a purchase on the outside of the vehicle – and the dark-grey, burnished surface was unbroken apart from the Department of Correction crest. A door at the rear swung silently open. Misha climbed inside, leaning heavily on the door. He must be worse hurt than he was letting on. Tom peered in. The interior was lit by a pallid glow, and was empty apart from a low bench moulded into each wall, and what looked like attachment points for restraining straps. Misha threw himself down on a bench.

'Get in.'

'Are we sure about this?'

Misha gestured impatiently. 'We are not sure about anything. To have got even this far is a miracle.'

Tom stepped in. Immediately the door swung closed behind him and the pallid light went out. It was pitch black. A rumbling vibration told him that the transport was in motion again. Tom staggered and hit his knee on one of the benches. Clumsily he sat down in the dark.

'Misha?'

'Mm?'

'Did you tell her, did you tell DogGirl our names?'

There was a silence.

'Misha?'

'Ah, shit,' Misha's voice at length came out of the darkness. 'No.' He sounded uncharacteristically weary and defeated.

'If it wasn't her, then –'

If it wasn't her then Oversight had infiltrated their link and they had walked into restrainment without a fight.

'It is probably too late. But you should disconnect. I will see what I can do.'

'No,' said Tom. 'It probably is too late. Whatever you're going to do, we should do it together.'

There was a small breeze on the back of his ankles. He reached down. Air was hissing out through floor-level vents. Gas, probably. Reflexively he clutched his respirator, holding it against his face.

'Gas, Misha.'

'I know.'

'Ok, so one contact, and if it doesn't sound right, we jump?'

'Ok,' said Misha, heavily. His voice sounded slurred.

DogGirl?

Hello, Tom and Misha.

Tom realised Misha wasn't with him.

Any chance of a light in here?

Sorry, we can't access the light. But everything's under control. We're going to get you there soon.

Where's there? Tom asked, but there wasn't an answer.

Ok, that told him everything he needed to know.

/disconnect/

'Misha?' he asked out loud, but there was no answer from Misha either. He felt along the bench towards him. He couldn't work out which bit of Misha he was touching. An arm, maybe. He groped along and found a wrist. Misha must have slumped down along the bench. He seemed to be unconscious. Dead, maybe. Then Tom pulled his mind away from that thought. Concentrate, man, he told himself. Misha still had his pack. He must be lying on it. Tom reached around Misha's body, trying to manoeuvre him in the confined transport interior. His breath huffed in his respirator. Misha was solidly built. He couldn't turn him on the narrow bench. He knelt down awkwardly on the floor, pulling Misha towards him. When he had Misha's weight on top of him he could reach the pack. He struggled to free it from Misha's shoulder. The strap on one side was sticky with something cold. Blood. Right, now he had the pack free. He tried to roll Misha back on the narrow bench but he fumbled it and Misha slid onto the floor with a thud. Tom extricated himself from under Misha, wriggling back onto the bench on his side, grasping the pack. He undid the top and felt inside, groping for something useful. Metal, stuff he couldn't identify, something rigid in a plastic wrapper. Vaping kit, must be, for fuck's sake, Misha. Then his hand closed around the elastic strap of a head torch. Thank god. He pulled it out and pressed the switch.

The small circle of light showed Misha lying in a jumble on the floor space of the transport. One arm had fallen across his face. Tom moved the arm aside, dreading what he would see. Misha's face looked worse now that he wasn't moving. The eye on the bad side was swollen shut. Tom reached to the side of his neck, feeling for a pulse. For a moment he couldn't feel anything. He started to panic. Calm down, man. Ok, there it was, not strong, but he could feel it. He lifted Misha's head to put it at a more comfortable angle, and the respirator fell away. Whatever had caused the blow to Misha's temple, had cut the respirator strap. So the unconsciousness was just sedation. Good. Or rather, not good, terrible.

The vibration of the transport stopped. Tom swung Misha's pack onto his back. The head torch wouldn't fit over the respirator. He pulled at the strap, stretching it, jamming it on askew. He needed to have his hands free. He took Misha's Taurus in one hand and, laying the rifle within hand's reach, he crouched down at the rear of the transport, straddling Misha's legs, facing the door. This was it, the end, he thought. If there was anybody human there when the door opened, he would show them.

/disconnect override/

Fucking shit, they could do that? Sweating, Tom disconnected again.

/disconnect override/

hold on guys its me they had us there but we're back

Tom lost any sense of strategy. 'YOU FUCKERS!' he roared. 'Come and fucking take me, come on! I've had it, I've had it, you shits, you fuckers.'

Guys we're opening the door but gotta be quick. Vehicle control abit shaky.

The rear door hissed and slowly started to open. Tom stayed where he was.

Fuck get out get out can't hold this & only picking up one of you??

His gun still clenched in his fist, Tom half-stood and peered around the edge of the opening door. It looked quiet. No welcoming committee.

Guys losing it gotta move now.

The door stopped opening. Then with a lurch it started to close again at the same deliberate rate. Tom made up his mind. Whatever, out had to be better than in. He leapt out, turning to drag the unconscious Misha by the feet. Now the door was only a quarter open. He couldn't get Misha's body all the way out. Desperately he reached back inside, wedging his back against the inexorably closing door, grappling with Misha's inert torso. He pulled Misha forward into a sitting position and by brute force heaved him out against the force of the closing door. They fell into a heap on the corridor floor. The door closed. With a purring noise the transport started to move off.

Tom looked around. The transport had taken them out of the emergency zone. The lighting in this part of the complex was the normal, motion-activated white light. They were at the junction of a corridor with a cross-corridor. In front of him were wide lift bays. Red lettering shone above the lift doors. Floor -5.

DogGirl? sent Tom, but there was no answer.

Killaq

/journeyschema/replace/

/exit/

Killaq sat back with a sigh. There, she hoped she had deleted the satellite trace showing the whereabouts of the little digger and overwritten a false trail. She rubbed her forehead. She felt like shit. There was a sour taste in her mouth and a headache was pounding at her temples. The aftereffect of the sedative, she supposed. She got it: Jean-Lou or his colleague, whatever she was called, Dog something, had told her to sedate herself before they triggered some sort of emergency alarm, fire maybe, and then because she was obviously unconscious, Oversight had been able to process her as cargo under their emergency protocol without drugging her further or binding her in VR. And then her console had been shipped out to a slaved truck just the way Consuela had explained. Consuela had said that in the event of a serious emergency, the escape vehicle would be programmed on the assumption that there was something badly the matter back at the main miner, and its twin aims would be to gain some distance from base, and to move along random vectors so that where it was going couldn't be anticipated. The vehicle wouldn't be recovered by Oversight until the emergency had been subdued and it was certain that it was safe for the occupant to return to the miner. And in the meantime Killaq had time to wake up and to hack the digger, instructing it to wipe its previous recorded route and giving it new co-ordinates.

She scowled. That had been hard, waking up so disoriented and groggy, and having to re-programme the digger's memory against the clock. And she was still no nearer to finding out what was going on. She didn't dare try to contact Ma or Amaruq from here. She had programmed the new journey, a looping, indirect trajectory, which would take her back in the direction of home, but not for many days. Once Oversight had realised she was missing, home was the first place they would look. For now she would try to find somewhere to hide up, make her console safe, and try to get in touch discreetly in VR.

First, she was thirsty. The digger didn't have a cab or any provision for human occupancy. She had done the programming lying in the console, but now she had swung the lid open and was sitting up. The lid was decorated around its lip with a line of tiny coloured lights, which dimly showed her the cargo bay where the console had been loaded and secured. There was nothing else in the bay.

Killaq's muscles ached from inactivity. If she wanted to drive the digger, she would have to do it from VR. She lay back down, ignoring her protesting back.

/module select/driver/

Now she was in the digger's virtual cab, sitting in the padded seat, high up above the landscape in the transparent control bubble. She knew that the real landscape that the digger was traversing was mapped onto the view in VR. It was light outside, a pale morning light, and the digger was trundling along the marshy floor of a shallow valley. Immediately outside pale stretches of water shone between lurid yellow-green mosses; she checked the terrain stats and saw that immediately under them was solid ground, at least for now. The digger was making its way along a raised gravelly band which ran down the length of the valley, with wetland either side. To her left there were birch trees in the distance, and to her right the valley wall ran up into low bluffs. East south-east was the direction of travel, not that it mattered for now.

Outside clouds of flies rose up, disturbed by the passage of the digger, and hung in simmering clouds in front of the virtual windscreen: it made her skin crawl to look at. Despite the flies she was going to have to stop and find water and something to eat. If this was a scenario she had written, she thought wryly, there would be an emergency locker which had food and first aid essentials, which you could find by following clues. This wasn't a scenario and the digger wasn't designed to have people on board. The idea behind the emergency protocol was that the rescue vehicle would be recovered from base as soon as possible: it wasn't provisioned for a journey. Couldn't be helped, she needed to piss, anyway. She put her hands to the heavy steering wheel and reached with a foot for the brake pedal. Her actions would be translated into programming commands, bringing the digger to a halt.

/open cargobay/

There was light from above, the digger must be loadable vertically. She swung open the console lid and sat up. The air was cold but it felt clean after the rebreathed atmosphere in the console. For thirty seconds she felt a surge of achievement. Then the flies found her. She flailed her arms, batting them from her eyes and skin. She needed to get out. She still needed to piss. The loading hatch was in the bay ceiling. She couldn't reach. She clambered out of the console. The insects were crawling in her hair and biting everywhere there was flesh exposed. She swung the lid shut and climbed onto the closed console, batting the flies away with one hand, reaching with the other for the hatch edge. First she thought it was going to be too far and then she managed to curl her fingers over the lip. She swung up the other hand and hauled herself up. The bugs were no better on the outside. She jumped down and had her piss, flinching as the bugs found new areas of fresh skin. Now she was surrounded by a cloud of insects. This was no good, she couldn't stand it. She didn't know if she could get back inside.

Where she had jumped down the outside of the digger was smooth, but further along there were robotic handling arms folded against the side of the machine. She leapt up and got her hand on one. She couldn't hold it. She fell back, yelling with frustration.

For a moment she stood scrunching her fists in her eyes, ah, it itched so badly, it was intolerable. Go again. This time she held on like a demented person, scrabbling her feet against the metal side, grabbing for holds further up the arm, until she could get a foot on something. Desperately she scrambled up, swearing aloud, onto the roof and along to the hatch. Hold onto the edge, drop back in. Shit, fuck, fuck. Back in the console. Slam down the lid. Little fuckers still in here with her. Aircon on full and fan to max.

That was better.

Right. The cargo bay was still full of insects and she didn't think there was any way of clearing it. She had come across a *full decon* in the command menu, but she didn't think she could run that while the console was still in the bay. Might as well leave the bay hatch open in that case. She needed urgently to find somewhere where the digger would be hidden from above: the birch woods over there would do, except they would be just as full of bugs, probably worse than here. An overhang under cliffs would do, or even better, a cave. Ok, back into VR.

/topographic search/parameter set/run/

She waited for the programme to do its work. There was nothing else to do. Here in VR she couldn't feel thirsty, but down in the corner of her view her real-body icon was showing red for dehydration. Couldn't be helped. She was aching to message someone, to make contact with Ma, or Amaruq, or even Jean-Lou, but she mustn't, she knew she mustn't as long as the digger could be seen from above. Loneliness washed over her, and behind it fear. She heard Ma's voice in her mind. *They're looking for your brother.* Maybe they had found him, SAPA Oversight had found him. Maybe they had already found everybody and there was just her, in an Ardsen slaved vehicle, in a swamp. Maybe at any minute someone would find the digger's true location and then they would send a drone for her. The first she would know about it would be the sound of the drone engine. She glanced fearfully above her, even though here in VR there was nothing to hear.

/ready/

She had set the programme to find a cave, or failing that, an overhang, or thick woods not in a swamp, within a 30km radius, with enough cover to hide the digger, or failing that, to hide part of the digger. She scrolled through the survey results. There weren't any caves. Some of the crags up on the bluff had a scooped-out base, but not enough to hide a vehicle, and she would be in plain view on the pale scree. The birch woods were interspersed with flooded areas and the digger might sink, according to the terrain stats. She expanded the radius to 50k. Ok, what was this? At the head of the valley the ground started to rise and there was a deep ravine running up at an angle into higher, more mountainous terrain. She couldn't tell if the ravine would be too narrow for the digger to attempt, or if the terrain would be too rough once she got there, and anyway they would still be visible from above, but at least the digger would be tucked away, not out here on the marshy valley floor.

/route select/exit/

It was dark in the console. The transparent face plate was black with bugs. Killaq shuddered. Now that she didn't need to piss, she was ragingly thirsty. She mustn't lick her lips, she knew she mustn't lick her lips. She licked her lips anyway. Damn, damn. Mustn't do that again.

She could feel the rumble of the digger's engine. They were on the move. Her back ached from lying in the console. She stretched and twisted in the narrow space, trying to find a comfortable position. Eventually she fell into a fitful, shallow doze, dreaming of the clutching talons of the creature that Noah had become. In her dream the Noah-Sanderson hybrid was tracking the digger on foot. The riveted metal plates of the cargo bay wall had somehow become transparent and she could just make out his faraway sinister figure bending intently over caterpillar tracks imprinted in the gravelly soil. Then in the next minute he was there, right against the glass, pressing against the window with his hooked beak and dark feathered hackles and fixing her with his terrible bird eye, and all of a sudden she woke up, gasping, staring at the bug-smothered faceplate. She shook her head, trying to stay awake, but she couldn't hold on to wakefulness and she slipped back into her shallow sleep. The dream was waiting for her again in the dark.

It felt as though time had passed when she woke up properly. It was still light, but it seemed like late-evening or even midnight light. The faceplate was clear of bugs: maybe they had left the swampy ground. The bad taste of the dream still lingered. She sat up and swung the console lid open, trying to clear her mind of the feeling of being followed.

There was a wind blowing and it was cold. She stood up on the console lid and looked out. The landscape had changed while she was asleep and now the digger was picking its way up a long, blocky, bouldery slope. It rocked on its treads, negotiating the difficult terrain, and as she watched it started to back up and go around, avoiding a steep jumble of boulders immediately ahead. In the distance the base of dark cliffs met the steep scree and on the face of the cliffs was a line of silver: water. Without thinking any more about it Killaq pulled herself up and jumped down. She could make faster progress up the rocky slope than the digger could, and she ran, pulling herself over boulders and jumping from rock to rock. Water! It was further than it looked, though, and by the time she had reached the cliff base she had slowed to an exhausted trot. Away behind her the digger struggled over the rough ground.

The stream fell splashing down the cliff face and rushed away down a channel it had scoured in the loose scree. Killaq scrambled recklessly down the steep channel side and plunged her face into the running water. It was cold and gritty. She drank and drank again. Then she sat back and gazed at the running water, and for a short while was entirely content.

The rumbling noise of the digger engine, straining on the steep slope, shook her out of her calm. She clambered to the top of the gully and for the first time saw the entrance to the canyon where the digger was heading, a dark gash bisecting the whole face of the cliff. She took a look at herself: her Ardsen liveried top was wet and muddy where she had thrown herself down into the stream. That hadn't been clever, these clothes were all she had, and it was chilly. More soberly she made her way back over boulders and shifting scree bands to the digger, now in the final approach to the canyon. As she came up to it she could smell a smell of hot oil and hear the engine labouring: it hadn't been designed for this sort of task. She poised herself on a boulder top and repeated the leap and scrabble manoeuvre to get back in. Then she stood, watching, as the digger crawled the final distance up to the canyon entrance, juddering wildly from side to side. She clung on and wondered if it was going to be able to make it. The last rocky step was steep and the digger stuck on it, engines screaming, before with a convulsive movement it propelled itself over the lip and stopped, steaming, right in the canyon mouth, half-in and half-out of a stagnant black pool. The light was dim under the great overhanging canyon walls and the wind howled.

Killaq jumped down into the cargo bay and crawled back into the console. She felt a bit lightheaded. If this was the best cover she could find, she would have to live with it. The digger wasn't well hidden and she might not have long before it showed up on some satellite trace. Whatever the way out of here was going to be, if there was a way out, it would have to be by calling for help in VR. There was no way she was going to be able to survive by herself, even if SAPA didn't find her straight away. For a minute she lost herself in a fantasy of building a shelter and catching fish in the stream. That was scenario-builder's stuff. She had no tools and the stream wasn't big enough to have fish in it. VR was the only way. She swung the console lid down.

She spent a long time writing herself a temporary cover address for the contact, backed up with the strongest security that she knew. Then she exited VR, leaving time for any waiting traps to be sprung. It was twilight. She made herself run through a full set of stretching exercises before she went back in. Apart from anything else, it stopped her feeling so hungry. Ok, no sense waiting any longer. First she tried the bear around her neck, the beacon that had saved her before, but the code was inert. She wasn't surprised, they had told her it was a one-shot. Next was to try and contact someone.

Amaruq?

The address you have used is not known. Please check and try again.

Jean-Lou?

The person you are messaging is not available. You are welcome to leave a recording.

Out of some feeling of superstition Killaq had left Ma till last. She couldn't contact Ma directly in VR but she could screen-call in the old-fashioned way. If Ma was there, she might pick up. She rechecked the temporary ID which she had set up to message Ma from and activated the sweeper programme which would erase the trace of her call in real time. Right, do it now.

'Hello? Ma?'

'Little bird? Where are you?'

Ma's voice was almost unrecognisable, choked with sobbing.

'I'm here on the miner, Ma, what's the matter?'

Ma could only gesture at the room behind. Killaq widened out the field of view. It was the kitchen at home, but it was full of people, soldiers, SAPA armour, and where the table ought to be there was a console, and cables, and now someone was taking Ma roughly by the shoulders, asking who she was talking to, and another voice came from across the room, 'No, no, it's the girl, hang on, we can get a fix.' Killaq should exit right now, but her eyes were fixed on the console, and now the second voice was saying 'Open it up, let her see her brother!' and a gauntleted hand was swinging open the console lid and oh god, it was him and

The link went black. Ma must have disconnected. Quick, out.

/exit/

Tom

A line of violent cherry-coloured light lit up the rough concrete of the opposite wall and the percussive sound of the laser echoed down the corridor. Tom shrank into the shallow cover given by the entrance to the cell behind them, squirming up against the locked door at his back, trying to pull Misha further in with him. Misha groaned. He was coming round a bit. Tom peered out cautiously. There was an armed droid at the top of the corridor, only one so far. Tom had tried to return fire with the Taurus but it didn't make much impression on the droid's armour. The Alienator was synced to Misha's palm print and therefore useless.

Hey guys, you still with us?

DogGirl!

What about your friend?

He's here, he's out cold.

What's his name?

Fucking shit, what was he, a dating agency?

WE'RE UNDER FIRE HERE! he sent.

The cherry light burned up the centre of the corridor, leaving a long smoking stripe. Tom leaned out with the Taurus and got a shot off. No fucking use, he knew, but it might hold the thing back, give him a minute.

Yeah right, got your schema.

Can you sync me to Misha's Alienator?

Misha, huh?

Can you fucking sync me RIGHT NOW?

Takes a minute. Door behind you ok now.

What?

Another cherry stripe burned along the wall on Tom's side.

Door. Behind you.

Tom lunged up, slapping his palm on the door lock in the centre of the door. The door mechanism whirred. The laser struck again, over Tom's head. The door split in half and started to slide back into the frame. Misha muttered something incomprehensible and made to fall forwards into the corridor. Tom grabbed him and dragged him into the cell and the laser struck again and the door surround vanished in flames. He leaned against the cell wall, shuddering.

Outside he could hear the droid's treads crackling along the burned corridor floor. He gripped the Taurus. There wasn't any way out. The crackling came nearer.

Gimme another palm print. Door will do.

Can't the door's gone.

Now the tread noise stopped and the dark body of the droid was stooping into the cell and Tom in desperation picked up the Alienator anyway and pulled the trigger and in some part of his mind he was aware of DogGirl sending *ok try that* and the droid's torso blew apart in a white explosion.

After a minute Tom realised that he was crouching on the floor, still clutching the Alienator with an unconquerable grip. He had been muttering under his breath, fuck fuck fuck fuck. Misha next to him groaned and started to pull himself up against the wall. 'DogGirl,' Misha slurred. 'Love you forever.'

Tom looked around the cell. It was occupied. There was a small pale White bloke on the narrow bed, his skinny arms wrapped around his knees. He was staring at them with incomprehension. His shaved head was carved with red scars: insertion cable tracks. Tom ignored him. He pulled himself to his feet, hefting the Alienator.

Ok, you got our schema?

His heads-up filled with the green lines of the building plan. Their location flashed. Two other cell locations were flashing: -5/714 and -4/023.

'C'mon, Misha.'

Tom grabbed Misha's arm and pulled him out of the cell, leaving the pale ruined man and the still-burning door-surround. Misha could walk now in a shambling sort of way, but god help them if they ran into more armour. Ok, start with the floor they were on, -5. The schema showed them the route. Desperately Tom towed Misha along the corridor, second left, no *second* left, third right, down identical passages past ranks of identical unmarked doors. This was it, 714.

DogGirl?

You're in. Got you a cover but can't say how long it'll last.

Tom felt a buzzing in his head as he stepped forward and placed his palm deliberately on the ID plate. The door started to open. Misha leaned against the wall and giggled.

It was her, Annie, she had flinched away when the door started to open, but now she was looking at him with what seemed like recognition. But oh god, she was so little and thin, with her hollow cheeks and shaved head. There was a curving scar over the white scalp but her eyes were alive. He realised he was standing, staring at her.

'Babe?'

She struggled to stand up but in a stride he was by the narrow bed and had scooped her up, holding her in his arms like a child. He couldn't tell what he was feeling. Maybe he was feeling nothing at all. Annie leaned her head against his shoulder and shut her eyes.

'I hate,' came Misha's slurring voice, 'to interrupt the touching reunion, but we cannot stay here.'

'Right.'

He handed Misha the Taurus and, still carrying Annie, ducked out of the doorway. DogGirl had said they had a cover, did that mean they were safe from interception for the time being? Gotta keep going. Next floor up. The schema lit up, showing the way back to the nearest stairs. The lift would be too risky now. Twice the schema halted them at a junction and they saw security going past: droids once, a group of human operators on a transport the other time. There was still an alert on; Oversight knew they were still here, somewhere, were hunting them.

He took the stairs two at a time, Misha backing up behind him, gun in hand. Misha seemed to be making more sense but his head wound still gleamed dark with blood and sometimes he would stop in his tracks, chuckling or muttering under his breath. Tom couldn't worry about Misha right now. Top of the stairs, check the corridor, straight along. Fourteenth door on the left. 023. Ok. DogGirl palmed them in.

He had thought it would be the same, it wasn't the same. Annie's cell had been a prisoner's cell, unfurnished except for the narrow bunk and the toilet. This was an interrogation cell. He couldn't take it in, to start with. One wall was taken up by a bank of screens and wiring. It took him a minute to identify the naked person in the middle of it. He couldn't recognise her. She was strapped upright to the wall and straight into the back of her head ran heavy knurled cabling.

'Gina? Shit, Gina?'

Annie stirred in his arms, hiding her head in his shoulder. He wouldn't put her down. He would never put her down again. Helplessly he looked around at Misha.

'Misha, what the fuck? Is it even Gina?'

Misha swayed, pressing a hand to his injured temple. Then he seemed to regain some of his crisp demeanour.

DogGirl? We need bio stats for -4/023, can you do it?

Not good, huh? Wait one.

Tom couldn't stop staring at the body, at the wiring. He cradled Annie's bald head. Misha palmed the cell door shut behind them. They waited. Nothing happened. Tom took a step nearer, staring at the slack face, the closed eyes. He could sort of see that it might be Gina.

Guys, I'm sorry. I really am.

'What?' said Tom wildly, aloud.

It's a flatline. You gotta keep moving.

'No!' Tom shouted, and then, turning to Misha, 'We can unhook her, can't we? Take her with us? Someone can help her, on the outside?' But Misha had already drawn the Taurus.

'Fuck, man! Are you crazy? What are you *doing?*'

'What Gina would have wanted,' Misha said grimly.

'No, wait! There's gotta be a way!'

'There is no way, and there is no time.'

Annie lifted up her head for the first time and looked around, taking in the room, the body, the cables. Her voice came as a whisper. 'Shoot her,' she said.

The shot echoed in the confined room.

Tom looked at Misha in horror. Gina's body looked exactly the same except for the dark stain spreading over the ribs. As they watched blood started to run and drip over the clustered cables, onto the floor. There was no change in the slack face.

Annie stirred in Tom's arms. 'Put me down,' she whispered. Slowly, leaning on Tom's shoulder, she took three steps to the body, reaching up to lay a hand along Gina's cheek. Then she bowed her head and turned away. Tom picked her up again, rocking her against his shoulder, and she closed her eyes. Tom looked at Misha over her naked head.

'Time to go.'

Silently they turned to the door and Misha palmed it open.

'Wait,' said Tom. Misha shrugged.

DogGirl? Do we have a way out of here?

Now he asks!

'Misha, what was the plan, originally?'

'We would find the girls.' Misha grimaced. 'Then we would improvise magnificently.'

His ironic tone fell flat, there in the cell with Gina's body hanging on the wall behind them. Tom sighed.

Annie spoke with difficulty. 'When someone dies,' she said, 'they send a clear-up bot. We just need to wait.'

'Annie, my darling,' said Misha, 'I am not ready for the mortuary.'

Annie had closed her eyes again, exhausted by the effort of speaking. Tom stroked her forehead. 'Babe,' he said softly. 'Babe, will the bot come with a trolley, something to take Gina away on?'

Annie managed a tiny nod. 'Maybe,' she murmured, eyes still closed.

Tom lifted an eyebrow at Misha. 'Might be a way?'

An expression of disgust crawled over Misha's face. Tom guessed what he was thinking.

'We don't have to go on the trolley with Gina. We could take the trolley from the bot. Mean I could have my hands free.'

'On the other hand, if the bot has a viz link, they will find out where we are.'

'They probably know where we are anyway.'

'All the more reason, my dear Tom, not to stay here.'

DogGirl! Misha sent. *Is there a trolley store, we can get to?*

Wait one. Stuff going on here.

They waited.

'We could, I dunno, we could find where the refuse comes out, see if we can escape that way.'

'Firstly, I have no intention of crawling through refuse and second, a facility like this will be on full-recycle.'

'Right.'

DogGirl?

Ok stuff you gotta know but get going now, clear-up team are on their way.

Team? Not bot?

Team. Trolley store on schema. Go.

The route lit up on their heads-up. They palmed the door open and left without looking back.

The ceiling lights lit up the empty corridor in front of them and fell dark behind them with an unnerving regularity. Tom felt vulnerable with Annie in his arms, as if at any moment, around the next corner, at the next junction, the air would explode into laser fire and they would be cut down and lie dying on the floor before he had had the chance to shoot back. They must still be labelled with whatever identifier DogGirl had hacked for them, allowing them free passage in the eyes of the system security. He wondered how long it would last.

When they got there the trolley store doors were locked and they couldn't raise DogGirl. Now the Alienator was synched to Tom, Misha couldn't use it. Tom set Annie down carefully, propping her against the concrete wall, and blew the door open. An alarm started to sound. Between them they wrestled a trolley off the stack and lay Annie on it. She curled on her side and shut her eyes. Tom wished he had a blanket for her, something cozy. They set off rapidly in a random direction, trying to put some distance between them and the smoking ruins of the door. A small bot scurried around the corner and Tom gripped the trigger of the Alienator but it ran straight past them on its whirring pads. Fire security.

'Where the fuck now?'

'Vehicle park.' Misha's face was grey. 'By the main entrance. If we can work out how to get there.'

'Shit,' said Tom, shaking his head. It could only be a matter of time, they couldn't go much further like this.

'Have to be the lift. Keep turning the same way, we'll get to a lift bay. Vehicle entrance will be at ground level.'

Misha was having difficulty catching his breath. He looked terrible.

'Here, lean on the trolley.'

Misha didn't argue.

Left, left, left. A dead end. Back up. Next left, left after that. Now a broader concourse, permanently lit. Must be a lift bay here, maybe in the middle. They were about a third of the way along when they heard running footsteps behind them. That was it, then. Suddenly Tom was immensely weary. He just wanted to lie down, lie down and weep. He'd done his best. He drew Annie's trolley behind him. The Taurus hung slackly in Misha's hand. There were three, no four, figures running down the concourse. Tom shouldered the Alienator, took aim. Then he hesitated. The runners didn't look like Oversight Security. He could see the man in the lead now: he was wearing a prisoner's trousers and smock and running with a gasping desperation. As Tom watched laser fire came from behind him and he pitched on his face and lay still. There was something mechanised, Oversight armour, behind them. 'Get to the side!' Tom screamed at them, and kneeling down waited. He couldn't get a clear sight. Another runner was hit, falling in a crumpled pile, and the Alienator hummed under Tom's hands and he took his shot through the space the dead man had made and there was the white blaze of a hit but Tom didn't stop to look. Whirling round he went to take hold of Annie's trolley but it wasn't there behind him. For a moment he was completely disoriented. Then he saw Misha with the trolley, further down the corridor, and ran for them. Behind him there was shouting and the snak-snak of more laser fire. His last stride took him to the trolley as a pleasant chime sounded and a door opened in front of him.

'I called the lift,' said Misha.

'What the hell, what the *fuck* was all that?' Tom gasped as he rolled the trolley inside and the lift doors slid closed behind them.

‘Vehicle bay please,’ said Misha. ‘My guess is, DogGirl and her team have created a diversion. But I can’t raise her, Tom. They must be keeping clear of talking to us, so the link can’t be corrupted.’

‘Like in the transport.’

‘Like in the transport.’ It already seemed like a lifetime ago.

‘At least, that’s what I hope. Alternative is, the prisoner escapes are just collateral from whatever’s going on in VR. Our guys, they must be in desperate danger.’

Tom nodded slowly. It was hard to imagine, while he and Misha had been running around like rats in a maze, DogGirl and her fighters had been locked in their own battle in VR, Oversight rebuilding security as fast as it was penetrated, links being corrupted and repurposed. The invaders ran the risk that Oversight would follow their coding back and find them in VR, find them in the body, even. None of this could have happened without them, he and Misha would have fallen at the first hurdle. Even now they were protected only by the cover identities that someone far away in Nunavut had written, that someone even now was probably fighting to maintain. He felt ashamed that he’d given it so little thought. His hand tightened on the fragile bones of Annie’s shoulder.

The lift chimed again. ‘Vehicle bay, executive level,’ said a cool voice. The doors slid open.

They rolled the trolley out of the lift, because there didn’t seem anything else to do, and stood looking at each other in a plushly decorated foyer. Stiff glossy plants stood against the walls in polished bronze containers and on the walls hung aboriginal paintings seemingly chosen to co-ordinate with the brown and gold colour scheme. Tom started to laugh, looking at the three of them covered in blood and dust, standing on the immaculate wheat-coloured carpet, and then choked it back when the laugh threatened to turn into sobs.

Annie raised herself on one elbow. 'Well hell,' she whispered, 'this is nice.'

In between each of the plants, long metallic oblongs were marked on the wall, two metres high and a body's width wide. Tom had thought they were just part of the décor. Now the flat reflective face of the nearest one began to churn and tremble like stirred paint. Rounded shapes started to protrude from the metal. An arm came free, reaching out from the bronzed surface; then the other arm; the beginnings of a face. Tom had heard of this sort of thing, self-creating androids. He swung Annie off the trolley and sent it spinning between the creature and themselves. The three of them backed up against the linen-effect wallcovering. The android stepped clear and they could see it was female, shaped in smooth anonymised curves like a mannequin on a shopping site. The dark green leaves of the plants shone reflected in its bronze skin. Misha raised the Taurus.

'Good afternoon, honoured guests, I am here to assist in your choice of vehicle. Can I offer you refreshments in the meantime?'

Tom did start to laugh now, but Annie raised a hand. 'Can I get a Pasito?'

'One Pasito for the lady, and the gentlemen? Sirs? No?'

'Can we get on with it?' Misha growled.

'Of course, madam and sirs. Shall I show you our range of executive vehicle choices with alternative livery and service options?'

'We just want,' said Tom, getting a grip of himself, 'whatever is at the top of the parking wheel and we can get quickly.'

'Ah,' said the mannequin conspiratorially, 'Sirs and madam are in a hurry. Certainly, sirs and madam. This way.' It gestured towards the end of the suite where doors were sliding open, revealing the long tapered outline of a silver Aldebaran. The passenger doors clicked open as they approached.

'What about my Pasito?' Annie asked.

'Madam will find that her request is already logged with onboard refreshments.'

Tom helped Annie into the leather-effect interior and slid in himself. Misha immediately lay down on the opposite banquette and closed his eyes. 'Have a good journey!' said the mannequin, waving girlishly. The doors hushed shut.

'Welcome to the Mark 3 Aldebaran, brought to you by Vista Hydrogen,' said the car's deep voice. 'We are now preparing for parking exit. Do you have destination co-ordinates for me?'

'Melbourne,' said Tom. It was the first thing that came into his mind.

'Very good, sir. Journey time will be five hours. Please do not hesitate to let me know if I can assist in your comfort or travel requirements in any way.'

Faux windows projected a view of the outside, and Tom saw that they were already powering down the exit ramp and the heavy security doors were grinding open. He threw his head back in relief, stretching his arms along the back of the curving seating. Then he looked at Annie sitting next to him, so tiny and frail, sucking fiercely at her soda. He couldn't bear it. He clutched his head in his hands and let the sobs come, uncontrollable, wracking his body. The Aldebaran slid onto the restricted freeway, and the view of grey containment walls rolling past was replaced by the first menu of the onboard entertainment programme.

Misha raised his head. 'Tom!'

'Leave me alone.'

'Are you getting this?'

Tom reluctantly wiped the back of his hand across his face and went back into his message feed. DogGirl had sent them viz. A shaky, hand-held view of someone in a console, looked like they were being kept under in VR. The view narrowed in on the sleeping face. Shit, it was him, the northerner. Tom glanced down at Annie oblivious by his side. She didn't have her portal chip, he realised, she wouldn't have VR access.

DogGirl had forwarded the message attached.

Do as we say if you want him back alive.

Killaq

She had woken up surrounded by a strong animal smell, a comfortable smell that made her think of hay and dung, stables, maybe. She had lain with her eyes closed, not thinking of anything, and after a while she had realised that she wasn't cold anymore. And then coming a little further back to consciousness she became aware that her head was pillowed on short, rough hair, and that the pillow was warm and moved slowly in and out under her cheek, like an animal breathing. She opened her eyes a fraction and squinted at the sky. It was daylight, although she had the feeling that it might have been dark, some time ago. She looked down at herself and found that she was tucked under a brown hide cover, and on her feet were fat hide boots, stuffed with – she reached a hand down – it felt as if they were stuffed with straw, or reeds. On her head was what felt like a fur cap. She raised her head and looked around properly, and saw the swept-back antlers: caribou, she was leaning on the flank of a grey-brown caribou, which was lying on the short grass and chewing peacefully, and all around were antlers and grey-brown backs: it was a herd, she was in the middle of a herd of caribou. It was too difficult to understand; she had no idea how she had got here. She closed her eyes again and tried to remember where she was supposed to be. Perhaps she was dead.

Gradually it came back to her. She had been in the digger, and there had been nothing to eat, and it had been cold. She had spoken to Ma – but her mind veered away from that thought. And she had wandered away from the digger and she had been crying, she had walked out into the tundra in her thin Ardsen tracksuit. She remembered being too tired to walk any more, lying down on a great flat rock, looking up at the sky. That was all.

She opened her eyes again. She still felt weak, and when she moved her head she felt dizzy and lightheaded. It was warm under the brown hide. There didn't seem to be anything she needed to do. If she was dead, someone would tell her what would happen next. She let her gaze travel out over the sea of brown-grey backs. They were restful.

She couldn't tell how long she had been lying like this when she felt a hand on her shoulder. She looked slowly round. It was a little man, shorter than her, she thought, with a light, wiry build, dressed in a poncho and trousers made of brown hides, and he had hide boots and a fur cap like hers. His face was brown too, and weatherbeaten, and lined with deep networks of wrinkles. He wasn't one of her people: he had a thinner face and round dark eyes. He squatted down next to her and looked her carefully in the face. Then she saw that he was carrying a bowl of milk and suddenly she was terribly thirsty. He raised the bowl to her lips and she gulped, drinking with difficulty through her dry mouth and cracked lips. The milk was warm, with a strong pungent taste, and there was the smell of some sort of herb. It was very good. She reached for the bowl again, but this time the little man held it away, making patting gestures in the air with his free hand. She understood: slowly, she must drink slowly. He held the bowl to her mouth again and she took another sip. After half the bowl was gone she leaned back and fell immediately into a deep sleep.

The next time she woke the sun had moved across the sky. She was lying on her back and the caribou she had been leaning on had gone. She raised herself on one elbow and saw the herd grazing around her. She was thirsty again. She started to struggle up to a sitting position, but before she had managed it she saw the little man making his way towards her between the beasts. He was carrying the bowl: that meant milk. She found herself smiling.

Today the milk was different: it was warm from the animal, but the herb taste was gone. She held the bowl herself and drank it all, remembering to take sips. The little man crouched next to her, watching her with a kindly intensity. She felt as if she might have been one of his beasts which had been taken poorly. She didn't doubt that they were his caribou, or maybe he was their herder.

She gave him the bowl back. 'Thank you.' He dipped his head in acknowledgement. Then he placed his hand on his chest. 'Saami,' he said. Yes, that made sense, he was a Saami reindeer herder. She copied his gesture: Killaq. 'Killach,' he said. Then a long sentence in a language she couldn't understand. She just looked at him, smiling again. 'Sorry,' she said.

Now he was moving a hand across the ground in a rocking, jerking movement. She couldn't work out what it meant. His other hand swooped over the hand on the ground. Then both hands flew violently apart. He looked at her for confirmation that she had understood. 'No,' she said, shaking her head. Again, the one hand showing something crawling, rocking. The other hand swooping. Then, bang. An explosion, maybe? A third time he mimed the crawling, jerking motion. It could be the digger, working its way over the rough terrain. Then something flying over it. Bang. Ok, she understood. 'Bang,' she said, copying his gesture. SAPA must have blown up the digger. He nodded solemnly, not taking his eyes off her.

The next bit was easier. This was her, on her back looking at the sky. Here were many legs walking. He walked his fingers in little steps, then gestured widely around at the herd and himself. He had seen the strike on the digger. Then he had found her on the rock. 'Thank you,' Killaq said, smiling a wide smile. There needed to be more; he had saved her life. Fumbling around her neck she found her soapstone bear and pulling the thong clumsily over her head, handed it to him. He took it gravely, with ceremony, and inspected the carving, turning it over and over, rubbing it between finger and thumb, bringing it to his nose to sniff. Then he looked up at Killaq and something had changed in his manner. He bowed his head, holding the thong before him, spread wide in a circle. Killaq understood: she was to place it round his neck. She grasped the thong carefully and reached it over the top of his cap; he settled the thong, tucking the bear under his clothing, and looked at her with a sort of appraising respect. 'Kunossa,' he said. Then he stood up in a quick movement and Killaq thought she was going to be allowed to sleep some more. She made to lie back down, but he laughed, and with a wide gesture showed her the herd around her already moving. He gave her his arm to stand up: she thought she wouldn't be able to, but it was ok, she could balance although a little lightheadedly. Then he put in her hand a stripped and polished wooden stave and he was off, vanishing among the caribou.

Killaq leaned on the stick and set off, putting one foot in front of the other, as the grey-brown backs streamed past her, the young ones penned in the middle of the herd, the swaying antlers of the older beasts ranging along the outside of the group. They moved together in accordance with some social rules which she didn't understand.

That had been the beginning of many days of wandering, following the herd on foot. Sometimes the caribou had been far ahead of her and she had followed their distant smudge on the horizon, over thin grass and mosses and past wind-bitten bushes and solitary lichen-covered boulders. Sometimes she had walked in amongst the herd as they paced alongside her. There had been a river crossing, deep and terrifying: the little man had shown her how to strip naked and wind her clothes into a bundle before entrusting herself to the black current, holding on to an antler, beasts labouring in the water all around her.

On the other side the caribou had pulled themselves out with ungainly, efficient movements and had started to graze, seemingly unconcerned, although one of the young had been washed out of sight downstream and its mother stood on the bank, calling after it with a deep lowing call.

Every night there had been a dark spicy stew, bidos he called it, and flatbread cooked in the fire with handfuls of flour that he kept in a pouch at his waist, and she had slept under furs in the little hide lean-to. It wasn't until afterwards that she had thought that of course that had been reindeer stew – meat – and the milk had been reindeer milk, and none of it was vegan. It didn't matter at the time and she never felt that it mattered, afterwards.

In this way they had come to the trading outpost. The land had risen up gently to a hilltop scattered with broken stones, and he had gestured for her to come and sit down next to him, leaving the grazing herd a little behind them, back down the slope. From their viewpoint they saw the wide valley of a winding river, which crossed the valley in looping curves, leaving behind it long raised gravelly beaches and impermanent-looking islands. Near to one of the beaches there were pale oblong box-shaped objects: Killaq had been out of the sight of man-made structures for long enough that it took her a minute to work out what she was looking at. Prefabricated pod houses; a scuffed brown track winding between them; an incongruous orange roadster; a jetty and boats bobbing. The little man made his gesture of patting the air: quiet, careful, it meant. He sat watching in silence for half an hour or more before, apparently satisfied by some evidence that Killaq couldn't make out, he got to his feet and started making his way down the hill, pausing only to signal to her that she should follow.

The people at the settlement were Inuit, unfriendly enough, but they had obviously seen the caribou herder before and were used to bargaining with him for meat and hides. Killaq could understand the version of Inuktitut that they spoke, although it had a twang that was strange to her, but she thought it was better to keep quiet: who knew what news they might have heard or what contact they might have had from SAPA Oversight. No one paid her any attention and she supposed they thought she was the herdsman's wife, travelling with him over the summer pasture grounds. They spent a day drinking tea from tiny, dirty cups and haggling, before, to Killaq's great distress, two head of caribou were slaughtered and the little man took in exchange what he needed from the store cupboard: flour, aspirin, a flat unmarked bottle filled with what Killaq thought must be home-distilled vodka, run off from a plastic keg. It didn't seem enough for two beasts, but then Killaq was made to understand that part of the deal was to pay for her; she was to stay, and she could have food, and console access, and a lift down river by boat when she needed it. She had a moment of fear, thinking that maybe she was being sold into slavery, but she looked at the little man with his round eyes and his sly, cheerful expression. She trusted him: after all, she had given him her bear.

So he had left, crossing the braiding river with the caribou, vanishing east into the distance, and Killaq was left at the outpost under the care of the surly grandmother of one of the two, or maybe three families who made up the settlement. Her first thought had been to get into VR as soon as she could. She had been walking with the herd without anxiety as if she had been dreaming, but now that she was back with people, however unhelpful and far from civilisation they were, her fear for Ma and Amaruq mounted in her throat and threatened to overwhelm her. So after a tiring period of arguing in sign language (she wouldn't let them know that she spoke Inukitut), the grandmother grudgingly hooked up the console and ran a power cable from the solar generator, and she was back in VR.

The first thing she did, with the greatest stealth and caution, was to access the Ambra character which she had hidden under many layers of security when she had first gone on the miner. She took a few sessions to do this, creating telltales, going back in to see if she had been followed or if her access had prompted any alerts or if there was any sign that the character had been corrupted. In between she ate unsatisfactory meals with the family and fended off the advances of the older son. Finally it looked all right. She would use Ambra to try to contact someone, Jean-Lou maybe.

/access/message/enter/

She gave her ID as Ambra Di'capria but she attached to it a tiny icon of the soapstone bear. Jean-Lou, if he picked up her message, might understand. Of course, no one would know what had happened to her. SAPA would still be sending out the pre-records on her blog and anyway she was sure SAPA would have had no difficulty in replicating the synthetic Killaq character. It would look from the outside as if she was still there, sending out cheerily inane messages of support for the mining mission as it left its ugly swathe of destruction across the tundra landscape. It wouldn't fool Ma or Amaruq, though; she hoped it wouldn't.

She went back to the message the next day. There was a trip wire. Well, of course there was. She inspected it carefully. It didn't look like SAPA work. No way of being sure. She couldn't stay forever in the dingy trading post with the hostile grandmother and the lecherous son. She drew Starmaker and, deliberately, activated the trip.

It posted her immediately into an indoors scene, an igloo. Round the inside wall ran a low bench made of snow blocks and there was a sleeping platform covered in seal skins. The wall and ceiling shimmered with changing images: a hunter in a qayak, paddling expertly between ice floes; steep shaly mountains hanging against the sky like the improbable edge of a breaking wave; a throat-singing contest; a stylised image of an owl looking out from a dense surround of pattern. There was nothing modern in the igloo at all; no ice drill; no skidoo paraphernalia; no console. It was a statement that this was Inuit space. Or, Killaq realised, it was SAPA's idea of what Inuit space should look like. She sat down on the bench to wait.

After a while she was bored. She walked up and down, hugging her arms around herself. Ambra's desert costume looked out of place in this insistently northern scenario. She had just about reached the point of having decided to try the entrance, even though it was probably barred to her, and if it wasn't barred it would be a trap, when she heard the scraping, sliding sound of someone else coming down the entrance tunnel. She took a firmer grip of Starmaker's leather grip.

She saw the furred paw on the floor first, then the long muzzle. It was a dog, a husky. But then the person pulled themselves fully through the tunnel and stood up, and she saw that they had a dog's head – no, a bitch's head – but a woman's body, close-covered all over in short white fur. A long plumed tail waved over her shoulder and a double line of small rounded breasts ran down her torso where the dog's dugs would have been. Crossed bandoliers carried a rifle over each shoulder and she wore an ammunition belt.

'DogGirl?'

The girl showed her incisors. 'Identify yourself.'

There was nothing to gain from secrecy. 'It's me, Killaq. You helped me escape from the miner.'

The girl looked at her for a long moment. 'Where is your beacon?'

'My beacon? Oh, my bear? I, ah, I gave it to a caribou herder. Long story.' Killaq was aware that it didn't sound good.

DogGirl took a quick step forward, inside Starmaker's guard, and reached a claw to Killaq's throat. Killaq stood still, looking the other girl in the face. DogGirl pulled and something broke. Killaq put her hand to her neck: she knew the bear couldn't be there, she had given it away. But DogGirl was inspecting something dangling from the broken thong. It was a soapstone carving, an animal, but where the bear had been all rounded curves, this was crowned with a flourish of spikes. Antlers. It was a caribou.

DogGirl handed her the carving back. 'Ok. Ready?'

Killaq was still gazing wonderingly at the little reindeer, but instantly her surroundings changed around her and she was in a long room full of sunlight, glazed with tall church-like windows looking over the sea, and there were people sitting around a polished wooden table.

'I've got her, she's not dead,' said DogGirl, and walked around the table to sit next to a blue giant with bulging muscles and a turban.

FALL

The hall in the sea

She scanned the beta. It was them, the Ozzies, or some of them: Tom in near body-normal, in board shorts; the thin, fierce tigress was Annie; Misha was the blue giant. There was one missing. Gina, it was Gina who wasn't there. Or Noah, of course. Killaq stayed standing.

'We need you,' said DogGirl, coldly, 'to give us assurances of your good faith.'

'Really,' said Killaq. She swept Starmaker over her shoulder in a fast hissing circle. 'I need *you* to tell me where my brother is.'

'Guys,' said Tom, standing up, holding his hands out with the palms turned down in a gesture of pacification. 'Guys. Take it easy, DogGirl. And Killaq, sit down. It's ok.'

'It's not ok,' said the tigress.

'No, I guess,' said Tom, rubbing a hand across his forehead with a weary look, 'but it's not gonna help if we fight amongst ourselves.'

'It seems to me,' said Misha, 'that what we need is a drink.' Suddenly there was a pitcher of lemonade on the table, with a tray of crystal tumblers.'

'Since when did we eat or drink IVR?' asked the tigress.

'Since,' Misha said, filling glasses and passing them around, 'we needed a symbol of hospitality and co-operation.' He put his huge blue hand over

DogGirl's furred paw and a look passed between them. 'Killaq, there are things we need to tell you.'

'Do you know,' said Killaq, still holding Starmaker in front of her, although there was a tremor in her voice, 'do you know what has happened to my brother?' She couldn't stop herself glancing at Annie.

Tom sighed. Lowering his hands he pulled out a chair. 'Killaq,' he said. 'Sit. Please.'

Cautiously she took a step sideways and seated herself. She laid Starmaker on the table, the leather-wrapped pommel within easy reach. She found she was trembling.

'The Captain is still in SAPA custody,' said DogGirl bluntly.

'Is he *alive*?'

'We believe so.'

'Look,' said Tom. 'Start at the beginning. Killaq, you probably know that the Captain captured one of the secretariat, someone who had been piggybacking on one of our group.'

'I know. I saw him. I was there.'

'What did you see?'

'I met the SAPA man, Sanderson, back in the winter, when he came to Iqualuit. In the body.'

'Whoring for mineral rights.'

'Yes.' Killaq shuddered. 'But then, I was there, I helped capture him. It was horrible. I think your friend was trying to break free, to get out. And Amaruq sent a message, to say if they wanted him back, to do as we said. It was still all part of the miner, the protest about the miner.'

Tom shook his head. 'Ok. So I don't know how much you know about what happened next.'

'I saw him, Amaruq, in the kitchen, in the console. Soldiers were there, SAPA armour. And Ma broke the link, to save me.' To her shame Killlaq started to cry. The others watched her in silence.

'Right,' she said, after a moment, wiping her eyes with the tail of her gauzy turban. 'Tell me the rest of it.'

'First,' said DogGirl, ignoring a warning look from Misha, 'we need to know where you are, and where you have been.'

Killaq raised her eyes to the high ceiling. The outside world seemed so far away; her journey from the miner seemed such a long time ago. 'I'm in a trading post,' she said, eventually. 'I've been travelling with a reindeer herder. He rescued me.'

'Are you safe?'

Killaq shrugged. 'Who knows. Tell me what's been happening.'

'Well, first, the mining protest is fucked, finished.'

'You think?' she asked, bitterly.

Tom intervened. 'She doesn't know everything.'

'Tell me, then.'

'The Captain, he had planned a real coup. Something that would put an end to mining in the North, for a generation.'

'Blowing up the miner? I thought that was only misdirection.'

It seemed to Killaq that no one would meet her eye.

'So you *were* going to blow up the miner? When was anyone going to tell me?'

'Well, ah,' said Tom. 'There *was* going to be a physical aspect to the action, but, uh –'

Misha interrupted. 'She might as well know.'

'The weak point,' said DogGirl levelly, 'of Oversight's anti-virus, was always going to be via the blog link.'

'My blog link?' asked Killaq, blankly.

'Yes.'

'In my *brain*?'

'The important thing was information,' said Tom, almost pleadingly. 'If we could've cracked their firewall, we could have broken out all the real-time data. Y'know, the actual cost of the remediation, the live stats. Published it everywhere.'

'Jesus,' said Killaq, and then she fell silent. She refused to believe for a minute Amaruq would have agreed to it, to use her own consciousness as a conduit to breach SAPA's firewall. Unwillingly she remembered him saying 'You might not like it much.' She would have to have it out with him, when this was all over. When he was safe.

'So,' she said out loud, 'what actually happened? As far as we know.'

'It's complicated. We had that fucker, Sanderson, we had him tagged in VR. To begin with we didn't know they had followed back the tag, they had Noah tagged in return.'

Killaq shuddered. 'Where is he now? Noah?'

Tom shook his head. 'He, Sanderson, I guess he took it personally. We got raided. Annie and Gina were taken. Noah too. We reckon, once they had Noah in the body, they slaved him to Sanderson, gave him a permanent link to us.'

DogGirl cut in. 'The Army co-operated in an operation to retrieve the three. Annie was found. Gina died. Noah was not recovered.' The tigress curled in her chair, hiding her head in her paws.

'What the fuck, what has all this to do with me? And tell me quick, I have limited console time. What fucking army?'

The others exchanged glances. 'The Army of the North,' Misha said. 'Which your brother commanded.'

Rage swept through Killaq. She leapt to her feet, leaning her clenched fists on the polished wood of the table.

'I didn't come all this way to listen to this horseshit. Amaruq wasn't – isn't the commander of any army. He thinks he can do a lot of stuff, is all.'

DogGirl leaned across the table in turn, baring her teeth. 'He is my Captain and I will fight for him. I will fight even you if I have to, Little Sister.' In answer Killaq set her hand on Starmaker's grip.

Misha's lazy voice broke in. Now he was puffing on a hookah and silver-blue smoke swirled about him. 'Much as I would be sorry to break up a good catfight, we have more important things to do. Killaq, you have no choice but to believe us. Tell me, was your brother not a man who had secrets.'

'He was. He is,' said Killaq, and choked. She turned away from the group at the table, looking blindly out of one of the tall windows at the sea. There was no beach, no land in sight, only the rhythmic white of wave crests travelling across a vast sunlit expanse of ocean. She remembered Jean-Lou calling Amaruq 'Captain.' She rested her forehead on the glass and closed her eyes.

After a long moment she turned back. 'Ok,' she said. 'Suppose I believed you, what then.'

'Killaq, you've been missing for two weeks, over two weeks,' said Tom. 'It's already September. We've been trying to negotiate for his release, but we haven't got anywhere. We wanted some concessions from them, otherwise it's all been for nothing, losing Gina, Noah even, it wasn't really Noah's fault. They say they'll exchange Sanderson for the Captain but then they're going to ramp up the mining operation, they want to rub our nose in it, I guess. And we don't have the firepower to spring the Captain, and anyway we don't know where Sanderson is.'

'I know where he is.'

Tom looked at her dubiously. 'You sure?'

'I know where Sanderson is.'

Annie spoke in a small voice. 'We should just get him back. Get him back now. We can't fight SAPA. We never should have tried.'

Tom reached gently to put a hand on her elbow but she flinched away.

'We can't abandon everything we fought for.' That was DogGirl. 'It's not just Gina and Noah. Noah was foolish and Gina was unlucky. But the Army has losses too. The Captain wouldn't want them to go unavenged.'

'They won't go unavenged.' Killaq raised her voice. 'Believe me, they won't go unavenged. But we need my brother back now. We should do the exchange, do it soon, now. When Amaruq is back, he'll know what to do.'

'Such faith, Little Sister,' said DogGirl ironically.

'Weren't you the one saying you would fight for him? I don't see you fighting! Who will come with me?'

DogGirl gave her a long, steady look. Then she laid a paw on the table. 'I will come.'

'I'm in,' said Tom. He looked over at Annie. 'Will you stay back, babe?'

'No, I'll come,' said Annie in a colourless voice.

'Misha?'

'I was not doing anything else just at the moment.'

'Set up the exchange,' said Killaq. 'How do you contact them?'

'I'm not going to tell you,' said DogGirl and then, looking around the table, 'What? How can we even try to keep her safe, if we do?'

'Ok then. I've got to go. Give me a link to this place, tell me when you're ready. I'll be there.

Misha held his closed fist over the table and slowly opened the fingers. Three written characters swam out, black and shining in the light from the tall windows. Something like a tall 'L'; a small 'P' on its side; a larger 'P' on its side. They made the word 'maanna': 'now.' Killaq held out her hand in turn and the characters settled on her wrist like butterflies. She nodded. Not subtle, but it would do.

/exit/

She spent the day fetching and carrying in the trading post, serving tea and vodka to a fat white man in an all-terrain who had turned up selling contraband VR inputs. The grandmother seemed to have dealt with him before: he probably wasn't Oversight, but who knew. Behind the crates in the storeroom the leering son pushed her up against some boxes, his knee pushing her legs apart, but with a brief flailing struggle she slipped past him and escaped back into the main room of the pod where the fat trader was loudly demanding more vodka. Killaq's hand patted the hilt of the knife she had stolen, strapped at her waist under her filthy trousers. If he tried that one more time, she would kill him, him and his evil grandmother. She shook her head when she realised what she had been thinking. She had changed, everything had changed.

She knew there was no chance the grandmother would let her back in the console that day so it was late at night, once the son and the fat trader had drunk themselves unconscious, and the old woman was snoring her little bubbling snore, when she crept back. She could hack the passcodes: this would be the last time. After that, Amaruq would come and get her, when he was free.

She let the dark syllables spill out of her hand and followed the link they made. Now the long table shone by the light of many candles, reflected in the tall windows, and beyond the glass was blackness.

'Ok?'

'It's on,' said DogGirl tersely. 'We've got a synchronous release programmed. When we let one go the other goes too. Can't be countermanded.'

'Want me to look at the code?' Killaq couldn't help asking, but DogGirl just showed her teeth.

'You just need to show us where he is. And god help you if he isn't there.'

'He'll be there.'

/TheReal/enter/

They were standing on the edge of a high cliff. Tom had a feeling that he might have been there before, but there was no fog this time, and a pale sun cast their long shadows over the cropped turf that ended abruptly at the drop. Far below the sea shushed and boomed.

'Key,' said Killaq, and it was in her hand, two foot long, its ornate silverwork tarnished and streaked blackish-green. She turned towards the land, and they saw that behind them was a high grass-covered mound. An entrance passage lined with tall uneven boulders, open to the sky, was cut into the face of the mound, and at the end of the passage was a slender door, too narrow to walk through except sideways, barred with a grille made of the same stained metal as the key. A cold underground smell came from the opening. With an odd sense of ceremony Killaq stepped up to the grille and put the key to the lock. She looked back at the others.

'Ready?'

They nodded. She turned the key stiffly in the lock. For a moment it resisted and she had to put two hands to it. The caribou carving at her neck buzzed and trembled. Then the lock gave way and the grille swung open. Killaq took a step back.

Nothing happened.

After a few minutes the Ozzies started to shuffle and fidget, but Killaq stayed fixed in place, her eyes riveted to the dark opening.

Still nothing happened.

Moving cautiously Killaq tucked the silver key into the belt of her robes and reached over her shoulder for Starmaker. The wide blade came noiselessly from its scabbard. She stepped forward to the door. One step. Then another one.

Misha had turned away and was watching the seagulls squabbling on the cliff face beneath his feet.

Killaq stepped in closer. Now the shadow of the passage walls fell across her face as she peered into the darkness. There was something there, maybe further in; she could see something, some slight alteration in the texture of the pitch darkness in front of her. She thought she could make out something gleaming, maybe far away down the passage. Then she realised what she was seeing. It was the stork's bill, the stork's dark shining eyes, within two inches of her face. He had been standing right in front of her, completely still and silent, as she had peered down into the dark tunnel. She screamed, leaping back, jabbing Starmaker in front of her in an incoherent, untrained movement.

'What the fuck?'

'It's him, he's there, right there.'

DogGirl stepped forward as Killaq backed trembling between the line of stones. 'You! Come out!' she called in a firm voice. As they watched a long dark claw reached forward into the hazy light of the passageway, then a black, ragged wing, and the stork unfolded himself and stepped in his high-stepping bird walk to where the group encircled him at the mouth of the passageway.

'Guys.' It was Noah's voice. 'Guys, it's me.'

'It's not him,' said Tom. 'Don't listen to him.'

'I don't understand,' said Noah's voice. 'Where are we? Where have I been?'

'You're not Noah!' said Tom.

'Tom, hey, man,' said the thing with Noah's voice, and then, changing his tone, 'but where's Gina? I don't see her. Is she back at base?'

Tom lost his temper. 'It was you, you fucker, you betrayed us. You know why Gina isn't here,' and he seized the stork's thin neck in a muscled hand. The stork started to chuckle. 'You can't hurt me,' he said, still in Noah's voice, 'not if you want your little Eskimo pal back.'

Misha abruptly stopped watching the seagulls. 'Entertaining though this is,' he said, 'perhaps we can do what we came to do.'

'Right,' said Killaq. She was feeling nauseous. 'DogGirl, do we just let him go?'

In answer DogGirl just snarled, stepping out of the circle to leave an opening between them and the cliff face. 'Go, traitor,' she said. Tom gave the stork's neck a violent shake and then, with an effort, uncurled his fingers. 'Go,' he said.

'Go,' said Annie. Tears were pouring down her face.

The stork stepped out of the circle, settling its feathers. 'You needn't think,' it said, 'that this little episode ends here.' It strutted to the cliff edge and spread its dark wings. Then it looked back over its shoulder. 'We can find you, you know. You'll regret this.' It took off, soaring away from the cliff edge.

Impotently they watched as the stork gained distance from them, ragged wings flapping in huge slow movements. Suddenly DogGirl put her hand to her temple. 'Christ, no, shit, stop him!' she shouted. Then she crumpled, paws over her eyes. Killaq had never seen her like this. She reached across and shook her, roughly.

'What?'

'The simultaneity failed,' said DogGirl, not looking Killaq in the eye.

Killaq spun around, pulling Ambra's crossbow from its holster on her thigh. The stork was still visible, a small moving object, swaying with its flapping motion, far away in the grey-white sky. Killaq fitted the long crossbow bolt, blew on it once, took aim and shot in one smooth motion. The small moving object faltered. The long wings beat another beat, then two. Then the stork's image blew apart into tiny feathered fragments which hung in the air, drifting in a small dark cloud over the ocean. A small breeze sprang up and brought a long black flight feather to land at their feet on the short grass. Killaq picked it up, inspecting it somberly.

'Didja get him?' asked Tom.

'I don't give a shit,' said Killaq. 'All I care about is what's happened to Amaruq.'

DogGirl just shook her head.

29th September 2062

Aubrey Sanderson, International Head of Mineral Interface for the Sino-Australian Pacific Alliance, dies unexpectedly aged 48.

Tributes have been paid to Aubrey Sanderson who has died aged 48. He was a high-ranking SAPA executive who was praised for his interactions with indigenous communities around the world and his determination to make the supra-national corporation a byword for inclusivity. 'Supranational doesn't mean we're a nation all by ourselves,' he was fond of saying, 'it means we have responsibilities above and beyond the narrow national interest.'

At the time of his death Aubrey held the title of International Head of Mineral Interface and was a long-established member of SAPA's Secretariat. His last project was, true to his nature, one of support and partnership to the Arctic Nation's Inuit people. The Iqualuit Interchange was a programme through which SAPA helped far northern communities, left behind in many cases by the march of progress during this century, to upgrade medical and educational facilities, and to exploit their natural resources for the benefit of all.

The cause of death is not known.

www.theTimesofLondon.com

Killaq

She opened her eyes. The console lid, which she had locked shut, was hinged open above her. Her top was pulled up to her armpits, exposing her naked breasts and belly. Disoriented, she looked around, and saw the fat trader from the all-terrain standing by the console. His trousers were sagging around his thighs and both his hands were stuffed down into his grimy underpants. Behind him stood the son and the grandmother. The son was grinning with a horrible doglike excitement, and the grandmother was covering Killaq with an ancient shotgun.

Killaq was filled with a cold fury. She reached to her hip and found the kitchen knife she had stolen, plunging it with an effort through the checked shirt into the fat trader's wobbling belly. His eyes opened in surprise. Swiftly she swung herself out of the console, keeping the trader between her and the shotgun. 'Ah, gah,' the man gurgled, and started to slump forward. She pushed him violently backwards, onto the barrel of the gun, and the shot rang out loudly in the confined space. The trader fell back on top of the grandmother, who crumpled under his body. The son stared for a second and then ran out the door. Calling in security, she expected. Nothing she could do about that, if he had already messaged his drone service. It would take a while for any drone to get here, although the location would be under immediate satellite surveillance.

She crouched by the body of the trader, ignoring the grandmother's muffled wailing from underneath him and the blood pooling on the floor, and searched his pockets. What she really wanted was a manual override for the all-terrain, but that would be too much to hope for. If she had time, she could hack the access. She didn't have time. Nothing in the left pocket. Right pocket: two condoms, some pills, and a half-eaten cheese roll. She threw them aside in disgust and ran out into the darkness, back to the main pod, knife gripped in her fist. She had no plan at all.

She had done programming work for a security service before. She was sure the emergency alert would be accessible direct from the son's heads-up. He would have activated it immediately. But when she burst in through the pod doorway, he was waiting for her. An image of the security icon was projected in mid-air, over the rat's nest of his stained bedsheets. It was shining green, unactivated. The implication was obvious. He started to unbutton his jeans. 'Come here, you little bitch,' he said in Inuktitut, 'and if you're *good* to me, maybe we can forget about what happened just now.'

She didn't have time for this. She forced herself to smile, lowering the knife down by her side. She dropped her head and looked at him through her lashes as if she was shy.

'Knife on the floor, bitch,' he said. She stared at him as if in incomprehension. He pointed at the knife, miming someone throwing something aside. She stooped down, keeping her eyes on his face, and made to put the knife on the floor. The emergency alert *would* have a physical override. There had to be a way for the subscriber to call in an alert if they had lost VR access. She had to find where it was. She crouched, keeping hold of the knife, frantically casting her eyes around the pod room. It would be on the wall somewhere, high up, she was almost sure.

'Time's up, bitch,' said the son, and pointed meaningfully at the projected security icon. He let his jeans fall to the floor.

She was almost sure, when he had pointed at the security icon, he had glanced on the wall behind her. She pointed herself, as if she wasn't sure what he was saying. He did it again. The security eye must be behind her, above the door. She grabbed the knife and spun around. Yes! She leaped up and thumbed the red-alert button. Then she ran towards the son. Confused, he started back from the knife in her hand. The security eye came to life, shining red in the disorder of the pod living space. Killaq sidestepped the son's groping arm and hid behind him, knife pricking in the small of his back. 'Au secours!' she yelled. 'Ils ont tué mon mari!' The security controller started speaking in reassuring French tones, but without waiting any longer she flung her arms up to cover her face and ran for the door. Security should have identified her as a victim; it should let her get out before freezing the door lock. Please, please. She fumbled for the door. She heard the eye starting to interrogate the bewildered son. The door swung open and she leaped out; the lock buzzed and the emergency lockdown light shone red above the door. Thank god.

Outside, she slid the knife up her sleeve and walked quietly to the other pod, letting herself in to find the trader's corpse and the wailing grandmother were still where she had left them.

There, that should have caused enough confusion. The security outfit would run face and voice recognition, but the eye hadn't had a full view of her, and she was hoping that there wouldn't be a voiceprint on file of her speaking French. And at least to start with, if they thought she was the trader's wife, they wouldn't be treating her as a suspect. She heaved the console over to barricade the door in case the son came back, then climbed in. She would have to use Ambra again to access VR; it wasn't a safe thing to do, but she couldn't use her own ID, and she only had a short time to hack the trader's vehicle.

/Darknet/vehicle search/

It took longer than she would have liked, but it was still quiet outside by the time she had found the vehicle passwords and erased its existence from the Overnet. It would take a while for a physical drone to get here from security even if that level of service was covered by the outpost's contract, but more likely the call would just have been routed to local law enforcement, overworked and probably corrupt, who knew how many tens or hundreds of miles away. She pulled the console away from the door, then paused. The grandmother had gone still. She didn't dare try to extract her from under the trader's body. Killaq pushed open the door and walked out confidently, pre-entering the access codes for the all-terrain. The son was nowhere to be seen. It was a murky pre-dawn twilight: here, further north than home, the daylight hours were already shortening and it was starting to be dusk for much of the day. She swung herself into the cab, which smelt of sweat and feet, pulled the all-terrain round in a tight circle and set off east without looking back.

She drove on manual for the first hour, jaw set and shoulders tense, expecting at any minute an intercept from a law enforcement drone. A grey light crept across the landscape and sleety rain started to fall. Then without warning she found herself pounding the steering wheel, and long shaking sobs came from nowhere. 'Amaruq! Amaruq!' she cried out.

After a minute the auto-pilot cut in and recklessly she let it take a satellite fix and carry on south by east, on into the pale rainy morning. Either her programming was secure, and she had successfully removed the vehicle from the Overnet, or it wasn't. It didn't matter anyway, none of it mattered, nothing mattered. She found a bottle of vodka in a locker and started drinking it in deliberate gulps. It was foul stuff. There were more bottles at the back of the locker.

The journey back to Iqaluit took three days, and all that time Killaq drank. Some of the time she passed out and lay across the steering column in a stupor and some of the time she was awake, shouting and weeping. There wasn't any food in the all-terrain cab and anyway she had forgotten the point of food. The all-terrain carried on its trundling way across the landscape, lights shining in all directions into the silent tundra, and outside the first snows of the long winter started to fall.

Then there came a time when she woke up. She had a piercing headache and she felt sick and weak. This was how things were now, everything was fucked. It seemed that something was different though. She reached for the latest vodka bottle but it was empty. She laid her head back down on the steering wheel, staring vacantly at the driver's side window. Through the window she saw things moving, lights. She watched them incuriously. Then she closed her eyes. Whatever it was, she couldn't be bothered to think about it. She tuned out, drifting into vacancy.

Something was annoying her. She couldn't place it. She screwed her eyes tighter shut. It didn't go away. It was a tapping noise, a voice. She peeled her eyes open and squinted at the window. There was a person's face framed in a furred hood. They were saying something. She couldn't hear them.

'Hey!'

Maybe if she shut her eyes again they would stop.

'Hey! Driver! Are you ok?'

The voice made her headache worse. She tried to find the way back into unconsciousness. The darkness, that was better. It didn't hurt in the dark.

'Driver? Can you release the door? We need to see if you're ok.'

It started to dawn on her that the all-terrain wasn't moving. She must have stopped it. Or it had reached the end of its programme trajectory. She couldn't work out what that meant. She scrubbed her eyes with her fists. The lids were all crusted and it hurt to open them.

'Driver? Can you hear me?'

For the first time in days she looked through the window, beyond the confines of the cab. She ignored the talking hood. Maybe it wasn't real. Outside was a dim snow-filled daylight and it looked as if the all-terrain was stopped in the middle of a street. Clumped flakes were falling fast in the windless air. Through the snow she saw the sweeping lines of a white edifice, round-domed like an igloo, but higher than any igloo, and from the summit of its dome rose a tall spire and a cross. It looked like St. Jude's; it was St. Jude's. A procession of dark-coated people was making its slow way up the metal steps. At the back was the bent figure of an older woman, clutching the railings: she looked bowed down, grieving maybe. Perhaps it was a funeral. The woman looked familiar. And then memory and wakefulness came together in Killaq's mind and she knew where she was and what she was looking at.

'Ma!'

Killaq flung herself out of the all-terrain and past the person tapping at the window, who started back from the stench in the all-terrain's cab. She staggered on her feet. 'Ma!' she called. 'Ma!' Her legs wouldn't obey her. She reeled and nearly fell, but caught herself and started running in a desperate shuffle. 'Ma!' She reached the bottom of the steps. The tapping person was still at her elbow but she ignored them. 'Ma!'

Ma turned round at the head of the steps, and for a moment she frowned, and then she focussed on the gaunt and ragged girl clinging to the railings beneath her.

'Little bird?'

Ma ran down three steps and Killaq struggled up two and Ma took her in her arms and for a moment Killaq felt that everything would be all right. Then Ma released her, holding her by the shoulders, and Killaq knew looking at her worn face that it was not ok and that all her fears were true.

'Little bird, I have to tell you ...'

'I know, Ma. I know.'

Tears rolled down Ma's cheeks. She took Killaq's hand. 'With you beside me, maybe I can do this. Come on, little bird.' They hauled themselves up the steps, the cold metal of the railings biting Killaq's ungloved hands, and together they walked through the great central doors.

It was dim inside. The wooden pews curved in front of them, following the outline of the rounded walls, and there seemed to be lots of people whispering and shuffling. Light fell from the great octagonal skylight and illuminated a circle in front of the altar. In the light was an open coffin; it was a young man wrapped in sealskins; it was him. Ma took a shaky breath and, leaning on Killaq, she walked up to the coffin.

Killaq couldn't make sense of it. It was Amaruq's body, but it didn't look like him. The flesh of his face looked pale and set. Somehow he looked smaller than she expected. His eyes were shut and he wore an expression she couldn't fathom, almost a frown. It wasn't him; it couldn't be him. She had such a strong sense that he wasn't there, that the passive body in the pine coffin wasn't him, that she nearly turned round to look for him in the congregation.

Ma reached out and stroked the cold cheek. 'My little boy,' she said, under her breath. Then she collapsed onto her knees, letting out a pure high wailing cry. Killaq crouched down beside her and clumsily tried to embrace her. Ma rocked back on her heels, to and fro, still crying a high inhuman cry, the cry of a seabird or a rabbit in a snare. Killaq didn't know what to do.

Then there were people and Ma was being helped to her feet and ushered to a seat and she was apologising and wiping her eyes, and Killaq stayed next to her and wouldn't let go of her hand. And there were words, but Killaq couldn't understand them; she could only hear the solemn liturgical tones that the words floated on. Welcome. Tragic. Blessed. Flourisheth. In the midst of life. Days like grass. They that mourn. And let our cry come unto thee. Killaq sat through it numbly, gripping Ma's hand.

Then there was music, and they lifted the coffin lid and settled it over Amaruq, and Ma hid her face in Killaq's shoulder. 'Wait,' Killaq wanted to say, 'wait.' There was something she had meant to ask him. She couldn't remember what it was. Small black spots swam in her vision. She stood up, reaching a hand towards the closed coffin; this wasn't the end, it couldn't be; there was something she had wanted to say. Then her eyes began to blur and darkness folded in from the edges of her sight. Her legs buckled and she fell unconscious into the aisle.

Tom

Light from the tall windows fell in oblongs over the dark amber gloss of the table. Outside a bright noonday sun shone over the endless sea.

'The Captain,' declared DogGirl, 'died the death of a soldier.'

'Didn't do much good, did it?' said Tom.

'We cannot say, at the moment,' said Misha. He looked up from the moving graph suspended in the air above the table, different parameters showing in green and red, changing in realtime. 'There seems to be some indication that the weight of opinion is trending more strongly against perma-mining. There may be some connection with the work we did.'

'There may not.'

'There may not,' Misha agreed, inclining his head in an ironic bow.

'It doesn't feel like enough, for what we risked.'

'It is not.'

'We lost comrades,' said DogGirl. 'We can only honour them by living our own lives.'

Misha looked at her with half a smile. After a moment the green and red graph flickered out of existence. He reached for her, running his fingers deep into the white fur of her neck and shoulder. She grabbed his other hand and swung herself into his lap, straddling him, and Misha sunk his face into the double row of pink nipples.

'Guys,' said Tom. 'Get a room.'

They vanished.

Tom looked down the length of the table, to where Annie huddled, a small shape curled in a chair, wrapped in a plaid blanket. She had abandoned the tigress persona and now appeared in something like body normal, although the eyes were wider and darker and the skin was tighter over the frail bones. He worried that she chose to look like this. Sure, he got it, she was a trauma survivor, it would take time. It looked like it was deliberate, though, like she was making herself into the image of a victim. He had preferred the tigress.

'You ok, babe?'

She nodded listlessly.

'Want to have a break from VR?'

She shrugged.

'Tell you what, want to go to the beach? In the body?'

This time she didn't answer, but stayed staring at the wood of the table, seemingly immobile.

Cautiously he got to his feet and went to take a chair next to her. He was careful not to pull the chair too close. Every time she flinched away from him, it broke his heart. He understood, he really did. But still.

'Been thinking, babe.'

She showed no sign of having heard him.

'It's all over, the miner, SAPA, everything. It's time we started thinking about you, how to get you better.'

She didn't react.

'I thought, might be a thing, I dunno. I thought

maybe we should stay out of VR for a bit, just take it easy, catch a bit of sunshine.'

He looked at her anxiously. After a moment she raised her head.

'I thought I might go back to my parents,' she said, in a flat voice.

Tom was knocked back. When she'd joined the group, she'd been running from her family. He'd never asked her what had happened; something bad.

'What else is there for me?'

Tom gazed at her, full of fear. This was worse than he had thought. He chose his words carefully.

'Well, babe, you have to do what's right for you. I know that. And sure as hell, we can't go back to the old life, that's all done.'

He paused a bit, trying to gauge her response.

'And I know, it's kind of hard to say what happens next. And,' he rushed on, 'I can't imagine, you know, what it was like for you, what happened to you.'

'No,' was all she said. 'You can't.'

'And I know, I know maybe there won't be a place for me, I'm not asking for that. I just want to help. If I can.'

Annie said nothing. Without having meant to, Tom took her hand. The thin fingers lay lifelessly in his grasp. Gently he stroked them.

'What d'you think? We don't have to decide anything today? Just maybe go and sit in the sunshine, in the body somewhere. I'll find you a wrap to cozy up in, something comfortable. Then if you want to go back to your Dad, I'll help you do that.'

He held the thin hand. 'Reckon we could give it a go? For an hour or two?'

Finally he thought her fixed expression softened a little. 'I guess,' she said.

/exit/

To start with when they had landed in Melbourne, Tom, Misha and Annie had moved through a series of safe houses, keeping ahead of the pursuit they thought must be coming after them. Then after they had released Sanderson – after they had *killed* Sanderson, Tom corrected himself – everything seemed to be chaos for a while and Misha had started going off on his solitary excursions again. Tom didn't know where Misha was now, in the body. They had been meeting up in VR, but Tom sensed that this was coming to an end. Misha would fall on his feet, wherever he was. Tom guessed he would be there if he was needed.

So Tom had ripped some fake ID off the Darknet and had rented a shabby unit for him and Annie, a way out of Melbourne, and that was where they were now. Annie spent most of her time in VR: he didn't know where she went or what she did there, but he only went into VR to meet the others. The rest of the time he tried to keep busy, tidying the mostly empty rooms, trying to get Annie to eat, finding things she might take an interest in. Last week he had picked some pansies growing in the verge of the road, an escapee from someone's garden, he guessed, and had brought them home and arranged them in a cup on the rickety table, but when he had come back to the room the cup and the flowers were on the floor. Now and again he took a day's casual work, the sort of thing you could get paid for on a temporary top-up card, but he didn't like being away from the unit for long.

He had felt like he was in limbo, waiting for a direction, or a sign: something to give him an idea what Annie wanted to do next. Now he had his sign, but he didn't feel better for it.

He sat up in his console and went over to Annie's. The lid wasn't locked, which was a start, and she was awake.

'Hey.'

'Hey.'

A wrap, he had promised her a wrap. He ran upstairs, but there was nothing but the duna on the pallet bed. That wouldn't do. His flannie, that might be something. He pulled the checked shirt out of a pile on the floor and ran back down. Annie had swung the console lid back and was staring at the wall.

'Ok, easy does it, babe.' Gently he took her weight, helping her up into a sitting position. He tried to ignore the shudder that ran through her when anyone touched her. If she hated him, he couldn't help it. He had to do what he could. He had tried leaving her alone but it wasn't helping, she was just vanishing further away from him. Not just from him, from everyday life. If what he was doing was wrong, it would have to be wrong. He wrapped the shirt around her shoulders.

'Ok?'

She nodded.

He helped her down and let her lean on him to shuffle to the bathroom. Then he let her be and jogged softly back downstairs. He was starting to put together what they had that he thought might be nice for a picnic – a bit of bread, the apples still looked ok, the hummus was past it, he would have to throw that out – when he looked over his shoulder and saw her standing in the doorway with her holdall in her hand. Packed, ready to leave. His heart sank.

'Aren't we going to catch a few rays somewhere, first?'

She just stared at him. For the first time he felt truly defeated. It was her life. What could he do, after all. He put down the hummus and the apples, and took the holdall from her, checking his heads-up that he had enough credit for the bus. He could get her back to Melbourne, at least. Then he expected Daddy would pay for an exec train berth back to the leafy gated community she had run from two years ago. Tom needed to stay with her now, if only to get her safely into town. They filed out of the house and he let the door swing unlocked behind them. He wasn't coming back.

There was a bus stop down the road. All the way back to Melbourne, would take all his credit. Didn't matter. They stood in silence until the bus arrived. It was coloured a vicious green, the livery of Victoria DriverlessSolar, apparently. Tom handed Annie in and paid, and found a seat where Annie could look out. The bus pulled away. He felt completely numb. This was it, it had been his job to look after her and he had failed, and what was there left for him now? The slow purr of the solar-electric engine was taking him and Annie towards the city, and there wasn't anything for him beyond that. He gazed in despair over Annie's dark head, watching the street signs go by. The bus stopped and the doors opened and people got on and off and the doors closed again. It would be a slow journey.

The bus had a primitive tourist info feed. You couldn't select it on or off, the images just ran, spooling across the interior front wall, displaying grinning families on beaches and fashionable dark-skinned young couples in swimwear, cocktails in hand. Come to Victoria and learn to surf! A young woman carved proficiently along the breaking edge of a modest wave. Sign up to watch the Surf Masters! Ride the Great Ocean Road! And here were the famous names: Castle Cove, Port Campbell, Princetown.

Where they had been staying was in the heart of the serious surfing area. When Tom had rented the little unit he had sort of thought, he supposed, that the pull of the sea might help Annie find herself again. She had loved salt water, in the old days. But as the days had passed by and she had become ever more inward and withdrawn, he had given up on the idea. He had even felt that if he took her to the beach it might have been too much to bear, a bitter reminder of earlier times.

The bus stopped again. He was dimly aware that the stop bore the name of a beach, somewhere he had always wanted to surf. The name itself was painful: it hurt him like a reproach. This is where you could have been happy, if you'd done everything differently.

The doors closed and the bus started to move off. You should have stayed with her, he told himself, you should never have let her be taken. Now everything is broken and it can't ever be better. Without knowing what he was doing, he stood up. Obeying its safety programming, the bus started to slow again.

'Come on!' He grabbed her hand. She looked at him, uncomprehending. He said the first thing that came into his head. 'Wrong bus! Gotta get off!' He grabbed the holdall in one hand and pulled her up with the other. 'Stop request! Sorry! Stop!' He dragged Annie along the aisle, past a grumbling old man in shorts and a sagging vest.

'Should request your stop before the bus moves off. Safety, see?'

'Sorry, mate.'

Annie moved after him like a drugged person. He lifted her down the steps, not giving her a chance to object. Then there they were on the footpath and the bus was purring away down the road. She looked at him with a faint frown. He scooped her up. 'C'mon, beach is that way!' (But Christ, she felt so thin and fragile in his arms). She laid her head against his shoulder and closed her eyes.

Turned out they weren't right by the sea. Tom set off down the narrow gravelly road, following signs; he would have walked the whole way, carrying Annie if he had to, but a farmer with a tractor stopped for them. Tom swung Annie up into the hay-filled trailer and she tucked in against a bale, and they lay swaying as the tractor rattled slowly down the road. The fumes stank:

idly he wondered whether the farmer had some sort of agricultural fuel licence or if it was illegal fuel, chip shop diesel or the like. The sun beat down on them.

'This's far as I go, mate.'

Tom turned to help Annie but she had climbed down by herself. He held out a hand to her; she let her gaze drift past him.

'C'mon.' He started down the road. After a pause he heard her light footstep coming hesitantly after him. He turned and waited for her.

He could hear the ocean now, the rhythm of the waves rolling in like a homecoming. There was a narrow dirt path running downhill between pole and wire fences. The steep sides of the cove were greened with low shrubby plants; at the bottom of the slope they gave way to dry, sharp dune grass. And then there he was, on the flat of the beach, and in front of him were the high breakers curling in majestically in procession and one after another flowering into foam: five, six foot, he reckoned the surf must be. He kicked off his thongs and felt the firm damp sand take up the shape of his bare foot.

Annie was standing silently at the foot of the path. A gust of breeze reached her and she huddled into the red and blue flannie. He felt an ache of pity; poor girl, so thin, so cold. Her eyes met his and he looked away. Gently, gently: it was like taming an animal. If he pushed her at all, she would be gone. She might go anyway. Resolutely he turned his back on her and walked down to the edge of the sea, kneeling down to watch the waves running in to shore. The water came accelerating up over the sand, only a few inches deep, and then came the pause, like a swing reaching the top of its trajectory, before the wave fell rushing back, leaving little bubbles winking out of existence at the boundary between the wet sand and the dry. As he watched the water piled itself up and returned with the froth and pressure of the new wave. Tide must be coming in, he thought. He took a long breath, drawing the salt smell deep into his lungs: he had missed this.

He didn't hear Annie coming down the beach behind him. The first he knew was the feel of her hand on his shoulder. He daren't look round at her. It was like when you first started going with someone, that thing where you were so aware of the person's skin, their nearness, and the lightest contact burned through you and filled your whole mind so that nothing else existed. He could feel each fingertip resting on the cloth of his t-shirt, as if each separate touch was sending fire into the muscle of his shoulder, blazing with possibility.

At last he lifted his face to her. 'Babe?' he asked.

2nd November 2062

Exciting new undersea venture from mining giant Ardsen

Ardsen today announces a move away from terrestrial mining to concentrate on its deep ocean fleet.

'Ardsen is thrilled to be part of this new wave of mineral exploration,' said Daphne Lauderman, newly appointed head of Resource Identification.

'Modern pressure containment technology will allow our fleet to access sea-bed riches at depths only dreamed of before.'

'In the next century, all of our resources will come from the sea, or outside the Earth. Ardsen will be one of the first corporations to be fully engaged in this rich harvest from day one.'

In order to fund the new fleet, Ardsen will be withdrawing its support from some outdated partnerships, such as their joint operation with SAPA in the far North.

'SAPA have been outstanding business partners,' said Daphne, 'and we look forward to working with them many times in the future, but this particular exploration has run its course.'

'Mineral exploitation is all about cresting the wave of future technology so as to bring benefits for everyone.'

Note to newsdesks: for further information please contact Sokuharu & Frank PR.

Killaq

'It's chicken soup. I got a tin from the QuikMart.'

Ma looked at her with nothing in her expression.

'Try a bit?'

Ma's hair was full of knots and her tracksuit wasn't clean. When she stood up Killaq thought she looked stooped.

'Come on, Ma. You've got to eat.' Killaq put the spoon in Ma's hand, and with a sigh Ma took hold of the spoon, and stared blankly at the beige lumpy surface of the reheated soup.

Killaq herself wasn't eating well, or sleeping much. After the funeral she had been unconscious for twenty-four hours and woken up in her bed in her old room, shaky and disoriented, still wearing the remnants of the filthy Ardsen joggers that she had crossed the tundra in. She had got up slowly, feeling nauseous at every movement, and had showered slowly, scrubbing herself repetitively, wrists, arms, torso, legs, over and over again, scraping off the smell of the journey. She didn't recognise her body: her ribs showed under the skin and she seemed to be smaller all over, thinner, wiry. All the old clothes she stuffed in a bag to throw away, wincing at the reek of sweat and alcohol. She ran a finger around her neck; there was something missing. The bear, of course, she had given it away.

She had tied her long wet hair back from her face and wiped a clear patch in the mirror. She didn't know what she looked like; she looked like someone else, someone older.

Now the days had started to go by. She stayed at home without having any clear sense of what was going to happen next. She had to look after Ma; that made her get up in the morning, go to the store, buy bread and food in tins. People came round, bringing casseroles, and sat in the kitchen and said sincere, warm things, and that if they could be any help, any help at all, Ma had only to ask. Killaq waited for them to go away. She didn't leave the house except to get groceries, and every time she went out there was less light, and she felt as if it was going to get darker and darker until they were living all the time in the darkness and the darkness would never release them. She and Ma kept the door to Amaruq's room shut and didn't go in there.

Killaq reached across and put her hand gently over Ma's hand holding the spoon. 'All right, little bird, I'll try,' Ma said. Without any purpose Killaq thumbed the news on. The space over the table filled with the presenter's insistent voice, her too-bright tailoring and sculpted hair. It was about Korea again. Killaq went to turn her off but Ma held up a finger. 'Wait.'

Killaq looked at her with surprise. 'Ok, Ma, whatever you want.'

It was about the almost-war, as it had begun to be called. North Korea were saying that they had been ejected with violence from the homelands of their ancestors. The viz showed an energetic stout man in a military grey suit with a round collar, punching his fist into the air, his face contorted with passionate anger. Killaq couldn't be bothered with the translation to start with. It was all the same; nothing mattered. Then for no reason she brought up the sound.

'... supra-national forces ranged against our patriotic state will feel the tempest of our anger! Collaborators in the capitalist swindle will regret ...'

Killaq turned the whole thing off. She looked over at Ma, thinking that if Ma had any response at all, she would share Killaq's exasperation with the jingoist rhetoric. Ma was nodding, though.

'They had weapons, little bird, and they were backed into a corner. We, all of us, we should have given them land.'

'Oh, Ma! Eat your soup!'

But Ma sat, spoon in hand, shaking her head. 'Don't you think, it feels like all the world is in pieces and we've got past the point where there can be any hope.'

Later, Killaq lay awake. Sometimes she turned off her heads-up and sometimes, like now, she looked into the dark and watched the time display ticking off the seconds. If she did this long enough she could fall into something like sleep, a sort of trance-like state where the red numbers spooled in front of her and became mingled with heavy, unsatisfying dreams. Tonight there was something she was trying not to think about, some memory; the news item about North Korea had reminded her. It must be something to do with Amaruq. She didn't want to remember. She picked her way around the thought in her mind, trying not to disturb it. A young Asian man's face swam in her memory; it was the soldier; Amaruq had put him in the bear. The full depth of her loss opened up beneath her like a dark crevasse that she could fall into at any moment. Grimly she reached for the sleeping tablets, swallowing two dry, waiting for unconsciousness.

This time she dreamed. In the dream she saw a featureless flat terrain of sedges with water gleaming between the plants, and ice around the bases of the reeds. A young woman was moving across the landscape with a wide-legged skater's motion; she had flat, oval snowshoes strapped to her feet, keeping her from sinking in the melting permafrost. She wore dark padded trousers and a coat and carried something cradled in her arms: a baby, perhaps. Her red headscarf was the only colour in the scene. Killaq had a sense of foreboding, of waiting. Now the woman's face sprang into focus: her wide cheekbones; her dark eyes; her expression of determination. Suddenly the sky was red. She cried out, hunching over to protect the child. For a second the air was full of flying debris. Behind her the mushroom cloud towered billowing into the high stratosphere.

Killaq struggled to wake up. It felt as if she was striving up towards consciousness through the muffled layers of medication holding her down like a weight of blankets. Eventually she opened her eyes and turned the light on. What had that been? She didn't usually dream when she took sleeping tablets. She strained her eyes wide, willing herself not to fall back to sleep. The dream had had an evil reality. Maybe Ma was right. Maybe they were past the point of no return, and there would be war, and the carbon deniers would win, and the seas would rise, and over her head where she was lying now, twisted in her duvet, would be nothing except the huge frigid waves of the angry Atlantic. She shook herself. Tea, she needed a drink. She disentangled herself from her bedding.

The next day she cleaned the kitchen floor. She coaxed Ma to have a shower. She arranged the commiseration messages in a tidy feed and switched the rest of the wall viz to a plain, soothing landscape cycle: small rocky hills; a braided river running over cobbles; a blue windy sky; assorted wildlife. It didn't really matter, she just wanted to bring some sense of the outside into the confined air of the kitchen. She walked past Amaruq's closed doorway without the feeling of horror that had ambushed her before. She knew he wasn't in there.

She realised, half-way through the morning, that she was working her way towards something. She didn't ask herself what it was. She wrung out the mop and started on the corridor floor.

After lunch – tinned soup and toast again – she told Ma she was going to rest. 'You do that, little bird,' said Ma, staring absently at the picture wall. It was birch forests at the moment. Killaq went to her room and unlatched the console.

She hadn't been in VR since she had got home. She had been avoiding it. Now she lay back with a set expression and bypassed the start-up and the message feed.

/den/enter/

She didn't know what she had expected. The den had an unused feeling. It wasn't like the last time she had been here, when she had known that this was their place of safety, weaponised and armour-plated, around which dangerous enemy forces raged. Now it just seemed empty. She wandered about a bit, picking Amaruq's old crossbow from the wall. It was a child's toy again: she wondered if it had ever been anything else. She put the bow back on the wall and her own sleeve caught her attention: it was Ambra's muslin undertunic. Killaq realised that she wouldn't come here again as the little Inuit girl with her puppy: that girl was gone now.

She didn't know why she was here. Maybe she should delete the den altogether. She turned, absently peering out of one of the little round windows. The circular window frame was made out of intertwined withies, and green buds were starting to show at the junctions where the springy twigs had been broken and forced into the new curved shape. Outside the window ... Wait. Why were there windows? The den had never had windows before. She lifted a finger to the smooth brown surface of one of the curved branches, feeling the young bark through her fingertip. Behind her, someone laughed.

She spun around. It was an image of Amaruq, lounging on the moss floor, looking as usual as if he owned the place. The sight of him, so carefree, looking so much as if he were alive, sent a wrenching spasm of grief and nausea through her. She doubled over, hands to her temples, sobbing and shouting aloud.

'Fuck! Fuck! He made a fucking *post-death avatar.* I can't bear it, the bastard, the bastard.'

'Hey, hey, sis,' said the image, getting to its feet. 'If you don't like the windows, we can change them.'

'And he gave it a cheap script because he *knew* I would be here! He had to be clever! Never gave a shit about other people, other people's feelings!'

She was choking in tears. Now she straightened up, pointing a finger at the image, shouting at it. 'Delete! Delete!' The avatar caught her finger and held it, looking serious now.

'Sis. Sis, listen to me.'

'Fucking hell! Am I that predictable? He wouldn't play a fucking trick like this on Ma.'

'You can't tell Ma,' said the avatar. The face had a horrible expression of overwhelming sadness, it almost seemed like a real person. 'You can't tell Ma, ever.'

'Too fucking right! She wouldn't believe that he could ever be this, this *cruel.*' Killaq dissolved in tears, holding her face in her hands, rocking and sobbing.

'Sis,' said the image. 'Look, sis, I'm sorry. I didn't mean it to be like this.'

'Did he leave,' Killaq asked the image, 'some sort of fucking *message*? To say, I told you so, look how cunning I am.'

'No, look, sis, I don't need to leave a message.' The avatar took a step towards Killaq and put its hand on her shoulder. 'I'm sorry, I truly am. I never meant us to have this conversation. It was just a fail-safe. I thought it would never come to this, I thought I could outwit him.'

'Sanderson?' Despite herself Killaq was talking to the avatar as if it was real. She had so desperately missed Amaruq, all that time; she had so wanted him to come back and make everything right. It was hard not to take some comfort from the pre-programmed image.

'Yes, him, Sanderson.'

'I shot him.'

The avatar smiled. 'Yeah, I saw he died suddenly. I get the news, y'know.'

'You mean, the programme that runs you has an updating function.'

'No,' said the avatar, sounding suddenly impatient. 'I mean I get the news. Look,' he continued, 'sit down, tell me what happened. Then I have something I need to get straight with you.'

'I knew there would be a fucking *message.*'

'No, not a 'message', just something I need to explain. So tell me what happened.'

'I went to your funeral,' said Killaq, looking the image in the eye. 'You looked all pale and squashed. You were frowning.'

Killaq had expected the avatar to have some smart retort, but to her surprise the image looked uncomfortable.

'You went to my funeral, huh? That's some weird shit. My funeral,' it said, wonderingly.

'Your funeral!' Killaq shouted at it. 'Because you're dead! Amaruq, my brother, he's dead! You're just a programme he left behind.'

'I guess,' the avatar said, 'I never really thought, I didn't realise there would be a funeral.'

'What the fuck, what did he *think* was going to happen? We were just going to leave his body under a pile of stones like in the old days?'

'No shit,' said the image. 'A funeral. I guess there really is no way back, I never got that properly till now.' Then he grinned, looking more like his old self. 'Did lots of people come?'

'Fuck you!' Killaq screamed, reaching over her shoulder for Starmaker. 'Fuck you!'

'Woah!' said the image, hands held out low in the gesture of someone calming an angry animal. 'Woah. Dangerous fighting woman, let go of ferocious scimitar, and listen to genuinely contrite brother.'

Without having meant to, Killaq laughed.

'That's better. Ok, sit down. This may be hard, hard for you to hear, to believe. Hard for me to say.'

Killaq uncurled her fingers from Starmaker's grip. Slowly she lowered herself onto the mossy floor. So many times they had played and fought here. Fresh tears came welling to her eyes.

'Ready?' said the image. Killaq nodded.

The avatar took a deep breath. 'This,' he gestured at his image, his sealskin jerkin, his high kamiks. 'It's not a post-death responsive recording. It's me.'

Killaq looked at him blankly.

'I'm not dead.'

For a moment Killaq continued looking at him blankly. Then abruptly she stood up. 'Fuck this shit,' she said. She brought up the exit menu. She found she was looking at him, waiting for him to stop her. He just shook his head.

'Not this time, sis. You can go if you want to.'

He looked so sad, sitting there on the mossy floor. If she wasn't so infuriated with him, she would put her arms around him. Instead she paused the menu.

'How can you … He can't have expected me to believe that. I saw him, dead in his coffin.'

The image winced. 'Look,' it said. 'Maybe this was a bad idea. But I'm glad to have seen you, face to face, at least. Just one last time.'

Killaq exploded. 'And that's it, is it? That's good enough? For Ma in pieces, all that shit with SAPA? The mining carrying on? We lost! We lost the fight! We lost you! And for you to leave some shitty recording saying you were glad to see me?'

The avatar cocked an eyebrow. 'Actually,' it said, 'I think you'll find the mining isn't carrying on. I do have some influence from inside here.'

'What the fuck?'

It brought up the news item. 'Sea-bed mining, who knew,' said Killaq when she'd viewed it. She looked at the avatar with a dry respect. 'He wrote it pretty well, your updating function.'

'For the last time, sis. I don't have an updating function. I have the whole of VR. Everything I want, except you and Ma. And I had hoped *you* would come and visit, sometimes. Once you understood.'

It looked at her pleadingly. Then, as if reaching a decision, it put an arm on her shoulder, propelling her around to face the den wall. There was a door there, where there had never been a door before. It was made of thin planks of knotted, weathered wood, worn soft with polishing, and instead of a door frame, braided withies ran around the lintel and the sides. There was a wooden latch. Amaruq lifted the latch and pushed the door open, standing aside to let Killaq step out first.

They were standing in sunshine in a grassy clearing, on a hillside. It felt like springtime. In front of them the land fell away into a vista of gentle rolling hills, dropping ahead into a long valley, with a river catching the sunlight away into the distance. The slopes were shaded with trees and everywhere there was the rustle and music of leaves. Amaruq put an arm around her shoulders.

'Let me tell you, sis, and then you can think what you like. I can't prove any of it.'

Killaq nodded, soothed by the green hills, by the sunlight.

'You know I've been working on VR, on a real, liveable VR, for a long time. The world is so fucked, so broken, and everything is recorded and monitored. There's no privacy, no freedom anymore. No real work for a man to do.'

'No danger, you mean.'

'Danger ... well danger, risk at any rate, is part of life, part of how we ought to live. We need it, you know, sis. It's what makes the rest of it worthwhile.'

She shrugged.

'Anyway, I've wanted to make a new world for a long time. I've been working on it.'

Killaq scrutinised his face. It looked like him, it did look like him: something about the expression, about the eyes.

'So you know this, most of it. I learned how to move someone, their mind, without using the port to interface with the physical body back in the outside. I moved that guy, that North Korean, before he died.' Amaruq's face twisted in a complicated expression. 'I know, I know what you said. You were right, kinda. I was experimenting with him, I shouldn't have done that. But he would have died, otherwise.'

'He did die.'

'His body, his human body, yes.'

Killarq looked at him for a long time.

'Are you saying,' she said, 'that you did the same? To yourself?'

Amaruq sighed, looking down at his hands. 'When they had me, sis – I don't want to tell you. It wasn't good.'

Killaq remembered the little tigress, crumpled in her chair in the hall by the sea. SAPA was ruthless. She nodded.

'I came in here, to escape, really, to keep sane. I kept an eye on what was going on, outside. I was worried about you. Everything was going wrong, all at once. I couldn't get in touch with anyone, it was too dangerous. And then it seemed like there was an exchange planned, and it was going to be ok.'

He stopped.

'I just wasn't sure, is all. I didn't trust them. I made myself a failsafe. So that if it was a trap, it would spring me into here.'

He looked at her, suddenly professionally alert. 'You didn't programme the simultaneity, did you? Please tell me it wasn't you.'

'No, they wouldn't let me near it. The army.'

'Yeah, makes sense. Except if you had written it, it would have worked.'

She smiled a small smile of pride.

'It all happened really fast. They woke me up, in the body; they'd been keeping me under in VR. They told me I was going to be exchanged for Sanderson. They were recording viz, evidence I guess. Then there was a doctor, with a needle, and he hooked me up, and, shit sis, it was terrible pain, like I've never felt. And then I was here, without anything in between, and I was so glad it had stopped hurting, I just stayed here and cried. And when I tried to go back, I couldn't. The ID, the pathway, wasn't there.'

Killaq turned to him and put her arms around him, leaning her cheek on his shoulder, and held him, rocking to and fro, in the sunshine.

After a while she stopped rocking and held him by the shoulders, looking him in the face.

'So, sis? Is it me?'

'I have no idea. But it's good to see you, anyway.'

'Gonna come back?'

'I think so.'

'That's ok then. You look after Ma. I'm off now, but I'll see you, right?'

'What d'you mean, you're *off*?' Killaq exclaimed, torn between love and exasperation. 'Where are you off *to*?'

'Tell you sometime.'

He was gone. Killaq hugged her arms around herself, suddenly lonely, and gazed out over the valley. She hadn't noticed before that a wide sandy track wound away from the hilltop, rising and dipping over and around hollows in the landscape. She could see two figures some distance down it, walking hand in hand. One of them looked like Amaruq. The other – she shaded her eyes, peering into the distance – the other seemed to be a woman: she could see a shining dress, and a long fall of black hair. As she watched they turned to each other, and Amaruq wrapped the silver girl in his arms.